IN THE DEPTHS OF CHTHON

A shape rose from the cavern floor. It came toward him, oddly suggestive and a little frightening, a beauty and a horror at once. Now Aton could see the outline of a woman's body, and a voice came from the figure, unctuous and yet appealing:

"You want to make love to me?"

PIERS ANTHONY

CHTHON

CHTHON (thōn), form of English adjective *chthonian, -ic,* pertaining to nether world; derived from Greek *chthon,* the earth. 1. A subterranean prison for incorrigibles, location classified. 2. A garnet-mine.

SECTOR CYCLOPAEDIA, §398

BERKLEY BOOKS, NEW YORK

CHTHON

A Berkley Book / published by arrangement with
the author

PRINTING HISTORY
Ballantine edition / July 1967
Berkley edition / March 1982
Third printing / December 1982

ISBN: 0-425-06260-0

CONTENTS

"In Heaven you have heard no marriage is. . . ."

JOHN CROWE RANSOM, *The Equilibrists*

Prolog:

N!
Nova Factorial
Stellar explosion so vast and swift that light falls centuries
                behind.
This is our setting: the nova of life.
It springs from the microcosm to the planet
In eons;
From the planet to the universe
In centuries;
And its duration is the inverse function of its magnitude.

§
Section, symbolic
Date of the emergence of man: propulsion to the stars.
All that has gone before is ancient.
Number the new years: Section 1, Section 100, and on;
Communicate through sophisticate Galactic—

Though colloquial convenience lingers.
Modify man's genes for space
But hide the strange divergences. Make myths of those. . . .

5
Family of Five
Fifth-ranked of the founding Families of Hvee
Who settled the garden world in §79,
Seeking their transcendental paradise.
But Five is decimated by the chill of §305.
Two lines remain, the eldest:
Aurelius (§348–402), betrothed to a daughter of Ten;
Benjamin (§352–460), celibate;
And the hopes of this highborn Family devolve on the child
         of Aurelius:

Aton (§374–400)
Aton, agonist;
Aton, protagonist;
Contending for the knowledge of the nature of evil;
Condemned for that contention.
Aton—while your body dies in prison, your emotion lives
         beyond;
Yet both are one: your death reflects your life.
Every episode you suffer here parallels your other existence,
Now
And in the past
And in the time to come.

Aton, Aton—child of the sun—
Come, come to our nether world:
We have need of the damned.

CHTHON

I. ATON

1

It was hot in that cabinet. Aton licked at the salt and grime on his lips as rivulets itched down his neck and soaked into the rough prison shirt. In the sweating surface of the book he carried he saw a dark-haired, clean-shaven man.

Normal features, average stature—was this the person of a criminal? Am I, he thought, am I . . . ?

It did not matter. Chthon was the prison of the damned, and the man incarcerated here was damned, whether there was justice in it or no. Legally damned and legally dead: no one escaped from Chthon.

The prison was a deep, natural cavity far beneath the surface of a secret planet and hidden forever from the stars. No cells were there, no guards; only the living refuse of man's empire, dying in unthought wealth. For Chthon was a garnet mine, the moderate value of its individual stones complemented by their enormous number. The manner of its enterprise was this: every twenty-four hours the single elevator went down, loaded with food. It came up again with several hundred garnets. If the value of the stones was not enough, the next shipment of food was reduced.

Aton understood this much of Chthon, and it was as much as any free man could know. Now he was to learn the other side of it, the underside. The close cage shuddered, grinding on down into the fevered bowels, and Aton rocked with its motion. He felt the heat increase; smelled his own reek.

Am I dreaming of the impossible? he thought. Is it foolish to believe in a physical escape, simply because of a rumor I overheard in space? Return from death. Freedom. Perhaps even . . . completion?

The motion stopped. The door opened to roaring darkness. Heat blasted in, oppressive, suffocating. Sweat drenched his light uniform.

Knowing that he had no choice, Aton stepped into the gloom.

"One side!" a voice bellowed in his ear. Rough hands shoved him away. He stumbled into the center of the room, his book clamped under one arm, barely making out the shapes of men as they moved between him and the lighted interior of the lift.

They worked silently, three of them, hauling out crates and stacking them against the nearest wall. When the elevator was empty they carried smaller metal caskets carefully inside. The garnets, Aton realized. The men were husky, bearded, long-haired, and naked, and each had a sloshing bag of some sort strapped to his back. The effect, in the poor light, was grotesque; they reminded Aton of hunchback trolls.

One of them slammed the door, cutting off the light. The noise in the room was so great that Aton could not hear the elevator ascending, but he knew that his only link to the outside world was gone. He was now at the mercy of Chthon.

There was light after all—a sputtering glow, green and strange, given off by the walls and ceiling, as though they were smoldering. His eyes adjusted. He would be able to navigate.

Now the men came at him. "New man, eh. Name."

"Aton Five."

"Five?"

"Take it or leave it."

They considered that, weighing him as wolves of the pack weigh the stranger. "O.K., Five—this's your orientation. Down here we don't ask questions. We don't answer questions. We don't care why they shipped you here, only don't do it again. Just don't make trouble, hold your end, and you'll get along. Get it?"

They waited for his reaction, hard, lupine.

"Where do I—"

One man stepped forward, swinging an open palm. Aton automatically caught the blow on a raised forearm. He was a hair late, and the hand hit the side of his face hard enough to make his head ring. He backed a step. "What the—?"

"Mind your business. We don't warn twice."

Aton fell back, angry. For a moment he toyed with the idea of repaying the advice in kind. That would mean fighting all three, probably at once. Was that what they wanted? But behind his mounting temper he realized that the suggestion was good. Don't make trouble—at least until you know your way around. There was no point in beginning his sojourn here as a combatant. Time enough for that later. He nodded.

"Good," the man said. He laughed. "Remember—we all got to die together!"

The others guffawed and went to pick up the crates. Aton would remember them.

"Advice," one said as he passed, not unkindly. "Strip. Like us. Hot."

They tramped off, leaving him alone. Were they typical? He knew there were women in Chthon, but in a prison without guards or any other exposure to the world, conventions must long since have bowed to the stifling heat. Abnormal mores were bound to prevail—unless he was being set up for some further joke.

Aton looked about him. The room was rounded, the walls irregular but not rough. Stone, coated with glow. Long ago some scouting party must have explored these caverns, or at least enough of them to locate the garnets and determine that there was no feasible exit. He wondered whether the air was natural or somehow piped in; its presence seemed too provident to be coincidence.

But surely this terrible heat could not be borne for any length of time. This was a stifling oven. There had to be cooler sections, or it would be impossible to live. He discarded his sopping uniform, took up his book, and made his way out of the room. At the exit he touched the wall cautiously: it was hot, but not burning, and the greenish slime continued to glow for a few seconds on his fingers. The heat was evidently not from cavern chemicals.

He found himself in a short tunnel. He had been told that Chthon consisted of a maze of lava tubes, and intellectually he knew that their formation had been completed many centuries before, but it was hard to be objective. The far end of the passage pulsed with heat, and the roaring sound grew constantly louder, as though the primeval forces were still in motion. But there was no other way to go.

At length he emerged into a large cross tunnel, a dozen feet in diameter—and was smashed into its smooth wall by a rushing mass of air. Wind—in closed caverns? This was the source of the noise; but where could such a draft be coming from? Somehow his vision of the infernal region had not included this.

Aton braced himself and forged back into the wind, letting it guide his body down the tunnel. The walls were featureless, except for the glow, and the passage was almost exactly circular in cross section. Could it have been excavated and smoothed by an untold era of wind erosion? Chthon was growing stranger yet.

The fierce breeze—thirty miles an hour or more—served nicely to cool his laboring body, giving him at least part of the answer to survival here. But almost immediately he felt its consequence: dehydration. He would have to have water, and quickly, before his body shriveled. Somewhere there should be other people, and suitable provisioning.

Moving along with one hand against the wall, Aton suddenly fell into an inlet. The wind subsided here, and the heat returned; but grateful for the rest, he decided to follow it on down. The passage was small, hardly high enough to clear his head, and opened into another cell or room similar to the one in which he had been deposited originally. A dead end.

He was about to retrace his steps when he realized with a start that this room was occupied. There was a mutter and a stirring, and a shape rose from the curving floor. It came toward him, oddly suggestive and a little frightening, bringing to mind an image from his past; nebulous, a beauty and a horror at once too tempting and too painful to handle fairly. The background howling of air seemed to shape itself into sinister music. It is the song, he thought, the terrible broken song, the melody of death? Is this my demon, my succubus, come grinning to snatch away my manhood?

A woman's voice issued from the figure, unctuous yet appealing. "You want to make love to me?" she asked.

Now he could see the outline of a nude female body. Conscious of his own exposure, he held his book protectively in front as she approached. He was uncertain of her intention, and she brushed the book aside and slipped into the circle of his arm. She was confident; apparently she was able to see things more readily than he, in this half-light.

"Love," she said. "Make love to Laza." Her naked breasts pressed up against his chest.

He was afraid of her and of his phantasm. Warned by the tenseness of her body, he jerked backward. Her hand came down savagely, the sharp stone in her fist just grazing his cheek. Twice in an hour he had been attacked. "Then die, you bastard!" she cried. "Die, die . . ."

Her breath caught, choking, and she fled to the far side of her cell, to fling herself down in a shuddering heap. He could still hear her tortured whisper, "Die, die . . ." Had she really intended to kill him?

He stepped back into the connecting hallway. Laza heard the sound and came upright immediately. "You want to make love to me?" she inquired, exactly as before.

Aton ran.

The main tube went on and on, intersecting numerous cloisters. Some seemed to be empty; others broadcast strange noises, grunts, scratchings. Aton passed them quickly.

Thirst drove him on. The cruel wind chafed at his back, wringing moisture from him. He had kept his shoes, but now he removed them and let his sweat-sodden feet breathe. And pushed on.

At last the sound of voices drew him into a larger cavern. The wind eased slightly, filling more spacious quarters, and the noise diminished. Aton's numbed senses came back to life. There were several people here, working and chatting idly. In the center of the hall was a large metal device on wheels with a spoked axle rising from the top. Two men were pushing at the spokes and slowly rotating the top as though it were the wheel of a grinder. Nearby two other people squatted against the wall, carving small objects with slender blades. Beyond them a single man flipped pebbles into baskets. All were naked.

Nearest to him was a ponderously genial woman who spotted the visitor immediately. "New man, eh?" she said, using the same greeting he had met before. More trouble?

"Aton Five."

"You came to the right place," she said. "Everybody comes to Ma Skinny."

She laughed at Aton's blank look. "Naw—it's 'cause I handle the skins. You'll be wanting one, 'fore you shrivel. Here." She went to the central machine. The men stopped their grinding to allow her to remove a bag hanging on a spout in the side.

She brought it to him. "This here's your skin. You don't never want to leave it behind."

Aton took it, uncomprehending. It was made of some sturdy fabric, weighed about twenty pounds, and had straps obviously designed as a body harness. Now he saw that every person in sight wore a similar bag—the only article of clothing. But what was the purpose?

Ma Skinny picked up an empty bag and suspended it from the spout, allowing the men to resume their labor. Slowly it began to fill.

At last Aton caught on. "Water!" he exclaimed, taking the narrow neck of his skin into his mouth and sucking thirstily. The liquid was cool, comparatively, and delicious.

The woman looked on approvingly. "Worth more'n garnets," she said. "We just grind it out of the 'denser, here, and everybody's happy. Just so long's they stay right side of ol' Skinny."

Aton got the message. This woman had power, in whatever subterranean hierarchy existed here.

She went on to introduce the others. "Folks, this here's Five. These two're my pushers, this shift, Sam and Horny. Down this way we got ol' man Chessy. He makes whole chess sets out of broken garnet stone, or whatever it is. Nice work." Aton nodded, surprised again. Outside, those figurines were worth a fortune, both for the material and the craftsmanship— yet here the artisan was revealed as a gray old man squatting nakedly and poking with a battered knife. "This other's Prenty to him. They got an understanding."

The apprentice was a young woman, hardly out of her teens, but quite well formed and pretty. Aton wondered what crime she could have committed to be sentenced to Chthon at such an age. He imagined that their "understanding" was more to gratify the old man's ego than his romantic prowess. Reputation must be most important here—a good point to remember.

Ma Skinny led the way to the man with the baskets. "Tally, here," she said. "Good man with figures, good eye for garnets. Don't cross him." Tally was sorting the little stones by color: a basket each for shades of red and brown, dimly distinguishable in the imperfect light. An attractive girl resorted them into graduated sizes. "That's Silly," Ma said. "Her name, I mean— Selene, Silly. You'll learn." The girl looked up and giggled.

"Everybody's got a job," Ma finished. "You run around a little, Five, get settled, and we'll fix you up with something. No hurry." Too casually, then: "You smuggled in some tools."

"Tools?"

Her alert eye was on his bound book. She wouldn't ask the question. Aton opened it. *"LOE,"* he said. "A text. They let me bring one thing." She turned away, wordless, disgusted.

That was the tone of it. Once acclimatized to the heat and wind and able to find his way around the interlocking tunnels by sound and sight, Aton found prison life to be suprisingly easy. Too easy—there could be no enduring drive toward escape, in such a situation. The inhabitants were contented, as he was not. He would have to find a catalyst.

The caverns extended down interminably. The garnets were brought up from somewhere below for sorting and trade with the outside world. They commanded a price far beyond their actual worth as gems. Artificial stones could easily surpass them in quality, but lacked the appeal of notoriety. These were the produce of condemned hands, originating in nefarious Chthon. Man always placed a premium on the morbid.

Aton found the attitude of the prisoners inexplicable. This was supposed to be the worst prison in the human sector of the galaxy, reserved for the criminally insane, the incorrigible, the perverted—those whom society could neither cure nor ignore. Chthon was pictured outside as the home of perpetual rampage and orgy, sadism and torture beyond belief.

Instead Aton discovered a crude but placid society whose members followed their own advice: make no trouble. The genuinely insane were isolated in their cells and cared for by volunteer wardens. Unless these ventured out, they were left to their own devices.

Even normal people could hardly be expected to get along so well. Were these really criminals? If not, why did they accept their lot so easily? There had to be a missing element, some binding force. He could not act until he understood its nature.

2

"Aton." The voice was a low, warm alto.

He came out of his reverie to discover the girl Selene, provocatively posed, not giggling. Her eyes had lingered on him whenever they met; but though aware of this, Aton had felt he should be wary of women until the other mysteries were solved. A woman was trouble anywhere.

She came toward him, breasts outthrust. "I ain't no Laza, Aton," she said, intercepting his thought. "It ain't going to kill you to come near me."

Aton was unmoved. "Tally's woman, aren't you?"

"Tally knows where I am. Tally knows where everybody is, all the time." She came to stand against him, soft and lithe and feline. "How long since you had a woman, Aton?"

She had scored. It had been too long a time. He had learned the way of things in space, and space was over, now, perhaps forever. Judging from the attitude he had seen so far, she was probably telling the truth about Tally. He might even have sent her, as a gesture of amity.

Selene moved away, hiding behind her water-skin. Certain that she had his attention now, she began to dance, with a rhythmic hop and swing fully as alluring as intended. Aton set his book against the wall and went after her.

She giggled and skipped away. Playing an intricate hide-and-seek with hands and body, she led him into a side passage. Aton checked, suddenly wary, but it was empty.

She brushed against him. He caught her and pinned her against her water-skin along the wall. Their lips met abruptly in a kiss, broke, touched passionately; then she escaped and pirouetted into the center of the cell. Her eyes glowed.

Aton stalked her, cutting off the exit and herding her into a niche; she dodged and wriggled with delight.

Selene began to hum a tune when she saw that she was fairly trapped. It was the final artifice: an innocent, indifferent melody, as though she were not aware of company. It should have launched him into the terminal effort.

Instead it drove him back, cooling his ardor instantly. It was the broken song.

She saw that something was wrong. "What's the matter, Aton?"

He turned his back. "Get out of here, Silly. You aren't half the woman I crave."

Shocked, then in flashing anger, she ran. Aton listened to the sound of her footsteps, a bare patter in the screaming wind. They merged to form the music of the broken song.

"Malice," he thought. "Oh, Malice—will you never leave me?"

* * *

It was a dream, of course, but only Aton knew it, and he, lured by the might-have-been it dangled before him, was foolish enough to forget that it was. In his conception he was not standing alone in the tunnel; the woman was not fleeing in anger. There had been a failure, yes, but not a total one.

She took his arm as they walked down the dim tunnel. She wore a light blouse and dark skirt which did more to enhance her figure than any nudity could do.

"Jill," he said, "I wanted to apologize for what happened. But you have to understand the impact the song has upon me. When that comes—"

She jogged his arm. He could feel the gentle pressure of her fingers through the coat. "My name is Selene," she said.

They turned into a side passage. It slanted down, expanding. "Your interest caught me by surprise," he continued, aware of the awkwardness of his explanation. "Somehow I never thought of you as a woman, Jill."

"Why do you keep calling me 'Jill'?" she demanded. "Look at me, Aton. I'm Selene. Silly Selene, cave girl."

He looked. "I suppose you are," he said. "I didn't recognize you, clothed."

"Thanks."

He guided her to a seat and found a place beside her. "I never realized there was one of these in Chthon. We had a theater for the crew on board the *Jocasta,* but I never attended . . ."

He faded out, alarmed. Her hand was in his lap, fumbling with the fastening of his trousers. Then her fingers were inside, reaching down to discover what lay there. He tried to protest, but immediately the people in the neighboring seats turned to stare, forcing him to silence lest his exposure be advertised.

The feature flashed on the big front screen. Aton's attention leaped to embrace that still scene. A man, toiling up a steep path, a strong man in antique costume, a young man garbed in flowing robes of indeterminate color. One man, but filled with meaning. Behind him the trail tapered away to a rockly, mossy slope, strangely attractive as a landscape.

The picture shifted, fading into another tableau. This time the foreground opened: a sheer drop with a horrifying hint of depth. The path had crested, as though running through a pass; indeed, one rounded hillock swelled in sight, while the surrounding land dipped away. Two men faced each other, having mounted on either side, meeting at the top. On the right was the strong young man of the previous picture; on the left, an older man, similarly dressed. They confronted, talking or debating. The old man's arm was raised in imperious gesture.

The third frame was more forceful: the young man's body was twisted, caught in violent motion, arms outflung, face contorted. The other person was poised in space beyond the precipice, arms raised as if to flail the air, bird-like, but falling nevertheless. They had had an argument, a falling-out, perhaps a contest of strength over the right-of-way. Who could say, since the images were fragmentary and silent? But the deed was done, irrevocably. Far below, out of sight, Aton knew that there was a narrow river bed—and wondered why he knew.

One more picture, seemingly unrelated to the prior sequence: a huge animal shape with mighty folded wings and the sensual breasts of a mature woman. Its mouth was open in a kind of question, as if to pose a riddle. That was all.

Unutterable horror seized Aton, a sick revulsion that churned his stomach and drove his senses back away from his naked face, recoiling from the monstrous import.

Now there was sensation in another area. He looked down and saw the female hand, clamped like calipers, stretching cruelly. But it was a cord, a serpentine length of it, blood-red in the half-light, connecting his belly to hers. He saw her face, and it was not the face of Laza, who would kill him, but another face, more lovely and more evil than any he could imagine.

He tried to wrench free, but could not move. The pain of his emotion was terrible as the stretching continued, a narrowing tautness wrenching the root loose from the flesh. Suddenly the melody steamed up from the horror and he knew fulfillment at last.

He woke, sweating, shaking, to the approach of footsteps, knowing that he had to get out of Chthon.

3

"Five." This time it was a man's voice. Selene had not taken long to spread the word. He turned to find Tally and two of his helpers.

"I didn't touch her," Aton said.

Tally was grim. "I know. That's why I'm here."

Aton kept a wary eye on the two other men. He knew their business, and he recognized one of them. "Because Silly made a pass at me?"

"Partly." Tally said with candor. "She shouldn't have had to do that. But then you turned her down."

"I wasn't making any trouble."

"No trouble!" Tally exploded. "You damned outsider! You made me the laughing stock of Chthon by proving my girl wasn't worth taking down. Teasing her so you could really make the point. You could have told her No at the beginning, if you didn't want it; but no, you had to—"

"It wasn't that. I wanted her, but—"

Tally's eyes were calculating. "'But—'? What were you afraid of? Nobody outside will ever see you again. You live our way now. There are no ceremonies, no two-faced rules. She wanted you, and I told her to have her fling. You can't spawn any bastards down here, not in this climate, if that's what got you. It just doesn't take."

"I knew that. I—"

"You cost me face, Five. There's only one way I can get it back."

"There's something else—" Aton began, but Tally had already signaled, and the two men were closing in. They were brawny; one was the member of the original greeting party who had struck him. They had taken off their skins.

Aton saw that there was no reasonable escape. He licked his lips, not bothering to remove his own water-skin. Had he really wanted to explain?

Timing. Coordination. Decision. Aton sprang. The first man had a naked foot buried in his solar plexus before he realized it. He was hurled back, collapsing bonelessly. Before he struck the ground, Aton was on his companion, wrapping a trained hand in the man's shaggy beard, jerking the original lunge into a headlong stumble. The calloused knuckles of Aton's free hand made a dull crunching sound on the other's temple.

One semiconscious, retching helplessly. One dying with a fractured skull. It had taken perhaps four seconds.

Tally stared down, amazed. "Spaceman," he said.

"You wanted it the hard way." Aton knew he had won the man's respect. "I tried to explain."

Tally got the men out and came back alone. "All right. I can't square things with you that way. Only one man I ever saw that could fight like that, and he's not . . . available."

"Spaceman?" Aton asked with interest.

"Krell farmer."

Aton wondered. The members of the guild that farmed the deadly krell weed had developed the ancient art of karate—kara-ate, the unarmed striking—in a different direction than had their spacefaring cousins. Both struck to disable, maim, or kill; but there was murderous power behind the spaceman's blow, lethal science behind the farmer's. Which school was superior? The question had never, to his knowledge, been settled. "Where is he?"

"Name's Bossman—down below. It isn't worth it."

"Nothing's worth it."

Tally changed the subject. "I'll take my loss and forget it. But I want to know one thing, and it isn't much of my business. I'll make a trade with you."

Aton understood the significance of the offer, in this place where information was more valuable than property. "I want to know something, too," he said. "Honest answers?" He saw immediately that the question was a mistake. The person who cheated on information would not live long.

"Let's match the questions," Tally said. The bargaining was on.

"The real Chthon setup."

"The reason you passed her up." Belatedly, Aton understood

why Tally had cut off his explanation before. He could not accept free knowledge. Easier to settle the grudge first, untangle the threads later. Here was an honest man, Chthon-fashion.

"You may not like the answer," Aton said.

"I want it straight, all of it."

They looked at each other and nodded. "Seemed too quiet for you here?" Tally asked rhetorically. "No wonder. This is only part of Chthon—the best part. We keep only the model prisoners: the harmless neurotics, the politicos, the predictable nuts. We have a pretty easy life because we're selected, we know each other, and we have the upper hand. But below—well, there is only one way to get down there, and no way back. Anybody we can't handle gets dropped down that hole and forgotten. That's where the mine is; we ship food down, they ship the garnets up."

"A prison within a prison!"

"That's right. Outside, they think we're all one big unhappy family, fighting and mining. Maybe that's the way it is, below. We don't know. But we like it quiet, here, and we have the same hold on the pit as the outsiders have on us: no garnets, no supplies. We get first pick of the food, and we don't have to work much, except to keep things running smoothly. We can't get out—but we have a living, and not a bad one at all. Every so often a new man comes down, like you, and makes things interesting for a while, until we get him placed."

"No way out," Aton said.

"Our caverns are sealed off from below. That keeps us in, and the monsters out. Below—no one knows where *those* passages end, or what's in them."

Unexplored caverns! There was the only hope for escape. It would mean facing a prison even the hardened inmates feared, mixing with men too vicious to accept any moral restraints. But it was a situation he could exploit.

"About Silly," Aton said, taking his turn, knowing his course. "It wasn't her; it wasn't you. She's a good girl; I would have taken her if I could. But something stopped me, something I can't fight."

"Stopped a spaceman at the point? You're a strange one. You and your damned book."

Aton said the word that condemned him: "Minionette."

Tally stared. "I've heard of that. Stories—you mean you met one? They really exist?"

Aton didn't answer.

Tally backed off. "I've heard about what they do. About the kind of man who—" His voice, friendly before, turned cold. "You *are* trouble. And I sent Silly to you."

Tally came to his decision. "I don't want to know any more. You aren't one of us, Five. You'll have to go below. I don't care how many men you kill; you aren't staying with us."

It was the reaction Aton had come to expect. "No killing," he said. "I'll go now."

One

Hvee was a pastoral world without pastoral creatures whose rolling mountains and gentle dales bespoke no strife. No dwelling lay within sight of another, and few of the angularities of man's civilization defaced the natural landscape. The population was small and select, hardly sufficient to man the smallest of cities on megapolistic Earth. There was just one major occupation and one export: hvee.

A small boy wandered through the circular fields of the Family of Five, careful not to tread on the green flowers yearning toward him. Too young to cultivate the crop, he could afford to be its friend. The hvee plants all about him projected, in effect, a multiple personality, an almost tangible aura that was comforting indeed.

He was seven years old, his birthday just one day behind, and he was still awed at the marvel of it, of that extra year so suddenly thrust upon him. The planet was smaller now, by a seventh of his life, and he wanted to explore it all over again and come to understand its new dimension.

In his arms he carried a large, heavy object, his birthday gift. It was a book, sealed in shiny weatherproof binding and closed by a bright metal clasp with a miniature combination lock. Ornate letters on its surface spelled out L O E, and beneath them, in script, his name: ATON FIVE.

The virgin forest of Hvee stood at the edge of the gardens, the trees less responsive to human mentality than the cultivated plants, but friendly all the same. The boy walked in the shadow of the wood, looking back toward the house of his father, Aurelius, far across the field. He stood beside the new garden shed, built within the year, looking winsomely up at its lofty peaked roof and thinking thoughts too large for him. Then he looked down behind it, where the hot black highway wriggled toward the distant spaceport—a pavement leading beyond even his present horizons.

At this moment of introspection the sound of music came, borne on the gentle wind, almost too fleeting to be real. The boy stopped to listen, turning his head this way and that, searching out the strains. His musical sense was untrained, but the compelling beauty of this melody could not be denied.

The song rose and fell in spectral ululations, the tenuous melody from some faerie instrument. There were bird-songs in it, and the rippling of hidden forest water, and the delicate sounds of the uncomplicated melodies of ancient troubadours. Aton was reminded of music he would later come to recognize as "Greensleeves" and "The Fountains of Rome" and older and younger pieces, and he was enthralled.

Unfinished, it stopped. The boy of seven forgot his other explorations, overcome by a desire to listen to the finish. He had to hear its end.

The melody began again, thrillingly, and he clutched the giant book to his chest and trailed his curiosity into the forest. The fascination grew, taking firmer hold on his mind; this was the loveliest thing he had ever heard. The great trees themselves seemed responsive to it, standing silently and letting it drift among them. Aton touched the bark of their trunks as he passed, drawing courage as he skirted the bottomless forest well (afraid of its black depth) and went on.

He could make out the music more readily now, but it had led him to an unfamiliar part of the forest. It was a voice—a woman's voice, full and sweet with overtones of promise and delight. The delicate arpeggios of a soft-toned stringed instrument accompanied it, counterpointing the vocal. She was singing a song, the meaning of half-heard words fitting the mood of the forest and the day.

The boy came to a glade and peeked through the tall ferns rising strongly at its edge. He saw the nymph of the wood. She was a young woman of striking beauty, so elegant that even a child just mastering seven could understand immediately, without question, that there could be no other on his planet to match her. He watched and listened, spellbound.

She sensed him, hiding there, and ceased her singing. "No!" he wanted to cry as the song was broken again in midrefrain; but she had put aside her instrument.

"Come to me, young man," she said, clearly and not loudly at all. Discovered when he had thought himself secure, he went to her, abruptly bashful.

"What is your name?" she asked.

"Aton Five," he said, proud of a proud name. "I'm seven years old yesterday."

"Seven," she said, making him feel that it was indeed the right age to be. "And what is this burden you have undertaken?" she inquired, touching the volume in his arms and smiling.

"This is my book," he said with diffident vanity. "It has my name."

"May I see it?"

Aton stumbled back a step. "It's mine!"

She looked at him, making him feel ashamed for his selfishness. "It's locked," he explained.

"But are you able to read it, Aton?"

He tried to tell her that he knew that the big *LOE* spelled *The Literature of Old Earth,* and that the rest was his own name, to show that it belonged to him; but the words got all tangled up in his throat as he encountered her deep and silent eyes. "It's locked."

"You must never tell the numbers to anyone, ever," she said. "But I will close my eyes and let you open it yourself."

She closed her eyes, her features as calm and perfect as

those of a statue, and Aton felt somehow committed and not a little confused. He fumbled with the lock, turning the dial in the pattern so recently memorized. The clasp popped open and the tinted pages were exposed.

Her lashes lifted at the sound and her gaze fell upon him once more, as warm and bright as a sunbeam. He pushed the volume into her waiting hands and watched, half fearfully, as she turned the fine sheets.

"It is a beautiful book, Aton," she said, and he flushed with pride. "You will have to learn to read the old language, English, and this is a difficult thing, because the symbols do not always match the words. They are not so clear as those of Galactic. Do you think you can do that?"

"I don't know."

She smiled. "Yes, you can, if you try." She found a place and spread the pages flat. "You are a child, Aton, and this book will have meaning for you. Here is what Mr. Wordsworth says about the immortality of childhood: 'O joy! that in our embers/ Is something that doth live,/ That nature yet remembers/ What was so fugitive!'"

Aton listened blankly. "It only seems obscure," she said, "because *your* symbols do not quite match those of the poet. But when you begin to grasp it, the language of poetry is the most direct route to the truth you can find. You will understand, Aton, perhaps when you are twice seven.

"And when you are twice seven—what will you be, what will you be doing?"

"I'll be farming hvee," he said.

"Tell me about the hvee."

And so Aton told her about the green flowers that grew in the fields, waiting to love, and how when a person took one it loved him and stayed green as long as he lived, and survived on no more than the air and his presence, and how when the owner grew old enough to marry he gave his hvee to his betrothed and it lived if she loved him and died if her love was false, and if it did not die he married her and took it back to himself and did not test her love ever again, and how the hvee grew only on Hvee, the world named after it or maybe the other way around, in the ground, and was sent all over the human sector of the galaxy because people everywhere wanted to know they were loved, no matter what.

"Oh, yes," she said, when he ran out of breath. "Love is the most painful thing of all. But tell me, young man—do you really know what it is?"

"No," he admitted, for his words had been rhetoric, a rehearsal of adult folklore. He wondered if he had heard her description correctly.

Then she said something else to him, something strange. "Look at me. Look, Aton, and tell me that I am beautiful."

He looked obediently at her face, but all he could see were her black-green eyes and her hair, a fire and a smoke, burning and swirling in the wind. "Yes," he said, finding unexpected pleasure in the saying, "you are beautiful, like the blaze upon the water when my father burns the swamp in the spring."

She laughed with the light echo of her music, accepting the compliment on its own terms. "I am indeed," she agreed. She reached out her hand and lifted his chin with her cool fingers so that he gazed into her eyes once more. The effect was hypnotic. "You will never see a woman as beautiful as I," she said, and he found himself compelled to believe it absolutely, never to question it so long as he should live.

She let him go. "Tell me," she said, "tell me—have you ever been kissed?"

"My aunt kisses me every time she visits," Aton said, wrinkling his nose.

"Do I resemble your aunt?"

He examined her. Women hardly counted in the primogenitive genealogy of Hvee, and the aspect of his father's sisters was lackluster. "No."

"Then I shall kiss you now."

She touched her fingers to his chin again and put her other hand on top of his head to tilt it sidewise a little. She held him, just so, and leaned foreward to kiss him softly on the mouth.

Aton, seven, did not know what to do. He felt nothing, he was ever after to tell himself, dwelling on this moment; but that nothing he did feel he could not understand.

"Have you been kissed that way before?"

"No."

She smiled brilliantly. "No one, no one else will kiss you that way—ever."

Her eye fell on a tiny plant almost at her foot. "This too is beautiful," she said, letting her hand drop toward it.

Aton spoke sharply. "That's a hvee. A wild hvee."

"May I not have it?" she asked, amused.

"May you not!" he said, unconsciously imitating her choice of words. "Hvee is only for men. I told you."

She laughed once more. "Until they are loved." She took it up. "See. See, it does not wither in my hand. But I will give it to you, my present, and it will love you and stay with you as long as you remember my song."

"But I don't know your song."

She put the green stem in his hair. "You must come back to me to learn it." Her fine hands took his shoulders, turning him around. "Go, go now, and do not turn back."

Aton marched off, confused but somehow elated.

•   •   •

He returned next day, but the glade was empty. The nymph of the wood had gone, and had taken her song with her. He dwelt on it, trying to recover the tune, but he possessed only a fleeting fragment. He touched the flat stump where she had sat, wondering whether the warmth of her body remained in it, beginning to doubt that she had been there at all. But he was unwilling to let the vision of the nymph go. She had talked to him and kissed him and left him the hvee and part of a song, and the memory was strange and strong and wonderful.

In the days and weeks that followed he continued to visit that place in the forest, hoping for some hint of the music. Finally he stopped and gave himself up to the more somber world of reality—almost.

Their nearest neighbor lived five miles down the valley. This was a branch of the low-caste Family of Eighty-One, farming poorer land and doing it less conscientiously. Aurelius never mentioned them. Aton had not known of their existence until his nymph indirectly introduced him to the children of Eighty-One.

Taken by a fit of loneliness when his tenth visit to the forest had been to no avail, Aton had either to assume the woman to be gone forever (because he found that easier than counting on into two figures with only ten fingers), or to begin a search for her farther afield. He chose the latter. Surely she was *somewhere*, and the logical place to investigate was the long valley, since he was not supposed to walk along the hot black highway. His aunt always arrived by aircar from that direction, over the valley, and while he did not conceive her residence in terms of place, nor wish to visit it, the fact added logic to his decision.

He set off, armed with his weighty *LOE*, and marched through many wonderous domains of field and meandering stream and dark stretches of forest. The world, it developed, was a bit larger than anticipated; but he shifted the growing mass of the book from arm to arm, and rested occasionally, and disciplined his little feet to be undaunted by the unthinkable distances they traveled, and found himself at last at the fringe of Eighty-One.

In this manner he came to meet, not the nymph for which he searched, but the twin boys his own age, Jay and Jervis, and their little sister Jill, and compounded a friendship that was to endure an even seven years.

"Look—he got a hvee!" Jay shouted, spotting the determined traveler.

The children of Eighty-One clustered around Aton, who responded to this interest in his mark of distinction with a condescending frown. "Why don't you take one?" he inquired.

Jervis skuffled. "I tried. It died."

"Where you get yours?" Jay demanded.

Aton explained that a lovely woman in the forest had given him the plant for his seventh birthday, and that he was looking for her now.

"I wish I could fib like that," Jervis said enviously. "Can you make a bomb?"

"We're making a bomb!" little Jill exclaimed.

Jervis slapped her across her bare chest. "No girls!" he pronounced. "This is man's business."

"Yeah," said Jay.

"Yeah," Aton echoed, though it made no difference to him. "But I need a safe place for my book. It's got Words-Earth in it."

"Is that like purple sand?" Jay asked. "Maybe we can use some for our bomb."

"No! Words-Earth is a poet. He makes rhymes about hot ashes. 'Oh, joy that in our embers—'"

"Who cares about that stuff?" Jervis said. "*Real* men make bombs."

In due course the three were ensconced in the twins' hideout, a hollow in the ground not far from the hog corral, concealed by thick bushes. They were fashioning a bomb from rocks and colored sand. Jervis had heard that the correct mixture of sulphur (which they could recognize because it was yellow) and saltpeter would explode, if dropped hard enough. But somehow it wasn't working.

"Must be the salt," Jervis said. "This stuff is just white sand. We need *real* salt."

Jill, hovering just outside, saw her opportunity. "I can get some salt!"

When she returned with a shaker snitched from the kitchen, she refused to give it up until granted a share of the enterprise. For the rest of the afternoon she attached herself to Aton, somewhat to his disgust. She was muddy all over, and her long black braids kept falling into the bomb.

Two

The years were left behind. Tutoring began. Aton became versed in the history and traditions of his planet and the great Family of Five. He learned to read the difficult mother language and gradually, wonderfully, worked his way through the mighty text of *LOE*. He learned to count far beyond ten, and to do other things with numbers; he learned the K scale of temperature and the § scale of time. He began the long hvee apprenticeship.

His free time, more valuable now, was spent largely at the farm of Eighty-One. The boys went on to other projects after giving up on the bomb. Jay and Jervis were not obligated to endure the extent of tutoring required of a son of Five, and had an easier time of it. Jill never relinquished her initial affection for Aton. The twins teased him constantly: "Kiss her and maybe she'll bring some more salt. *Good* salt." But he saw her as the sister he had somehow never been granted, and contented himself with yanking her braids just hard enough to make her behave, while time acted subtly on all of them.

At home, the farming of the delicate green flowers was an intricate matter, comprised of science, art, and attitude. It was soon evident that Aton had the touch. The plants he worked with grew larger and finer than average, and his pilot plots flourished. His future as a farmer seemed assured.

His future as a mechanic might have been otherwise. He learned to operate the Five aircar, pinpointing planetary co-ordinates on the machine's geographic vernier. The location grid was calibrated in standard units for easting and northing, with the superimposed vernier scale throwing everything out of focus except the correct reading. This was where Aton had endless difficulty. He seemed to lack mechanical aptitude, at least as a child. "Don't ever join the Navy," the tutor warned. "They'll be certain to make a machinist out of you. They have uncanny ability to select exactly the wrong man for the job." But once Aton mastered the technique he came to respect it well. There was something about the sudden sharp focus, after interminable struggle, that was exhilarating.

Perhaps, he thought, the beauty of that focus could be ap-preciated only *because* it came after struggle.

One thing continued to dull his appreciation of his destiny: the lingering image of the nymph of the wood. He could not be entirely complacent while that mystery remained. As he worked in the field, sweating in the hot sun to remove the encroaching weed-plants (he thought of them as krell, though they were hardly dangerous) from the valuable hvee, the broken song ran through his mind, insistent, tantalizing. Where had she come from? What had been her purpose? What could she have wanted with a small boy?

Gradually, age dimmed the memory. Only the central core of dissatisfaction remained, keeping him ever so slightly off-balance, making him wonder whether the life he contemplated as a farmer of hvee was actually the very best available. Yet—what else could there be?

He was a young man of fourteen, transplanting infant hvee

near the edge of the property, when the distant melody came a second time. His hands shook. Had she—had she returned at last to the glade?

He set his plants aside and followed the magic sound, now eager, now holding back. Excitement pounded in him as he circled the disused deep well within the forest. Was there really a nymph? Did she summon him?

He arrived at the glade, which was almost unchanged from his memory of seven years. She was there! She was there, sitting and singing, her quick fingers rippling over the little instrument—an offworld, six-stringed lute—lovely beyond belief. The ancient image in his mind faded before the new reality. The forest, the glade, the very air about her was beautiful.

He stood at the edge, absorbing her presence. It seemed only a moment since he had stood this way before; the intervening time a lonely dream—a moment and an eternity. She had not changed—*he* was the one who had aged seven years. And what he saw now was not what he had seen as the child of seven.

She wore a light green dress, translucent in the spot of sunlight, laced up the front in a bodice unused on Hvee. Her face was pale and fair, framed by the luster of hair which flowed deep red and deep black in fascinating alliance. There was a gentle fullness in her figure, not voluptuous, not slim. Her aspect represented a juxtaposition of opposites that Aton had never consciously realized he was searching for. Fire and water, so often at war, here merged into exquisite focus like the crossing scales of the vernier.

He stood entranced, forgetting time and self in the delight of that study.

She spied him, as before, and put aside her song. "Aton, Aton, come to me."

She knew him! He stood before the lovely woman, embarrassed, flushed by the first ungainly surges of manhood. She was man's desire, and in her presence he felt great and crude, conscious of the earth on his hands and the sweat on his shirt. He could not stay; he could not leave.

"Fourteen," she said, putting her magic into that word.

"Fourteen. Already you are taller than I." She stood, unfolding as a flower, to show that it was true.

"And you are wearing my hvee," she said, reaching up to take it from his hair. It nested in her hand, its green blossom hardly darker than her dress. "Will you give it to me now, Aton?"

Speechless, he gawked at her, unable to comprehend the offer. "Ah, it is too soon, too soon," she said. "I will not take it from you now, Aton. Not yet." She noted his curling, empty hands. "Where is your book, Aton?"

"I was in the field—"

"Yes, oh, yes," she said, twirling the hvee. "You are twice seven and you are a farmer now. But do you remember—"

"William Wordsworth's 'Intimations of Immortality'?" he blurted, immediately shocked by his own loudness.

She caught his hand in hers, squeezing it. "Never forget, Aton, what a wonderful thing it is to be a child. There is that immortal bit of light in you, a ray of that sun for which you are named. You must cherish that ember, and never let it die, no matter how you grow."

"Yes," he said, unable to say more.

She held the hvee to her cheek. "Tell me, tell me again, Aton—am I not beautiful?"

He gazed into the black and green depths of her eyes and was lost. "Yes," he said. "The forest fire, and the still water. You drown me in fire—"

Her laugh was the echo of candlelight and thicket streams. "Am I then so devastating?"

You compelling creature, he thought. You play with me, and I am helpless.

She reached her arms around him, standing close to replace the hvee in his hair. The light perfume of her body intoxicated his senses. She was timeless; she was perfection. "You have found no woman to compare to me," she said.

Protest was useless; even her vanity was rapture. No mortal woman could rival the splendor of her person.

"You must not forget me," she said. "I shall kiss you again."

Aton stood, hands rigid at his sides, feet rooted, half afraid that if he moved a muscle he would topple. The woman of the forest placed those cool fingers on his elbows, the gentle pressure evoking a responsive tingle from tight shoulders to clenched fists. She raised her sweet lips to his, holding him in ecstasy. The kiss: and desire and chagrin suffused his mind.

Gossamers pinioned his body. Only his voice found volition: "But tomorrow you will be gone," he heard it say.

She dismissed him. "Go, go now. When you find me again, you will be ready."

"But I don't even know your name."

She waved him away, and his clumsy feet turned him around and marched him from the glade.

•   •   •

What had occupied Aton's idling imagination up to this point now became more urgent. His attitude changed. Interested in the distaff sex only in a speculative way, until awakened by the forest nymph, he now contemplated a program of self-education that went somewhat beyond that provided by his tutor. He planted hvee in a preoccupied manner—the plants flourishing even so—and pondered ways and means.

He waited impatiently for dusk, then pounded along the old trail leading to the farm of Eighty-One. The wild plants had grown up thickly, obscuring the way and reminding him of the infrequency of his visits to this place, now. How long had it been since he'd laughed and fought with the dissimilar twins, Jay and Jervis? Since he'd let young Jill tag along, recipient of masculine unfairness? The childish games had fallen off and the barriers of status had grown, though he told himself that such things made no difference to *him*. And wasn't he coming, at this time of problem and dissatisfaction, to talk it out and make plans with his friends? The twins were more worldly than he. Man-talk would get it out of his system, make the strangeness go, set his confusions to rest. The old companionship would dissipate the nameless unrest he felt.

The house of Eighty-One rose out of the darkness; thin squares of light edged the closed shutters. Aton skirted the steaming hog pen, his passage eliciting the usual incurious porcine grunts. The warm animal smell brought a sympathetic wrinkle of the nostrils, though he had long since ceased to find it objectionable. He came up to the rear of the house and tapped the twins' window with the measured signal of old.

There was no response. He poked a finger behind the loose shutter and pried it open, peering in as far as his angle of vision permitted. The room was empty.

He banged the wall in futile anger. Where were they? How could they be gone when he wanted to talk? Knowing himself to be unreasonable and a trifle snobbish, he grew angrier yet. He knew that there were other things in the boys' lives beside himself, particularly since it had been months since his last visit, but the proof of it was irritating. What was he to do?

The shutters parted on a window farther along the dark wall and light flared out to strike the bushes and beam into the night sky. Aton stepped up to it, then hesitated. It could be one of the parents. They, perhaps more conscious of the difference in Family status, and not wanting trouble with the forceful Aurelius, discouraged the association of the children. Aton waited, holding his breath, as a head poked out: ebony outlines, features indistinguishable. Then a long braid flopped over the sill and dangled its ribbon below.

"Jill!"

She spun her head toward him, trying to penetrate the gloom. "That you, Aton?"

He ducked below the spilling light and caught the swinging hair, giving it a sharp tug.

"Ouch!" she yelped, exaggerating her pain. She caught at his hand and disengaged his fingers. "That's Aton, all right. I'd know that jerk anywhere!"

He got up to face her squarely. "Jerk, am I?"

Her face was very close to his. Her even eyes, pupils black in the shadow, looked back with unexpected depth. "When you jerk my hair—"

He had missed the pun. Embarrassed, and unwilling to admit it, he leaned forward and touched his lips to hers.

The contact was light, but that unpremeditated action surprised him as much as it did her. Jill had always been the tagalong, the drag, the interference in male affairs, the baby sister. Her unconcealed interest in Aton had always bothered him, his irritation accentuated because he was never able to admit his displeasure. He had responded with cruelty, angry at himself for that, but able to think of no alternative.

This was no forest nymph. These lips, while not wholly unresponsive, were untrained. They lacked finesse. There was no magic—except that he was kissing Jill and finding her unrepulsive. He wondered whether he should stop.

She was the one to terminate it, finally, lifting away her head and taking a breath. "Too late for that salt, now," she said. "You already banged the bomb."

"I was looking for the twins." He was unable for the moment to rise to the repartee. Had he, in reality, been looking for this girl? The thought upset him.

She nodded, one braid brushing his face. "I figured it. They're playing checkers with Dad, up front. Want me to fetch one of them for you?"

"Checkers? Both of them?" Aton asked, trying to keep the conversation going while he settled an obscure but powerful internal conflict.

"Both together. They keep losing, too. Jerv is getting mad."

Aton had no comment. The silence lengthened between them, awkward, uncomfortable. Neither moved.

Finally he put out a hand, holding it there, letting her interpret his meaning, and not certain that there was any meaning there.

"Well," she said, and this seemed to make the decision. She took his hand, leaning on it as she brought her foot up to the sill. Her firm legs and thighs showed through the material of skirt and slip in silhouette, stirring a guilty excitement in him.

"Wait a minute," she said, withdrawing. Had she changed her mind already? He seethed with disappointment and relief. But in a moment the light went out and she was back. "They'll think I'm in bed."

Aton helped her down, placing both hands on her waist just above the swelling hips and lifting her away from the high sill. She was heavier than he had thought, and they stumbled together and almost fell as her feet touched the ground. She was nearly as tall as he.

They walked together past the pigpen, this time drawing no remarks, and went on down the remembered trail, selecting this direction by silent consent. Aton's mind was whirling. It seemed impossible—yet she *was* a girl, with a body budding into womanhood. She had always liked him, and now she had chosen to express that liking more directly.

They found themselves beside the ancient hideout. The bushes had overrun the entrance, but the main space seemed to be intact. Aton squeezed through first, feeling carefully in the pressing dark, in case there were lizards. He brushed away a few loose burs.

She joined him silently. They would talk now, and she would try to get close, as she always had, and he would push her away automatically, and she would toss her head and giggle. . . .

She found his head, turned it, and placed her mouth against his. His hands came up to push at her chest, touched, and jumped away. Without interrupting the kiss, she caught hold of his shirt and pulled herself closer.

They broke, and she lay back, her form just visible as his eyes acclimatized. "I thought you were just teasing, before," she said. "But you aren't, now, are you? I mean—"

"No," Aton said, uncertain whether he was being mocked.

"All my life, it seems, I've been waiting for you to do that. And now it's done." Had she meant the kiss?

Aton studied her as well as he was able. She was wearing a summer blouse, gently mounded, and a darker skirt that blended with the ground. She had kicked off her slippers and her white feet stood out, the toes wiggling. "I might do more," he said, half afraid she would be angry, though he had never paid any attention to her anger before.

"Aton," she murmured, "You do anything you want. You—" Her voice cut off, as though she were afraid she had said too much.

"Jill, I won't make fun of you any more—ever," he told her, trying to stave off an excitement he did not understand nor wholly trust. He was sure, now: this had been her original intent. But did she truly know what it involved?

"You never made fun, Aton. Not really. Not so I minded."

He placed his hand on her blouse, deliberately now, pressing on the softness beneath. She did not object. He stroked, interested but not satisfied, and afraid, despite his bravado, to do more. Then, carefully, he tugged the material loose from her waistband. "Do you mind if I—?"

"Anything you want, Aton. You don't have to ask me. Here." She sat up. He lifted the blouse over her head, seeing her small breasts rise as her arms went up. She wore no bra.

Aton cupped one breast in his hand, feeling its delicate texture, running his thumb over the nipple. Holding her that way, he brought her sitting torso to his and kissed her again. This time there was fire. His tongue reached out to taste the sweetness of hers.

She sank back slowly, and he followed her, kissing her cheek, her throat, her breast. She brushed her fingers through his hair. "Salt—who needs it?" she inquired softly.

He forgot caution and put one hand on her knee, just below the spreading skirt. Her legs parted a little, and he slid his hand up over the kneecap and against the inside of her thigh. The flesh was smooth and very warm.

Throbbing anxiety took him. She had let him go this far; had he reached the limit? If he should expose himself, if he dared, would she take flight and bear a story to her parents that he could hardly deny?

His hand moved on, sliding past boundaries he had hardly dared imagine before. Abruptly it met the junction of her thighs. The soft down told him that she wore no underclothing here, either. Shivering with tension and excitement, he explored farther—and found a thick moisture.

Blood! he thought, shocked. I have trespassed and I have hurt her and now she is bleeding!

He snatched his hand away and lay beside her with the drumbeat of his heart filling the hideout. What have I done! he thought.

Visions of consequence obsessed his mind. The outrage of Eighty-One, the shame of Five. "Why did you do it, you lecherous juvenile!" they would say. "Don't you know you must never never touch a girl *there?*" Would they have to take her to a hospital? How would he ever get her back to her room?

The passion in him died, blasted away by his crime. His eyes stared into the faint cross-lace of branching shrubbery above, limned against the starry sky—a sky not one whit colder than the clutching terror in his heart. What have I—what— she's only thirteen!

Jill's hand touched his arm. "Aton?"

He jumped. "Believe me, I never meant to—"

"What's the matter with you, all of a sudden?" she demanded, rolling over to peer into his face.

Didn't she *know?* "The blood. There's blood."

She stared. "Blood? What are you talking about?"

"Down—between—I felt it. I never—"

"You're crazy. It's not the time of the—" Suddenly she giggled. *"Blood?* You mean you thought *that* was—? Haven't you ever done this before?"

He lifted his head, finding her hot breasts close under his chin. "Before?"

"You don't know!" she exclaimed, the thoughtless child in her ascendant over the dawning woman. "You really don't! And here all the time I was looking up to you, waiting for you. I thought you were the big boy."

Aton cowered behind his raging shame, unable to reply.

Abruptly she was the woman again. "I'm sorry, Aton. I guess you don't get out much. Here—I'll show you how—"

But he was on his hands and knees, scrambling away from her, barging out, finding the open night and running, sick with shock and embarrassment.

Three

Aton became a handsome, outwardly confident young man of twenty. He never spoke of his plans; on Hvee it was taken for granted that the son of high Family would advance to his father's fields. At last he received the summons he had known would come.

The living room of the house of Aurelius was generous and comfortable. A substantial hard-backed wooden chair, almost a throne, sat in a corner, parallel to the entrance; no one could exit without passing under the survey of that grim relic. A plush full-length couch lay against the far wall, seldom used. Above it, placed on the wall so that it faced Aurelius's chair, was a color photograph of a handsome young woman: Dolores Ten, dead these twenty years and more, in childbirth. Aton had never been able to face that picture without experiencing a deep and painful guilt, compounded by another and rather different emotion that never found conscious expression.

Aurelius Five was old, far nearer to death than his chronological age required. In health he would have been a powerful man, competent, determined, and scheduled to live another fifty years at least; but he was not in health, and only the power of his mind remained. He had exposed his body to the foul spring swamp ("spring" by convention only, on seasonless Hvee) too many years, and the incurable—locally—blight had taken hold. Aurelius, being what he was, had refused to spend a long convalescence on far-distant Earth, away from his farm. He had left the planet once, only once, and vowed never to do so again, and now he was in the process of dying for that vow. Aton, knowing something of the prior circumstance, agreed with the principle, though he never took it upon himself to tell his father so. They were not that close.

Aurelius might work three more years, and live five. Already he spoke slowly, tired too easily. He was the shell of his youth. The hvee tolerated him, but not gladly; too much of the swamp infested him now, anathema to the tender plants. His frame was gaunt: there seemed to be too little flesh between the hanging skin and brittle bone.

"Aton," the worn man said. "Soon—"

Aton stood beside his father, expecting to find no pleasure in the interview, but knowing that this had to be. There was too much of sorrow in their relationship, and each saw it in the other, with a premonition that that sorrow had not yet reached its nadir. They shared a cross that could not be put down until more than death had come to pass.

"Soon you must farm the hvee yourself," Aurelius said, speaking with all the certainty he could muster, pitiful in the implied insecurity of it. "Soon you must take your wife."

It was out—the condition he had feared. Farming was not a solitary occupation. The death of the daughter of Ten, wife to Aurelius, had damaged the crops of Five, and only Aton's early success had prevented complete ruin. The emotional climate had to be correct for hvee, and here it was not. The successful farm was run by a family, and the matches were most carefully made. The matter was far too important to be left to the idiosyncrasies of the young.

"Who is she?"

Aurelius smiled, taking the question for assent. "She is the third daughter of eldest Four," he said.

Four, eldest. This was a good match indeed. Aurelius deserved his tinge of pride. The possessors of First names preferred to have sons to carry on the lineage, but they protected their daughters by wifing them as prominently as possible. Many times the highborn daughters declined to marry at all, rather than drop in station. The ranking of Five was a favorable one, but there were many eager daughters below, and few above. There must have been complex negotiations.

Aton felt a pang, knowing that the effort had gone for nothing. The Families of Hvee were regarded by offworlders as aloof and cold, and in many ways they were; but within the formalistic structure the bonds were deep. Aton seldom spoke to his father, and the relationship between them was something less than usual even for this culture, but it did not surprise him to discover that Aurelius had gone to great pains to arrange an advantageous marriage. The line had to be continued honorably, and Aton was the only man bearing the name of Five who could accomplish this.

"No."

Aurelius went on. "For you, with a wife, a good wife, the hvee will grow. For you the farm will prosper. . . ." He drifted to a stop. Aton's answer had penetrated. He closed his tired eyes to shut in the hurt.

"I must take another," Aton said.

The old man did not try to argue, overtly. "She is strong, she is fair," he said. "I have seen her. On all of Hvee there is not a finer match. She is not like the—the degradingly promiscuous sluts of the latter Families. You would . . . love her."

Aton bowed his head, ashamed for himself and for his father. Aurelius had never stooped to pleading in his life, but he seemed close to it now.

"She is a song, a broken song in the forest," Aton said, trying to explain what could not be justified. Was he indeed afraid of a liaison with a local girl? He suppressed the thought immediately. "She kissed me and gave me my hvee; I can love no other."

Aurelius stiffened. Aton had not told him about the forest

nymph before. The matching procedures of the Families did
not deny the need for love; rather, they insisted upon it. The
ritual of the hvee guaranteed it. Aton could not marry without
his father's approval, but he did not have to accept a woman
he did not love.

"Show her to me," Aurelius said at last. He could not yield
more. If Aton could bring home his nymph, she would be
approved; if he could not, he was honor bound to give the
arranged betrothal a chance.

•   •   •

Twenty-one, and the music for which he longed came once
again. It was fleeting and haunting, but clear enough to his
eager listening. He made for the forest, cruising through the
several fields as rapidly as he could without damaging the hvee.

Aurelius signaled from a nearby field. He was not able to
work outside every day, but this time he had arranged it. He
intended to meet the nymph, and Aton had in effect agreed.
Aton waited in an agony of impatience for his father to catch
up.

It was the broken song, bending the very trees to its enchantment. It swelled, chord and descant, stirring Aton's blood
with its ultimate promise. This time, this time—

It ceased.

Aton sprinted for the glade, hurdling the well, leaving Aurelius behind. He burst upon it.

Too late. It was empty.

He stood absolutely still, listening for the sounds of her
departure, but he could hear nothing above the noise of the
man behind. She was gone.

Aurelius came up, panting and staggering. But his eyes
darted around the glade, fixing on the stump, the ground, the
circling trees. He pointed.

The dry leaves had been scraped away from one side of the
rotting stump, exposing the spongy loam below. Symbols had
been inscribed on the ground, hastily and crudely done by some
pointed instrument.

Aton studied them. "M-A-L-I-C-E," he spelled out. "What
does it mean?"

Aurelius eased himself down upon the crumbling stump, scrutinizing the mystic letters. His breath grew ragged and his hands trembled; Aton realized with unacknowledged compassion that the strenuous exercise had intensified the man's ague. "I was not sure," Aurelius whispered, his tone oddly apologetic.

Aton turned a questioning gaze to him.

Aurelius wrenched his eyes from the ground. He spoke with difficulty. "It is the stigma of the minionette."

Aton stared into the sky of Hvee, upset and confused by the nymph's flight. What had frightened her? Was she actually a creature not for the eyes of the skeptic? "Minionette?"

"Man took his legends with him when he went to space," Aurelius said. "Like man himself, they changed; but the stock is the same. You have heard of the terrible Taphids that consume entire spaceships; of the Xestian spidermen whose webpaintings penetrate an illusion; of the living hell of Chthon, where ultimate wealth and horror make eternal love. But this is the—the fable of the minionette.

"The minionette is a siren, an immortal sprite of untold beauty and strength, able to read a man's inmost passion. It is certain misery to love her—if love is what you can call the fascination compelled by her comeliness. It—it is said that if a man can only hold back his emotion long enough to force a kiss from her, the minionette will love him—and that is the most terrible fate of all."

This was the longest speech Aton had ever heard his father make, and the least pretentious. "But she was here. This—can't be true."

Aurelius sat still, his eyes tightly closed. "It is a mistake, Aton, to disparage the legends too readily. The minionette was here. Malice—she came for you, Aton—"

"Thanks," Aton said sharply, growing angry. "This ghost, this spook, this myth came to collect her little boy, the one who believes in her—"

"Try to understand, son—"

"I do understand! A girl was here, yes—a girl playing a game, all dressed and posed, ready to charm a simple country boy—"

"No, Aton. I must tell you what she is—"

"Damn your explanations!" Aton exploded, heedless of the

pain in his father's face. "I won't have you defending my
foolishness or the lewd posturings of an offworld siren. A
beautiful woman does not take up with a rustic innocent—
unless she intends only to lead him on, laughing at his animal
naïvete, his inexperience—"

But while he rattled his sabers at his helpless father, Aton
knew, underneath, the dark truth: he loved his nymph of the
forest, no matter what she was, what she had done. Next to
her, all other women were as rag dolls with painted smiles and
breasts stuck on in front, foolish giggles and disgusting moisture. He had had enough of this; at least the nymph had shown
him the futility of his existence. He had to go from here. He
would go to space, seek her out, and satisfy himself as to
exactly what she was—when the act was over. Fourteen years
of longing could not be dispatched so carelessly—not when
the Family was Five, not when the man was Aton. He would
force himself to face it, to face the truth, this time.

Aurelius, so unaccountably talkative moments ago, now sat
still, rigid, shriveled. Was the final seizure upon him? No; the
man lived. Was the conventional betrothal of his son that important? It was; it had to be—but it would have to wait. "If
I return . . . ," he said.

The old man did not pretend confusion. "We shall wait for
you, the hvee and I," Aurelius said, opening his eyes at last.

II. GARNET

4

The cavern passages went down, down, twisting wormlike through the stone. Hot lava had honeycombed this structure long ago, and been folded under, again and again, and powdered out at last to leave the endless passages.

Can all this really be sealed off, Aton thought, when the wind booms through so readily? Surely this hot blast comes from somewhere, and seeks its freedom somewhere. And where the wind escapes, so may a man.

But Tally's strong, narrow back, half hidden by the waterskin, was unresponsive. No use to inquire there. Even in this buried prison, mention of the minionette brought fear and hate. Safer not to bring up the matter, below.

At the lowest level a guard sat on a great flat slab of rock. A heavy rope was anchored beside him and tied to a large basket. Tally spoke sharply and the man stood up. Together they strained and ground the stone aside, exposing a sunken hole: this was the orifice leading to the nether prison.

Tally tossed the basket in, letting the cord writhe after it. Aton climbed into the hole, gripped the rope, wedged his book between his thighs, and handed himself down into the other world. A final glance at the peering face above: Will I ever see you again, you superstitious high-brow? Not likely.

He went carefully, unbalanced by the full water-skin and the book, unable to look down. *Was* there a landing here, or had he been tricked into a descent into a furnace? Had he been a fool to trust the man whose girl had—

Thirty feet below the hole he touched the floor. Rope and basket whisked up the moment he let go. The slab of rock ground over again, and for the second time he was isolated in an unknown hell.

There was light, at least—the same phosphorescent product of the walls. There was the wind, too; he had fought it on the rope without even thinking about it. The lower caverns were, after all, habitable.

"Garnet here. Take it."

Aton spun to face the speaker. This was a large man, topping him by three inches. His body, though running slightly to fat, displayed impressive musculature, and he shouldered a heavy double-bitted axe. His bushy hair and beard were brown.

Aton raised a hand to catch the glistening pebble tossed at him. It was a red translucent crystal, rather pretty: a garnet. He waited.

"You'll be working Garnet's mine. Any trouble, I'll settle it. Bossman. Come on."

So this was the farmer Tally had warned him about. Aton followed, watching the motion of the man. He did not appear to be in condition to fight, at least not Aton's way. Perhaps his reputation had made him soft. Or his axe—how had he managed to bring that with him?—might have provided a foolish security. There would come a time to make certain; but for now Aton planned to stay well clear of trouble while he scouted the situation for himself. Information was far more important than physical triumph. Knowledge, in time, would become mastery.

And—escape?

The wind abated as the passage expanded. A woman squatted to one side, a hunched monstrosity; but it was only the distortion of the water-skin on her back. She was sorting food into piles—rough bread, salted meat, other staples relayed from above—and wrapping each in a long dirty cloth for protection. Sanitation was not a concern, in Chthon—there was no illness here—but dehydration was. She stood as they approached.

"Man for you," Bossman said. He turned to Aton. "Give Garnet your stone."

Another time, he might have smiled. He held out the stone and Garnet took it, studying him intently. She was a solid, supple woman, too hefty to be good-looking. In a good light her hair might have been blonde. She picked up one of the food packages and gave it to him.

"That's how it is," Bossman said. "One garnet, one package. 'Denser's over there; you grind your own," indicating a spot down the hall. Aton made out the machine in a recess. "Time's your own, too—but don't mine anybody else's territory." He ambled off.

Garnet beckoned, and he followed her to an offshot cavern. She ushered him to a section of wall, well scarred and pitted. She left him there.

Aton looked about him. Men and women were working down the line on either side, chipping at the face with bits of broken stone. Some were sifting through rock dust with their bare hands. Others slept. Two were sitting together, eating and talking. The pace was hardly frenzied.

He studied the wall. No garnets were visible. He thought of pounding loose large chunks with a heavy stone, then realized that this would probably powder any garnets in the way. It would be necessary to go very carefully.

He found a niche for *LOE* and his lunch, picked up a sharp stone, and tapped the middle section of his mine experimentally. He was rewarded by a choking puff of dust and grit. How many had died here from silicosis? He held back his head and tried again. This time it was difficult to see what he was doing. He could destroy a valuable stone before spotting it. This mining was not the easiest of tasks.

In the next mine downwind a small wiry man observed the

proceedings, a faint smile tugging at his features. "Got a better way?" Aton asked, frustrated.

The man came over. He borrowed Aton's stone, held it to the wall, gently tapped it with his own. The surface began to scale away with a minimum of interference. He leaned over and blew out the dust, careful to keep his face upwind from the cut. He returned Aton's tool and went back to his own domain.

Aton stared after him, suspicious of this act of instruction. Were these the fiercest of humanity's prisoners? But he experimented with the new method, gaining proficiency.

After an hour of fruitless chipping he retired to eat his meal. The food tasted uncommonly good. He went to refill his waterskin, then came back to attack his mine again.

Several hours passed. He excavated a fair-sized hole, but found no sign of a garnet. The scattered pocks left by the removal of earlier garnets mocked him. He resented the facility of the unknown person who had succeeded where Aton was failing. He began to understand why the other miners did not bother him: the business of making a living was too important. This was grinding, mind-deadening labor, cramping his forearms, tiring his legs. When he shut his eyes he saw a vision of the blank, pitted, pitiless wall; when he opened them, they smarted and blurred.

At length there was a general exodus, and Aton followed, picking up the routine by observation. They went to Garnet's office, where she was handing out new packages. The men and women formed into a rough line, each in turn offering a single gem in exchange for the meal.

Aton, of course, was empty-handed.

Garnet accepted no explanations. No garnet, no food.

"Don't cry on my shoulder, Five," she told him irritably. "You've got to learn to work down here, newcomer. You don't get nothing for nothing. Better go look for a stone."

Aton left, tired and angry. His hands were raw and blistered, his lungs choking from the dust. He was hungry, but the vacant wall offered no hope.

His little neighbor approached: coarse black hair, bright black eyes. "No food?" Aton nodded. "Look, pal, she won't never give you nothing to eat 'less you got a stone. You got to have a garnet."

Aton was unimpressed with the news. "I know that," he snarled. "I forgot to pick one up."

The man dropped his voice confidentially. "Well, look, see, like if I was to do you a favor, would you be my pal? Name's Framy. Like if I was to give you a stone . . ."

Aton studied him, not certain of the gist. What kind of proposition was this? The man was cringingly eager. If he were a pervert—

"No, I ain't!" Framy exclaimed. Aton made a mental note to be more careful of his expression. The man's petulance seemed genuine. What could he want, then? Company or protection? Was he a pariah? Was his friendship dangerous?

Aton's stomach growled. The man might very well be useful, if he had garnets. Protection was a useful commodity. "Maybe," he said, and introduced himself.

Framy poked a dirty finger into his mouth and popped out a glittering stone. Aton concealed his surprise. How else could a naked man safely store a semi-precious jewel? "Here," Framy said, proffering the moist garnet. "I got an extra. You take it and get a package. Then you come back to me. Remember, I done you a favor."

Aton accepted it. Moments later he turned it over to Garnet. She took it and examined it suspiciously. "Well, I guess you got one," she conceded reluctantly. She kicked the last package over to him. "You can have what's left."

He moved off, tearing it open hungrily. The cloth unraveled and fell free, empty. "There's nothing here," he said, showing it to her.

"I forgot to tell you, mister. You came too late. Food's all gone." She turned her back to him.

"But my garnet—you took my garnet!"

She didn't bother to look at him. "Too bad. No refunds."

Aton fought down the urge to grab the tangled mat of hair and drag her through the coarse gravel. The incongruity of the situation struck him: here he was, quite naked, facing a similarly unclad woman—and his most immediate ambition was to knock out her teeth.

But he didn't dare. He could not be certain that Bossman would meet him alone, in case he were to offer careless resistance to the crude hierarchy. Massed force might destroy him. Escape was far more important than immediate satisfaction.

He could not take vengeance physically. But there were other weapons. Many times would Garnet regret the enemy she had made this moment.

5

There was a certain feel to garnet hunting, a talent that permitted some to discover the stones easily, almost intuitively, while others strained all day (Chthon definition) only to finish hungry. Framy had it. He seemed to smell the precious quarry, and his appetite for riches was insatiable. Aton developed a fair talent; he did not go hungry again, but his reserve never grew large. Each man maintained a private cache, and Framy, at least, labored regularly in the mine more for the sake of appearance than need. A man too quick at finding garnets could become unpopular, and he and his cache were in danger from the hungry ones. Framy had done well to befriend a man like Aton; this was soon apparent.

There were many types in the lower caverns. Not all of the inhabitants were wholly sane, but once their idiosyncrasies were known life was compatible. One fought when one had to, never for amusement; one yielded upon occasion to unreason and stayed clear of trouble unless one wanted it.

One man stood out amid the steady grind for garnets. He was notable because he was a nonsurvival type who managed to survive nicely. This was the grossly obese Hastings: intelligent, knowledgeable, cheerful, quick with his hands, but with a complete vacuity of talent for mining, and perpetually unlucky. He survived as an entrepreneur. He won his garnets from men, rather than from stone.

"I need a blue garnet as I need Laza's love," fat Hastings expounded during a break. The others gaped at him, rising to the bait.

"Hasty, Hasty—you know what a blue garnet *is?*" Framy

asked incredulously. "You know what a blue garnett'll *do* for a man?"

The other edged in, anticipating a show.

"I know what it'll do for a man," Hastings said. "It'll kill him so fast the chimera wouldn't pick up the pieces." The "chimera" was the cavern name for a deadly predator of the fringe caverns that no person had ever seen—and lived.

"I'll take that chance," a man said. "Just gimme the garnet."

Aton was curious. "I've never heard of a blue one."

"Oh, Fiver," Framy said, dusting himself off in the center of the group. "Lemme expoun' to you the facts of life. You know how the little ones we find are red, and maybe a brown one once awhile? Well, there's other kinds too, we don't latch on to often. Worth more. Like if you got a black one, you tap ol' bitch Garnet for a week's chow, maybe more. And if you got a chunk of pure white jadeite—well, ol' man Chessy upstairs is hard up for the stuff, and he'll pull for you something awful, you sneak him a message. 'Nuff of that stuff, you don't have to mine no more.

"Well, these'r little fish. You ever grab hold a blue garnet, it's your ticket to freedom."

Aton's interest abruptly intensified.

Framy was enjoying himself. He scratched his hair. "Yep. They'll let you go. You won't be punished no more. Free as a bird in the big outside."

The others nodded agreement, sharing the dream. "But you'll never see one," a woman said.

"That's right," another put in. "Ain't none of us seen a blue garnet. Ain't none never will. Ain't none."

"That's a lie!" Framy screamed.

"Don't call me a liar, you little liar!" the woman said angrily. She had sharp features and black hair winding down her back. Few of the women in the lower prison were pretty, but this one was; she still looked deceptively young and soft. "I'll poke your beady little eyeballs back into your dirty little brain," she continued.

Framy cringed, then came back boldly. "Not with my pal Fiver here, you won't. He'll get you good."

It hadn't occurred to Aton that the woman's threat might be literal. But it was; she had nails like talons. She now eyed him speculatively. "I reckon I can handle him awright," she said. She inhaled to make her fine bosom stand out. "How about it, mister?"

This too was literal, and not entirely unattractive. But not now. Aton attempted a return to the subject. "What's so deadly about the blue garnet, Hasty?"

"So your last names's Five," Hastings mused, as though he had just discovered the fact. "They call that the pixie number, you know. Dangerous. Only name I ever heard that translates into itself."

"What're you talking about?" Framy demanded.

Hastings held out a fleshy palm.

Framy fought his curiosity and lost. He spat out a small garnet and handed it over. Hastings considered Framy his prime customer.

"Science of numerology," Hastings said, and the people around settled back comfortably, listening. "Every number from 1 to 9 has its vibration. You add up the vowels—*A* is 1 because it's first in the old English alphabet, *E* is 5 because it's fifth, and so on—you add them up, and add again, until you have a single number. Each one has its influence—1 is the beginning, 2 is slow, and so on down the line."

"But how does 5—?"

"Spell it out. F-I-V-E. That *I* is worth 9; the *E*, 5. Add them up to make 14. That's too big, so add the one and the four to each other to get your number: 5."

Framy's face lighted. "Five is 5!" he said, delighted with the discovery. Someone snickered, but he was oblivious. He would be translating people to numbers for many shifts to come.

Suddenly he sobered. "You say 5 is dangerous?"

"Full of surprises. 5 can bring a fortune out of the blue—or sudden death. Really has to watch his step."

Aton steered the subject back once more. "You were talking about the special garnet."

Hastings settled his belly back comfortably. He waited. The others chuckled: it was Aton's turn to cough up the stake.

"Well, take a look at it this way," Hastings said after the transaction. "A blue garnet is valuable. So valuable that a man might bribe his way to freedom with it. That's a commendable price. Perhaps there are no blues, so the authorities believe they're safe; or it may be their subtle way of telling us that there is no such thing as a reprieve. But if there *is* such a thing—a blue garnet, I mean—it is certain that it is a lot more valuable than a prisoner or a principle. Now all of us here are criminals—"

"I ain't!" Framy yelled. "I ain't no criminal. I was—"

"FRAMED!" the group chorused.

"Well, I was," Framy said, hurt.

". . . Criminals, imprisoned here for the rest of our unnatural lives. There isn't any one of us here who doesn't want to get out more than anything else he can think of. There isn't any one of us who has a chance at all, unless he wants to take the Hard Trek. Except for the one who happens to uncover the blue stone.

"Now if I had a blue garnet right here in my hand, like this"—he extended a closed fist—"and I said, 'Gentlemen, I have found eureka and I'm going to leave you now . . .!'"

The fingers of his hand slipped apart a little, accidentally, it seemed. A touch of blue showed through. They watched in shocked silence.

Hastings made as if to rise. "Well, freedom is calling me!" he sang out gaily. "Be seeing you—never!"

Three flying bodies crashed him to the floor, as two men and a woman launched themselves simultaneously. One grabbed his outflung arm and wrenched the hand open with cruel force. A fragment of blue cloth fluttered out.

They turned him loose silently, the avarice in their faces fading. Hastings heaved himself upright, rubbing his arm. "Maybe you get my meaning now," he said. "You can't go free unless you make your garnet known. And when you do . . ."

·   ·   ·

Garnet was hard on Aton. She reviled him every time she saw him, and lost no opportunity to make him miserable. His meals were difficult. Garnet claimed that his offerings were too small or had flaws, or merely denied he had given her one, thus forcing two or even three for a single package.

Aton took it. He never argued with her, always thanked her

for the food as though she were doing him a favor. He stood silent while she yelled at him, simply looking at her. At times he would come to her for no apparent reason, just to sit and listen to her scream at him.

Framy couldn't understand it. "What you want to hang around her for?" he inquired incredulously. "There's lots better women'n her. Nice bodies and soft tongues, and they got the eye for you, Fiver, oh, my, they do. Like that sexy slut with the black hair. Why fool with the biggest bitch in the pit?"

Aton didn't answer.

Garnet grew progressively more violent. It was not uncommon for her to strike him with her fist, or to kick him. Something was driving her to fury. Aton accepted it with equanimity, sometimes even smiling.

There was no night or day in Chthon, but the prisoners tended to slip into a typical cycle of labor and rest oriented on the regular meals. Most worked in company, though the mines were fiercely individual, and retired to private caves to sleep. Aton chose his own hours, and so happened to be working alone when Garnet came upon him as he was chipping out an unusually large gem.

She began cursing him immediately. "Keep working, you dirty bastard," she shouted, as he stopped to give her courteous attention. Aton only smiled—in the caverns, strictly speaking, everyone was dirty. Washing was done by the action of sand and wind. The standard epithet referred to more than physical status. "This ain't no vacation."

"I know, my dear."

Her mouth fell open. Speechless with rage, she scooped up a stone and bashed it against the gem in the wall. Aton glanced at the ruin and took hold of her.

"It seems you have taken your payment," he said, a new note in his voice. "Now it is time for you to render service."

She struck at him. He knocked away the stone and took her down on the cavern floor. He was far stronger than she, as his genes were derived from the modified stock of the heavy-gravity Hvee colony. Quick blows to selected nerves made her stiffen with pain; shock made her passive for the moment, though she retained full consciousness and sensation.

Then realization came, and she struggled violently, but there was nothing she could do. No broken song stopped him this time, and Garnet had the protection of neither clothing nor experience.

It was over at his convenience, and he let her go. She stumbled away, cursing in a whisper and not knowing how to cry. He knew she would never speak of the matter; her shame was not the forgotten role revisited upon her, but the fact that he had been the one to master her, in every sense of the word.

The image of Malice was in his mind as he brushed away the blood-red fragments of the shattered garnet. I had no pleasure from you, he thought, not even that of conquest.

6

"Five, Fiver, you got to come with me right now!" Framy was more excited than Aton had ever seen him before. "You got to come, you got to see it, you got to."

Framy was a high-strung individual, but this was something out of the ordinary. Aton went.

Framy led the way upwind, far outside the habited caverns. "I been exploring," he explained breathlessly. "I been looking for something. . . ."

He had been looking far afield. Aton was glad for the chance to scout the outlying area; he had not had a pretext before. The strength of the gale increased as they went, and the heat blasted into their faces fiercely. They paused often to gulp huge quantities of water.

The journey seemed interminable. For more than an hour they plunged into the furnace draft, fighting mounting pressure. At last the little man stopped.

"Around that corner," he gasped. "Put your head around, careful, so you can see it."

Aton obliged, gripping the ridged wall as well as he could. The heat and wind intensified, and his eyes burned and blurred almost immediately. He wondered, fleetingly but not for the first time, what possible origin there could be for a subterranean holocaust such as this. He'd probably never know; the secret was protected by its own temperature.

The cave ahead was like any other, with a high ceiling and an opening at the far end from which the wind howled ravenously. The luminescence from the walls was brighter here, and of a different texture. The greater heat and agitation might be responsible—except that the glow had been decreasing up to this point. Aside from this mystery, the scene was not distinctive.

Something caught his eye. Aton studied the ceiling. There, from long corrugations, water was dropping and evaporating into the rushing air. This was where the moisture came from, for the condensers. That evaporation probably also exerted considerable cooling power. It might be the only thing that made these caverns bearable at all.

"The floor! Look at the floor!" Framy was shouting in his ear. Aton forced his bleary eyes to focus and looked.

There, at the far edge of the grotto, on the verge of the tunnel beyond, was a single glowing blue garnet.

They withdrew to relative shelter to consider the situation. "I saw it," Aton said. "I saw it. But remember Hasty's warning—"

Framy was practically dancing with excitement. "I don't care what Fatsy said. I got to have that rock."

"It would be better just to leave it alone. You'd never make it out of Chthon. That gem is death."

Framy turned on him fiercely. "You want me to leave it so's you can take it yourself. You want to get out worse'n anybody. I know you—"

Aton stared him down. "I'm sorry, pal," the little man said. "I know you wouldn't do nothing like that. But look—I just got to have it. I got to."

Aton said nothing.

"Look," Framy began again, desperately. "It ain't like I was a criminal like everyone else here. I don't mean nothing against you, Fiver. I don't know what you done. But I was framed. It ain't right I should be down here. I got to get out.".

You fool, Aton thought, don't you know that you are better off here than you could ever be outside? Your own mind has framed you into suicide.

Seeing his companion still deep in thought, Framy spoke more rapidly. "It ain't as if—ain't like anybody'd know I had it. I'd hide it in the skin 'til I had a chance to smuggle out a message. Tally, upstairs, wouldn't cheat—"

Would you offer your heart to the chimera? thought Aton.

Aton came to a decision. "All right. Who's going to fetch it?"

It was a good question. They huddled against the wall near the bend, increasingly aware of the enormous heat rushing by, knowing how much worse it would be on the other side of the water-drip. Already their drinking supply was low. It would take a strong man to reach the garnet and return.

But Framy was undismayed. "That's why I needed you," he admitted. "I'da told you anyway, Five pal, but—I figured if I run for it I can make it to the stone. But in case I don't make it, I got to have someone to pull me back. Remember, I done you a favor—"

You should not have done that favor. The wage of carelessness is death.

"I think I've heard that reasoning before," Aton said. "But if you're fool enough to try it, I'm fool enough to haul you back. We'd better get on with it before we fry."

"Thanks, pal," Framy said simply. He plunged ahead immediately with a bravery that belied his reputation. Aton saw him rocked back against the wall by the hot gust. Framy shielded his face with a forearm and forced his way onward. He was out of the full current, driving along the side wall, but his progress was still agonizingly slow. He was leaning forward against the pressure, feet placed and braced most carefully. The skin of his arm reddened with the heat.

At length he reached the edge of the far tunnel. Here the draft abated, missing the small pocket formed by the projecting rock surrounding the opening. But Aton knew that the channeled flow would be ferocious directly in front of the tunnel. That was where the garnet sat, trapped in a minor declivity. It must have rolled there from the room beyond, perhaps many years ago.

Framy put a tentative hand out into the blast and withdrew it quickly. Here it was really hot. The drops from the ceiling vanished into the wind several feet below this spot. Then, gathering himself for a final effort, Framy dived for the garnet.

Aton saw the man's body caught by the current and hurled

sideways. He felt the terrible pain. But one hand was on the garnet, gripping it tightly. Framy had his blue ticket to destruction.

He rolled with the wind and struggled to pull himself out of it, into the shelter to the side. But his efforts were weak, haphazard, disorganized by pain; soon they ceased altogether. He was unconscious, and would soon be dead.

Aton charged into the room. He too was caught by the power of the air and tossed back against the nearer wall. He dropped to hands and knees, ducked his head behind his shoulder, inched toward the prone figure. His knees skidded against the smooth surface as the center stream took hold. It was hard to breathe.

Aton lowered himself to his belly and heaved forward. He no longer tried to look where he was going, as the wind buffeted head and body; human eyes could not endure the strain. He concentrated on his blind direction, his head cleaving the holocaust. He did not know when he reached the body.

Realizing that the thing he was crawling over was an arm, Aton took hold and tried to reverse. His eyes smarted painfully the moment he opened them; it was better to be blind. But he was unable to turn around while hanging on to the arm. He sat up.

The blast of wind caught him again and flipped him over. For one brief moment his eyes popped open, bringing him a tormented but perfect picture of the cavern beyond the garnet's spot. Then he was on his belly again, feet in the wash, toes blistering, hands dragging a pinioned arm as he wriggled, like a sightless, dehydrated worm, away from the kiln.

He found himself emerging from the hell room, unaware of anything that had transpired since the vision of the far cavern. He must have been only partly conscious himself, dragging on by instinct. He twisted around to sight along the arm he clasped, and discovered that Framy was still attached to it. Framy's other hand still clutched the garnet.

Aton gulped water feverishly from the water-skin that was propped in an alcove, then put both hands to his mouth to stop the invaluable fluid from spewing out again. His bag was now empty; he found Framy's and forced the last of that supply down the man's barely conscious throat. The need was imperative—there were blisters and bruises all over Framy's body.

Why didn't we think to pour all the water into one skin, and use the other for a shield? he thought, too tired to be angry.

Framy revived at last. "We got to get out of here," he rasped. He clutched his treasure and leaned on Aton as they stumbled down the passage.

Both men regained strength as distance eased the sirocco. Once the wind diminished and cooled, their progress was better. They could afford to let it boost them along. Half an hour saw them well on the way home.

But it was not over yet. Framy skidded to a precipitous halt. "Five. Look!"

A small monster barred their path. Animals were few in Chthon, and almost never seen by man, but they did exist and were invariably formidable. The chimera was the worst, but there were other terrors, too. This one was a nine-inch lizard-like creature, red as a garnet. Deep-set and evil eyes glared burningly; a wrinkled jaw opened and closed with spasmodic intensity.

"Salamander!" Framy whispered.

Aton had heard of them. The miniature fire lizards inhabited the upwind caverns. They were fast and vicious and could leap high, and their tiny jaws secreted deadly poison. One scratch, even one squirt of it on blistered skin, and it would be over.

"We could outrun it," Aton said.

"Where? Back there?"

The salamander did not allow them time to discuss the matter. It charged, fat little legs scratching on the rock. Awkward it might appear, but it was making a good five miles per hour against the wind.

They wheeled as one and ran back up the passage. The wind seemed to strike with renewed force, pushing them back. The lizard followed with grim determination, losing ground, but grudgingly. It was evident that it could maintain the pace a lot longer than the suddenly exhausted men. The feeling of strength engendered by downwind travel was illusory.

Ordinarily a man could outrun a salamander, since its cruising speed was limited and largely independent of the wind. But

Aton and Framy were trapped in unfavorable conditions, and had neither space nor strength to make an escape upwind. Yet it would be foolhardy to wait; bare hands and feet were no match for a creature that could jump and bite at will in close quarters. The passage was too narrow; the weapons impotent. Oh, for Bossman's axe!

Framy ground to a halt. "I'm beat," he gasped. "I can't go no more."

Aton tried to help him along, but was too fatigued himself to do enough. The salamander was gaining. The adventure in the cave of the blue garnet had taken too much out of both of them.

"No use," Framy said. "Just one thing to do." With a supreme effort he held out the garnet. "You got a good arm?"

Aton didn't argue. He took the glinting gem, hefting its two-ounce weight carefully. He fired it at the oncoming lizard.

His aim was low. The stone bounced on the floor directly before its target and cracked into two pieces. One of them sailed over the creature's head; the other caught it in the middle of the body, skittering it sideways a few inches. Stung, the salamander pounced vengefully on the fragment, jaws clamping in a vicious bite.

They did not stay to watch the result. There was little question what a garnet fragment would do to a set of clamping teeth. They hurdled the thrashing monster and ran on down the passage to safety.

"It wouldn't have been any good anyway," Aton said when they slowed, knowing the emotion Framy felt at the loss of his prize. "It had a flaw. Garnets don't break like that."

"We could've used the skins," Framy said.

This was the second time Aton's mind had betrayed him under pressure, the second time proper use of the water-skins would have reduced their risk. Throw one at the lizard, bury it, if only for a moment—what had prevented him from trying that?

Now the garnet was gone. The blue garnet that could never bring freedom, except in the most devious way. The caverns would riot if they knew of it; no integrity was secure in the face of such a lure.

"Best not to tell—" he said.

"Who'd believe me?"

The secret would be kept, for a time.

And what of the larger secret? Aton asked himself. The one that could generate such chaos as to destroy both worlds of Chthon? Am I to tell them what I saw in that one brief glimpse of the far cavern, as the wind flipped me over?

Must it remain unknown: an entire passage lined with lustrous blue crystal?

Four

"Machinist Five to Hold Seven, Cargo. Emergency." Aton shut down his machine and grabbed his shirt as the foreman waved him on.

"That's the Captain! Take priority routing."

Why should I jump when the Captain calls? Aton thought. I'm not in the Navy any more. Three years, and they taught me two things: machinery and personal combat. Now I'm twenty-four years old and still looking for my woman—the darling bitch who charmed me so easily in the forest. I don't have to jump for anybody, except for her.

He stepped into the nearest trans booth, fastened himself inside the waiting capsule, punched the code for Hold Seven. As the vehicle began to move down its track he hit the PRIOR-ITY stud and hung on.

They made me a machinist after all. I had to have a trade to travel in space, and that meant taking what the Navy offered.

I had to wait through that enlistment, with that love burning inside. But I learned how to search for a camouflaged woman, oh, yes.

The sealed capsule popped into the vacuum tunnel and accelerated. Its internal relays clicked as it plotted a course through the labyrinth, flashing past intersections and other traffic. It was a miniature spaceship, traversing this hidden network as the *Jocasta* traversed the hidden network of the stars. For this capsule, the walls did not exist; it could reach any outlet in moments. For the larger ship—

The § drive—more properly called the F.T.L.—(Faster Than Light drive)—whose discovery dated man's novalike fling into space, was more of an effect than a science. Professor Feetle, the smiling legend said, had discovered it one day as he eased himself into his villa pool. As the water rose to accommodate his descending corpulence, and apple flew over the roof and bounced on his head. His poolside recorder, triggered into action by the key words "displacement" and "gravity," faithfully monitored the ensuing harangue. In due course this excerpt was transcribed by the robot-secretary, who made tasteful substitutions for frequent blasphemous expressions and references to neighboring juveniles, and forwarded the product to a technical bulletin whose robot-editor printed the report verbatim. Fifteen free-lance research companies attempted to construct the device outlined. Twelve gave it up within a year, two discovered serendipitous side effects and forgot about the original specification, and the last had a diode misconnected by an incompetent robot-employee and came up with §.

At first the device was not recognized as anything more than a perpetual-motion machine. It was bald and corpulent and tended to run around in circles while emitting angry squeals. An inquiry to Professor Feetle brought a furious suit for character assassination. Tested in space, it accelerated from an initial impetus of something less than an inch per second to something less than a foot per second in the course of an hour. During the second hour it attained a velocity several times as great. Eventually it caromed with such vigor that only instruments could track it. Finally it disappeared: although it had never left its self-determined orbit, it was gone.

Almost gone: the instruments picked up strange trace radiation—Cherenkov rays, the wake left by an impulse that exceeds the speed of light through a given medium. In this case the medium was a virtually perfect vacuum.

Professor Feetle withdrew his suit and took an active interest in his creation. But after that, the legend continued less benignly, censorship cast its mantle over the proceedings. It was rumored that the § device, once activated, drew its power from some unknown source—some power limitless in nature; that ships were constructed around large § devices and sent into some limbo that light itself was too coarse to penetrate; that not all of these ships returned; that there were malignant ghosts in far space, or nonspace.

Out of all this emerged the standard § ship; a full-sized vessel with a crew of thousands and a drive that could take it anywhere. Such a ship was the *Jocasta;* her velocity was governed by logarithmic ratio. The number of hours in which she accelerated could be taken as the exponent of that power of 10 required to express her speed in miles per hour. Thus when the ship's § clock registered 2, it meant that the drive had been functioning for two hours and that the speed of the ship relative to her starting point was 10^2, or one hundred miles per hour.

Oh, yes, Aton thought, as his capsule banked and spun, the § ships started slowly. But 8.83 on the ship's clock was faster than the speed of light, 186,000 miles per second. Thirteen on the clock represented a full light-year per hour, and 16 was the signal to begin deceleration, since the drive could not be disengaged while any number showed on the clock and higher speed would fling the ship out of the galaxy.

A day and a half, objective Earth time, could take such a ship anywhere in the galaxy.

The capsule slowed, bringing Aton's mind back to practical matters. He pushed through the seal, re-entering normal pressure. His journey, whether of rods or of lightyears, was over.

Five

Captain Moyne was waiting impatiently for him. He had never met her before in person, but it was not possible to mistake her. She was a handsome woman of indeterminate age, sleek and severe in the merchant service uniform. Her lips were almost colorless; her hair was bound in a tight skullcap and hidden under her helmet. Her face showed no trace of the ravage of twenty-four years in space. She was cordially disliked by the crew: a dislike she cultivated assiduously.

Why was she alone? An emergency should have the officers of the ship flocking impotently about her. And what was she doing in an obscure cargo hold?

"Five," she said without preamble. "Seven's refrigerant has broken down. We have thirty minutes, no more."

Aton followed her to the hold. "Captain, I think you ordered the wrong man. I'm a machinist."

She broke open a locker with practiced competence and removed a set of space suits. "I have the right man."

"Look, I can't fix a cooling system with press and die—"

The Captain whirled and caught his shirt with a slender hand. She yanked the fastenings open, reached inside, flipped out a thin booklet hidden in an inside pocket. "Is this not an illegal copy of the ship's lay roster?" she asked.

She had him. Prosecution on that score would net him two years in prison and a lifetime proscription against space employment. The lay roster of a merchant ship was a classified document.

"You're the captain, Captain," he said.

She flung a suit at him. "Put this on."

He hesitated. His heavy overalls would not fit inside the light suit.

The Captain caught his thought immediately. "Strip. We can't spare the time for modesty." Matching action to word, she stepped out of her own uniform, the scant underclothing revealing an astonishing well-proportioned figure, and climbed efficiently into her space suit.

Aton followed, still uncertain what was to be required. She did not leave him long in doubt.

"Our margin may be twenty minutes, but we can't take the chance. We've got to move this cargo in Seven over to Eight, where the cooling mechanism is functioning. We'll work together as long as possible; then I'll cover you with the hydrant.

Don't waste any time at all, but don't shake up the caskets any
more than necessary. Let's get to work."

"Cover me with the—*what's in that hold?*"

She picked up one of the boxes and marched out of the
room. "Turlingian Aphids."

The box in his hands quivered as her meaning sank in. The
Taphids! The eaters of spaceships!

Captain Moyne explained the situation in snatches as they
worked. "They're insects, grubs. Considered a delicacy on a
number of planets. Have to be shipped live, but the low temperature keeps them in hibernation. When it warms, they begin
feeding. First their own casing, then the cargo. Then anything
else, including the crew. Can't stop them; they'll bore through
metal, in time. Have to keep them cold and quiet. Clock's at
13 now. We can't bail out."

That was a considerable understatement. It was not physically possible to leave a ship traveling beyond the speed of
light. The outside universe simply did not exist for it. Five
hours deceleration could drop them into sublight—if the hunger
of the Taphids could wait that long. And the economic and
political consequences—

"Is this a legal cargo?"

"Don't be naïve. Why do you think I sent for you?"

Why, indeed. The Captain, it appeared, was a ruthless busi-
nesswoman. Strictly speaking, no interstellar commerce could
be considered illegal, since no planet could enforce its laws
beyond its immediate sphere of influence and no jurisprudence
existed formally on a larger scale. But a certain body of common law had grown up and gained steadily in power, and
individual policies were similar enough to encourage travel and
trade, particularly among those planets which took pride in
reputation. Sector law and the sector police force existed in
name only; the idea of such power alarmed the fiercely independent colonies far more than that of criminal behavior.

But violation of the common-law code was apt to blacklist
the offender on many prosperous worlds. No merchant ship
could afford that. The Captain had reason for secrecy.

Half the caskets were moved without event. Then it began.
The box Aton was carrying bulged. Pinpricks speckled the

surface, then nail holes. His heavy gloves transmitted unmistakable motion from within; then horny white maggots spewed out. The Taphid menace had awakened.

Aton stared at the sandpaper-surfaced arthropods for a perilous moment, then dropped the box. It burst open immediately and foamed with slimy bodies. The maggots sensed him unerringly and advanced across the floor in a white wave.

"Faceplate!" the Captain snapped behind him. He fastened it barely in time; a stream of freezing foam was already on the way. She had turned the hydrant on him. Now he understood the reason for the suits. The foam would have killed him in minutes if it had caught him without protection.

The creatures on the floor curled and subsided, reflexing into hibernation. But already the remaining caskets were writhing. "Hurry!" the Captain's voice came in his earphone, over the sigh of the suit's air circulation. "I can only cover one at a time."

His mind and body recoiled from the contact, but Aton understood too well the consequence of delay. He picked up the burst container and carried it into the refrigerated hold. The Captain stood in the doorway and sprayed him intermittently with foam, alternating with shots at the stacked boxes in Seven. The Taphid was not dangerous while frozen—but the margin was thin. If the hydrant failed—

Aton hurried.

·   ·   ·

He cleaned up in the Captain's apartments. He could not afford to be questioned about the nature of his duty at Hold Seven, and his uniform, forgotten in the rush, had been soaked in foam. There were also certain other matters to discuss before they parted company.

He emerged from the lavatory to discover the Captain reclining in a simple dress. Her hair was unbound and hung in dull-brown tresses. She looked young, too young to be capable of the nerve and power he had seen. Appearance was illusion; she was tough, and there was a battle to come. It would be fatal to let her pose undermine him.

Aton evaluated his assets: he had done her a service that could very well have saved the ship, and he had information that could force her resignation from the merchant service. But she was still the captain, with a captain's powers, and had similar goods on him. Stalemate, unless one of them made a mistake. Or lost his nerve.

"Sit down, Aton," she said, indicating a place on the couch beside her. Her voice was soft, almost musical. She was, he realized with a start, playing up to him. Was she in search of more than a handyman? Or had she coolly elected to use sex appeal to improve her position? What were her limits?

"The lay system," she said, beginning the fencing, "is a most convenient method for the arrangement of equitable remuneration for the members of a merchant voyage."

It was. The system had been borrowed from the practice of ancient whaling and sealing ships on old Earth. The members of the crew received, in lieu of pay, a certain share of the profits. Fiftieth lay represented one fifieth of the total, and so on. Even a two-thousandth lay could come to an attractive figure, if the voyage was good. Every crewman had an interest in the economic welfare of the enterprise.

Aton nodded and applied the precept of best defense. "Shipment of Taphids must remunerate well indeed."

She smiled. "The owners, of course, take second lay—half the profit."

"What lay does the Taphid take?"

The Captain refused to give way. "The *Jocasta's* lays go on down to four-thousandth for the recruit crewman—"

"Two-thousandth, for experienced machinists," Aton said, moving closer. "But sometimes there are hazardous duties—"

"Fractional lays have to be figured at every port—"

"And the refrigeration checked—"

"In case a crewman resigns and demands his share—"

"Or his next-of-kin demands it—"

Her eyes were gray, almost green. "Therefore the lay roster is a comprehensive manual identifying every person on the ship."

"And all legal cargo." Her hair seemed brighter, coppery.

"Possession by unauthorized persons is felonious—"

"As is shipment of the maggot," Aton finished.

Her lips were firm and close. "However—" she said.

Aton kissed her.

He moved into it shrewdly, conscious of his power over this woman, prepared to complete the tacit understanding by whatever token was required. He knew that something more than mutual liability was in order; neither one could allow the other to go forth with damning intent. But this was no more than the intellectual machination of survival. On the emotional level his heart was weighed by the disappointing search for the minionette—if, indeed, she existed as such. The Captain interested him only as a complication, not as a woman.

But a strange fire took him as his lips touched hers. What had been calculated art became guileless reality. He wanted her as the woman.

She twisted free. "Why did you do it?" she asked.

Aton suppressed the frustration of sudden rejection and chose to interpret the question as business. "The lay roster? Call it the same reason you smuggle Taphids." The debate had no interest for him now. He was angry, angry that he could be aroused and cut off so readily. But what he had said to her was the truth: their understanding did not require that their deeper motives be advertised. The two of them had a balance of a sort. It had to remain.

She leaned toward him, applying the lure again. What was the matter with her? He had to admit it was effective; already the yearning for her was reappearing. This was no woman to trifle with. He had never been subjected to such a campaign, never been susceptible to it. He declined to play the game, this time; he would not kiss her again.

"What is it that you wear," she asked, "in your hair?" There was a slight pause in her question that disturbed him. She had been intending to say something else, or perhaps to say it in a different way. He had assumed that the slight affectation in her speech was a function of rank—but she was not playing Captain with him now, and it remained.

He took down the plant. "This is my hvee. It lives on air and love—its love for its companion. If it were to be taken from me, it would die."

She lifted it from his hand. "I have heard of the hvee fable," she murmured, studying it. "Charming."

Again Aton was angry, unreasonably. He had thought the Taphid a fable, until this day. It was not surprising that others did not give credence to the unique property of the hvee. "I'll demonstrate," he said, taking it back. He set it on a table across the cabin and stepped back.

The hvee held its bloom for a moment. Then its leaves began to wilt. Aton returned quickly and picked it up, and strength came back to it, making the plant green and fresh and whole again. "No fable."

The Captain's eyes were bright. "What an enchanting liaison," she said. "Your mother gave it to you."

Aton's jaw tightened. "No."

She touched his hand, smiling. "I hurt you."

"No!" But beneath her understanding gaze, he felt the need to justify himself.

"My father," he said, "married a girl of the Family of Ten. She lived with him two years, and the hevee flourished as never since. She was kind and she was loving and she died in childbirth."

The Captain kept her hand on his. "I do not need to know, Aton."

But now he needed to tell her. "After that, Aurelius went to space. His cousin, Benjamin Five, acted as caretaker of the farm, so that the hvee would not die. Aurelius traveled to far planets, trying to forget. His ship put down for emergency repair on an unidentified planet. He—associated with a native girl, and he took her with him when they left. He brought her to Hvee."

The Captain gazed into his troubled eyes. "It is not necessary to—"

"She stayed with him just one year—and deserted him. I suppose she returned to her backwoods planet. Aurelius did not travel again; he farmed the hvee and brought me up alone."

"But she gave him the strength to continue—"

"She did not love him!" Aton shouted, casting off her hand. "She left him. No Hvee daughter would have done that. And I *had* no mother, real or step."

"Perhaps she left him *because* she loved him," the Captain said. "Could you, could you not understand that?"

"No!"—raising his hand as if to strike her—"If I ever meet that woman, I will kill her. And I claim my lineage from the Family of Ten. From the woman that was worthy. Ten!"

"So vehement!" But the Captain changed the subject. "In thirty-six hours I will show you where the Taphids are delivered. Now go, quickly."

Aton left.

Six

Four shifts later, in the cargo hold, Aton and the Captain loaded the Taphid caskets into a planetary shuttle. "No one else is going?" he inquired.

"No one else."

Aton completed the job in silence. This strange woman would tell him what was happening soon enough. Apparently she had cleaned up the hold herself in the intervening period. The damaged caskets had been repackaged.

The little shuttle cast loose in the shadow of the mother vessel. The unwinking stars were visible through the shuttle's port. Aton idly studied them while the Captain handled the controls, trying to guess what part of the galaxy they were in. "When I was a spaceman," he said, referring to his recent years in the Navy, "I learned never to look at the naked stars. When you stare at them too long they are apt to burn holes in the retina."

She snorted. "When I went to space, I learned to tell fact from fiction."

Aton laughed. The shuttle came around the ship, into the sunlight. A hood slid over the port, protecting them from the more severe radiation and leaving only the internal screen for guidance. The Captain piloted the little ship down from orbit, into the traces of atmosphere.

"This is the Xest outpost," she said.

"I still haven't learned about fact and fiction. You mean there *are* such things as Xestians?"

"Xests. Everything exists, if you travel far enough," she said. "They seldom communicate with human worlds, but the Xests may be the strongest nonhuman influence in our region of the galaxy. They happen to believe in live and let live, and they don't need us. But this outpost is so much closer to human trade routes than to their own that they elected to do business with us. The *Jocasta* is one of several merchant ships handling private orders."

"And *they* eat the Taphids!"

"They may. They may raise them as pets. We don't know. At any rate, they ordered this shipment. They pay well and their credit is excellent."

Aton shook his head. "Every time I think I'm used to space, it amazes me again. Yet if so many myths are true . . ." He left the sentence unfinished, thinking of the minionette.

She glanced at him. "There is one problem."

"Naturally. That's why Machinist Five was invited."

"The Xests are nonsexual creatures. They have great difficulty comprehending the human system. Traders have succeeded in a partial explanation, but misunderstandings remain. They believe that two beings, one male and one female, make up the composite human entity."

"Don't they?"

"The Xest mind misses the nuances." She frowned. "As Captain, protocol requires that I vist in person. But to them—"

"By yourself you're only half a captain!" Aton slapped his knee. "Grievous violation of etiquette."

"Precisely."

•   •   •

The Xests were small by human standards, under a hundred pounds if scaled by Earth gravity. Here, however, weight was only a quarter Earth-normal. Eight delicate appendages sprouted from the aliens' globular bodies in phalangidean symmetry. Communication had to be by galactic signs; they had no conception of sound.

Protocol further required the entertainment of the human for a specified period and the exchange of gifts. The Xests were semitelepathic, able to respond directly to emotion but not meaning, and believed that the honor paid to the visitor was automatically appreciated by the species. Captain Moyne presented them with several cylinders of emergency oxygen—a commodity as precious to them as to man—and in return an artisan contracted to produce a portrait of the human.

It was not long before the Xest spokesman got off on the favorite riddle: the binary nature of man. "Two species to make one Human?" it signaled.

"One species, two sexes," Aton returned.

"Yes, yes—Male of one species, Female of other."

"No, no—male and female of same species, Homo sapiens."

"Of same unit?" the sexless creature signed.

This would be another term for their conception of blood relationship. "No, too close," Aton began, but gave it up.

Captain Moyne watched this exchange with a half-smile, but made no comment.

"Will never understand," the Xest finished, perplexed. "Fire and water mix to make Human. Inevitable destruction—but that is your problem. Let us talk of trade."

●   ●   ●

The hosts understood the need for occasional estivation. A generous accommodation was provided for the Human: one bedroom, complete with bathroom fixture, kitchen fixture, appurtenances, bed.

"All right," said Aton. "Who gets it?"

"I do," the Captain answered firmly.

"Don't you think it should be share and share alike?"

"No."

"Should I make a complaint to the innkeeper?"

"Protocol forbids. You may absent yourself while I prepare to retire."

"But where will *I* sleep?"

"When you return you may make yourself a lair on the floor."

Upon that return, he found her sitting up in bed clad in the filmiest nightgown he had ever seen through. The game, it appeared, was not over yet, and she had certainly come prepared. The surprising rondure of the woman behind the uniform was once more evident beyond any reasonable doubt. She both intrigued and frustrated him, and he was not entirely pleased by the suspicion that she understood this well.

Aton sat on the edge of the bed. "What is your secret, Captain? You have the body of a young girl—a mature young girl—yet you must be fifty, at least."

"The years in space are brief," she said. She retained the skullcap; no trace of her hair showed.

"Not that brief."

"Leave a woman her secrets, and perhaps she'll leave you yours."

There was an implication here. "What do you know of my secrets?"

She leaned forward, letting the sheet drift to her slim waist, letting the nightgown pull tight. "The lay roster. You've been using it to search out every female crew member on the ship. You are seeking a woman."

She knew. Suddenly he wanted very much to talk about it, to lay bare the secret that had driven him from planet to planet and ship to ship for four years. The enormous futility of that search, that difficult seeking through stolen passenger lists and pay rosters for an imitation siren, that almost certain disappointment, brought a crashing misery about his soul. It was too much to bear.

He became aware of himself cradled in her arms, his head against her beating breast. She held him closely, stroking his hair, while the sorrow and pain of his memory flowed from him. "I'm in love with an illusion," he whispered. "A girl with a song played a game of love in the forest, and I can't rest until that song is complete. I have to find her, even though I know—"

"Who is she?" the Captain asked softly.

Again the agony washed over him, a sea of despair he had dammed back too long. "She called herself Malice," he said, "and I suppose it was allegorical. The name of a siren, a minionette, who lives to torment man. In that guise she gave me the hvee. If she exists, I am lost; if she does not, my life has been a dream, a tender nightmare."

She bent down and touched her lips to his with the tingle of fire. "Do you love her so much, Aton?"

"I love her! I hate her! I must have her."

She kissed his cheek, his eyelids. "Can there be no other woman? No other love?"

"None. Not until the song is finished. Not until I know what no person knows, what no text reveals. Oh, God, what I would do for love of Malice . . . only to have her with me."

She held him, and in time he drifted fitfully to sleep, still fully clothed. "It was so sweet, so sweet," he thought he heard her say.

·   ·   ·

Negotiations for additional trade were completed the following day, and Aton and the Captain made ready to return to the *Jocasta*.

"We thank you, Human," the Xest spokesman signaled. "We now offer our gift to you, our portrait of yourself."

They brought forth a large covered framework. Aton wondered when their artist could have done the work, since neither he nor the Captain had posed. Unless the technique were subjective. . . .

The portrait was unveiled. It was, after all, a web-network, colored threads woven across the hollow frame, passing each other in intricate parallels and skews and slants, touching and tracing three-dimensional patterns in a kind of gossamer fascination. It signified nothing, at first; then, as his emotions began to respond to the sense of the design, lured inside by clever signal-strands, the whole crept into focus, a weird and vivid picture of a forest scene.

Two people were depicted, coming alive through the alien magic, human, similar, yet oddly opposite. One, a strikingly beautiful woman, her hair the texture of a raging fire. The other, a small boy, a giant book in his arms, naked wonder in his face.

Aton stared at it, hypnotized. "This is—the two of us?"

"Our artistry is not easy to explain," the Xest conveyed.

"We do not understand the true nature of the Human. We have fashioned the portrait of you as you saw the two Male-Female parts of your being, when first you came together with comprehension. We hope this is of value to you."

Aton turned slowly to Captain Moyne. He saw the tears glisten in the depths of her deep green eyes.

"Perhaps she *had* to hide," she said. "The—the love of this man would cost her everything, in conventional terms, everything."

Slowly he put his hand to her tight cap and pulled it free.

The billowing fire cascaded down around her shoulders.

Aton touched the living hue of her hair. "You!" he said.

III. Chill

7

Hastings plumped down beside Aton, his huge body steaming. "I tried," he said sadly. "I tried—but I simply *cannot* pry a garnet out of that vacant wall in one piece. I'm jinxed."

"You're fat," Framy muttered helpfully from the other side. "Your stomach always beats you to it. Lucky you can even *see* a garnet, let 'lone reach it."

"I could reach it if I were able to see through the sweat," Hastings said, smudging the moisture from his eyes. If Framy's jibes bothered him, he never showed it. "I'm quick with my hands, but that heat—sometimes I long for a bout of the chill."

"The chill! I heard of that. You don't get no stone from me this time, Hasty. The chill'd kill you."

Hastings' eyes narrowed. Aton sat tight, knowing that the man would never have attempted to mine a garnet on his own unless his supply was low, and that he smelled a profitable encounter. Entertainment broke up the monotony of prison life when Hastings got hungry—and perhaps Framy, subdued for several chows after the disappointment of the blue garnet, was ready to play again. "Are you certain you know enough about the chill?" Hastings asked gently.

"What's there to know?" Framy picked at a broken toenail. "My buddy died of it, back on—never mind. He stopped over to settle a score on some planet and didn't know the chill was going around. Didn't know he had it himself, until it was too late. I thought sure I'd catch it from him, and I couldn't no more go to the doc'n he could. He just got colder and colder and he died."

"There was an epidemic on Hvee—that's my home—back in '305," Aton said, since he saw the signs that Framy had already been hooked and would pay the toll. "It came in the first month of the year. My great-grandfather Five was orphaned by it. Wiped out a third of the planet."

"Pandemic, not epidemic," Hastings said. "Did you know that it occurs in regular cycles just over 98 years apart, and that just about half the worlds of the human sector have been struck by it at one time or another? That it is not contagious? That Earth itself is being struck right now?"

Framy's silence in the face of each artfully posed question had been determined but his resistance broke at last. His weakness was that he couldn't bear to have anybody know something that he didn't, even if the subject had no inherent interest for him. "You been here longer'n me!" he exclaimed. "You don't know nothing about Earth."

Hastings settled back comfortably. "But it seems that I know something about the chill." And waited smugly.

"I already know about the chill. My buddy died of it. If there'd been a doc who'd keep his mouth shut—"

"There is no cure for the chill," Hastings said. Aton frowned at this.

"You're lying," Framy said without conviction. "Lots of people been saved. They got to catch it in two days, though."

"Even then, there is no cure."

Inevitably, after desperate rear-guard action, Framy lost his garnet, the others gathered around to swell the audience, and the flow of news began.

"Man," Hastings said, adopting the tone that made the standing listeners find seats, "leapfrogged light to plant colonies hundreds and thousands of light-years from his home. But he was caught unprepared for the chill. In §25 a brand-new colony almost 700 light-years toward the galactic center (no point in going into proper galactic coordinates here: that will be saved for another garnet) reported the first case. A young laborer on the cultivating squad stopped at the clinic with a complaint of sudden shakes. They had lasted only a minute or two, he admitted, but surely he was coming down with something. The medic aimed a thermal gauge at him, found no fever, and packed him back to the field. Colonization was rough work and the indolent were not to be coddled. The matter was duly entered in the record and forgotten.

"Five days later (Earth-time, naturally—this garnet doesn't cover comparative chronology) he was back, with a slip from the foreman: his efficiency was low and he was too cheerful about failures. What was the matter? The medic gestured again with the gauge, found no fever—on the contrary, the man's body temperature was several degrees on the safe side—and referred him to the disciplinary squad.

"Three more days passed. A friend brought the victim in this time. It was impossible to rouse him sufficiently for useful performance. The man was in an amiable stupor, and it was known that he had drunk no bootleg in two days. He no longer ate at all. And as long as he was here, the friend mentioned, he'd felt cold for a moment himself, a couple of days ago. As though a cold wash of air had descended on him, making him shiver, though no one else had felt it. It had passed in a minute and he felt fine now, better than ever, as a matter of fact, but. . . . The medic automatically played the gauge over him, found no fever, dismissed him, made another entry in the record (for he was a good medic), and took the slack laborer in charge.

"The man's body temperature was 297°K and dropping. This was an unusual departure from the human norm of about 310°K, and the medic was intrigued. The man had no symptoms that could not be accounted for by the chill itself; what caused the chill was a mystery. In due course the patient died and the fact was properly noted. A report was sent routinely to Earth where it was lost in clerical tape and forgotten.

"Meanwhile three more men, including the friend, were

down with it. They were not sick—that is, they had no fever—but the medic, catching a glimmer of a problem requiring a technique for which he was not competent—that is, serious thought—held two for observation and shipped the third directly to Earth for study. That one was intercepted by the efficient quarantine station and retained for proper dispensation. He was dead by the time the medic Officer of the Day had been notified, but Standard Operating Procedure had been upheld to the letter of the death certificate. Autopsy revealed the cause: malfunction of vital tissues owing to insufficient temperature. The body's natural regulatory mechanism had lapsed. No cause for *that* had been determined.

"A month later over half of the colony's 2,000 person complement was dead, and more were dying. The planet was quarantined. Earth shipped supply capsules, charging their cost against the colony's Earthside performance bond, but refused to accept any person or anything from the settlement itself. Thirty-six days after the onset—officially fixed at the moment of the first victim's initial shakes—ten additional men and women suffered the warning siege and set their affairs in order, each in the manner befitting himself and his religion. On the following day no new cases were reported; nor were any on the days thereafter. The ten recovered, and the epidemic (for so it was then regarded) was over, as mysteriously as it had commenced. The colony was held in quarantine for five years, during which time it accumulated a debt it would take a centrury to exonerate, but there was no recurrence, either there or anywhere else.

"Fifteen years later the chill broke out again, however, at a colony twenty-five light-years distant from the first. The pattern was identical, with the exception that the authorities alertly slapped on the quarantine within hours of the first death. Half the pioneers had been fatally infected within thirty-six days; the rest lived. Humanity breathed a collective sigh of relief when no contagion was detected.

"Now the debate of the first century § raged hotly over the chill. What was it? How did it spread? For the first question there was no satisfactory answer. For the second question there were several. One vociferous group held that the chill propagated by etheric waves traveling at the speed of light, a kind of death ray engulfing entire planets and moving on after a suitable interval to others. This was quickly labeled the Wave theory. Another leading group claimed that the contamination spread by personal contact, transmitted by some short-lived virus that rapidly mutated into impotence: specifically in thirty-six days. This was known as the Particle theory.

"The Wavists were challenged to demonstrate just how a wave traveling at lightspeed could traverse twenty-five light-years in just twenty years. But they rationalized that the inciting beam emanated from some third point, twenty years closer to the first afflicted colony than to the second. They waited eagerly for a third colony to be struck, so that triangulation could locate the origin. And in turn they challenged the Particlists to explain why no member of the moon-based quarantine party had contracted the illness, since many had been exposed before the full danger was understood. And why the chill showed no abatement whatever prior to its fixed termination, if it were really mutating its steady way into oblivion. The reply was that the quarantine experts had been exceedingly careful at all times, as proven by their ability to avoid contagion by the chill; and that the chill itself abated even though the symptoms displayed by man did not. When the causative virus weakened so that it dropped below the threshold of effectiveness, the body's natural defenses were able to repel it.

"Five years later both theories had their trials. A third colony was struck—but because its medic had been too busy publishing the learned tracts required for tenure and promotion to keep up with the medical literature, he failed to recognize the chill until several deaths had occurred. Infected colonists by this time had visited five other planets, including Earth itself. Moon station had been bypassed. Yet not a single case appeared outside the stricken colony, though the sick travelers cooled and died in public hospitals. The Particlists strained to explain the paradoxes, and could not. One of the victims had happened to be a popular call girl who continued her practice until her clientele complained of her literal frigidity. She died; the clients lived. The particle theory had been exploded.

"The Wavists pounced on the third coordinate with enthusiasm and triangulated for the fabled source. The third point was seventy-three light-years from the first; location was elementary. A ship of experts was dispatched. It found only empty space. If there had been a source, it had departed long since. And the disgruntled Particlists were quick to point out that a number of unaffected colonies lay between that so-called source point and the affected planets. How had those other colonies been missed? Was the wave discriminating? But in any event, the particular beam to strike the third colony could now be extrapolated. Volunteers planted themselves squarely in it— and were not affected. There was no beam, and the Wavists had been swamped.

"Time passed and the mystery deepened. Additional colonies were devastated, yet any victim removed within a day of the first symptom recovered promptly. If the chill were a contagious disease, why did time and location set such capricious limits? If it were a wave, why did so many escape?

"Gradually the unwilling answers appeared. Compromise gained the day. The chill *did* travel in lightspeed wave formation—but that wave was neither singular nor local. There were many waves, approximately a light-month in depth and ninety-eight light-years apart. The intersection of any wave with any colony meant pandemic until it passed. But within that wave there seemed to be random particles of infection that struck solely by the law of averages. Presumably there was a nutrient ether that guaranteed the progress of the illness unless the victim was promptly removed from its field. As with the ether of yore, none of this was detectable by instrument of man. He understood its presence by dying.

"The source was simply the center of the galaxy. There were other intelligent forms of life between man and that center, forms that also suffered variants of the illness, and it was rapidly understood that investigation was useless. The larger band of the chill impulse was twenty thousand light-years deep, and the source had been demolished long ago by a species now defunct. Yes, the chill was of artificial origin; no more was known.

"Meanwhile the waves were locally charted and schedules set up. The rich saved themselves by vacationing elsewhere during the critical month, while the majority simply waited and ferried the stricken out of range, if they found them in time. Great numbers were discovered too late.

"And Earth," Hastings finished, "populous Earth, with far too many billions to transport, could do nothing but wait for the first of the waves to strike. This is the time: the year §400. I'm glad I'm not there."

The crowd drifted off. Hastings had made light of the threat, but the chill was frightening, deep inside, to all of them. For no prisoner knew where Chthon was located.

The chill could strike tomorrow.

8

"Hey Fiver, pal—know what Garnet just done to me?" Framy was bursting with news.

"I can guess." Aton halted his chipping and sat down.

Framy rushed right on. "She gimme a whole chow for free. I held out my garnet and she never took it. Just handed over my meal and went away, sort of dreamy. She ain't never been so careless before."

Aton reclined against the wall, rubbing grit off his forearms as Framy ate. "It wasn't carelessness."

Framy spoke around a mouthful. "But she never took the— you mean she done it on purpose?"

Aton nodded.

"She'd be crazy to do a thing like that. She hates me 'most as much as she hates you."

"Does she?" said Aton. Hate is such an interesting thing. I hate the minionette. . . .

Garnet appeared, interrupting their discussion. "Got your stone?" she gruffly asked Aton. Wordlessly he held it out. She took it and dropped the package on the floor.

Framy stared after her until she was gone. "God of the Pit! I never seen it before. She soft on you, Five."

Aton opened his package.

But the little man was still puzzled. "That ain't no cause for her to be doing *me* no favors. I ain't no woman's idol. Why don't she give *you* no chow for free?"

Aton explained carefully so that the other would understand. Framy was incredulous. "You mean she don't want to show

how she's soft on you, so she takes it out on me? 'Cause I'm your pal and don't know nothing anyway?"

"Close enough."

"It just don't make no sense. No sense at all."

•   •   •

They brought the half-eaten corpse in for everyone to see. A man had wandered too far out alone, downwind. He might have been searching for garnets, or perhaps for an exit from the lower caverns. The chimera had come. Help had come ten minutes after his agonized scream—but he had been dead ten minutes. Stomach and intestines had been ripped open and eaten; eyes and tongue were gone. Long dark streaks showed on the cavern floor, they said, where he had been found, where the blood had flowed and been licked up.

"Remind me never to go on the Hard Trek," Hastings said sickly. "I'm too tender a morsel to be exposed to that."

The black-haired beauty gave him a sidelong glance. "I hear there's worse 'n that downwind on the Hard Trek," she said. "Ain't no one ever made it out. You can hear the howls of the beast-men that once were people like us, before they got caught."

"They live?" Hastings asked, obligingly setting up her punch line.

"Naw—but they howl."

There was general laughter. It was an old joke, and not without suspicion of accuracy.

This is my opportunity, Aton thought. Now—while it seems natural. Feign uncertainty, but get it out.

"I'm not sure, but it seems to me I heard about someone getting through," he said.

Framy took him up immediately. "Somebody got out? Somebody made the Hard Trek?"

"There must be a way out," Hastings said. "If we could only find it. The chimera had to get in *somewhere*."

"Maybe them animals never did get in," the black-haired woman said. Aton had never picked up her name. She had been subtly interested in him since that first discussion, but refused to make an overt play. Possibly she was afraid of

Garnet—or just smarter. She certainly interested him more; she was able to fling her hair about in a kind of dress that hinted at the sensuality of clothing. Nothing, he had discovered here, is quite so sexless as complete nudity. "Maybe there ain't no animals," she continued. "We never see none."

"I seen a salamander—" Framy began, then cut himself off.

"Salamanders, yes," Hastings said. "But that's about the only one a man can see and survive. That's why we speak of the 'chimera'—that's what the word means. Imaginary monster. But we sure as Chthon didn't imagine *that.*" His eyes flicked toward the corpse.

"It was a doctor," Aton said judiciously. "He was quite mad—but free."

Heads turned in his direction. Conversation stopped.

"A *doctor?*" Hastings breathed.

Aton held out his hand for a garnet, and everyone laughed. "About five years ago, I think. They never found out how he managed to escape. They had to put him in a mental hospital."

"Bedside!" someone cried.

"He swore he'd get out—"

"That means there is a trail."

"You sure about that?" Hastings asked Aton. "You remember the name?"

Do I remember the name I pried so carefully from the prison librarian, knowing that this was the word that might free me? "It wasn't Bedside," he said "Something like Charles Bedecker, M.D. Of course he lost his license when they sent him down."

"Yeah," Framy agreed. "They defrocked him."

"I knew him," Hastings said. "I had almost forgotten. We never called him by his real name, of course. He stayed about a month; then he set out with hardly more than his doctor's bag. He said he'd make a trail for the rest of us, if we had guts enough to follow. But he was such a small, mild character. We knew he'd never get far."

"How come you let him go?" the woman asked. "Him a doctor—"

"No sickness down here," Hastings pointed out. "We're sterilized—by the heat, perhaps. And death is usually too sudden. And he was a bad man to offend. Small, but what he could do—"

"That's not surprising," Aton said. "Didn't you know what he got sent down for?"

Hastings cut him off. "You remember a lot, all of sudden. We never ask that question here. That's none of our business."

"But there's a trail," Framy said, savoring it.

"A trail to madness," Hastings pointed out. "That's as bad as death."

"But a trail. . . ."

The magic word was out. Aton knew that it would spread like the hot wind through the caverns. Proof—proof of a way out. They could never be fully satisfied now, until they found it.

9

Ten chows later Bossman called the meeting. Since the meals were distributed every twelve hours or so, governed roughly by the schedule of delivery through the elevator above, this meant five days, outside time. Aton found the distinction pointless; short intervals were measured in chows. Seven hundred chows came to about a year.

"Must be something big," Framy said as they gathered. "Awful big. We never had no blowout like this before."

Aton ignored him, observing for the first time the full complement of lower Chthon. There seemed to be hundreds of people, and many more women than men. Most were from other garnet mines—people he had never seen before. Tall, short, hirsute, scarred, handsome, old—every one an individual, every one condemned both by his society and by his fellow prisoners. Here was the ultimate concentration of evil.

Every person was unique. Aton had become adjusted to a smaller circle, as though this were all there was to know of cavern society—but the people he knew had been selected by circumstance and not decision, and were representative. Bossman, Garnet, Framy, Hastings, and the black-haired one— bitter and violent, yes. But evil?

If there is evil here, he thought, I have not seen it. The evil is in the minionette. The evil is in me.

Bossman strode to the center of the spacious cavern, double-bitted axe over his shoulder. He stood on top of a small mountain of talus. Above him the intersection of a half-dozen ancient, gigantic tubes traced the history of the formation of this violent nexus. How many times had the rock been rent to form this jumble? As many times as human sensitivity had been rent to form this group. The wind eddied from several tunnels, now and again stirring up little dust devils which were in turn sucked screaming into the mouths of others. This room reflected the essence of subterranean power. It was a fitting meeting place.

Bossman hallooed, establishing his claim for the attention due the leader. The call reverberated across the passages and mixed with the sound of the wind. Once more, cynically, Aton sized up the man. The chatter stopped.

"They're giving us a hard time upstairs," Bossman said without further preamble. "They want more garnets."

There was a general bellow of laughter. "We'll give the bastards all they want!" someone shouted derisively.

"All they have to do is trot down and fetch 'em!" a woman finished.

Bossman did not laugh. "They mean it. They're cutting down our rations."

Now the murmur was angry. "They can't do that."

"They can," Bossman said. "They are. Each one of us got to give three stones for two meals to keep up the pace."

"They ain't that many stones!" Aton looked around and saw faces suddenly haggard with fear. There would be hunger.

"Why?" Hastings called out. A few snickered bitterly; he would be the first to suffer from a tight market. "What set them off?"

"Because they gone crazy," Bossman said. "They got some fool notion we got a blue garnet down here—"

"Tally knows there's no such thing. What's the matter with him?"

"Tally swears he's got proof."

Framy looked at Aton and leaned over. "You didn't tell nobody—"

Aton shook his head. "Never said a word." *The evil is in me,* he thought.

"Me neither. I went back after the salamander was gone and

found one of them pieces. It must've ate the other. But I thought about what you 'n Hasty said, and I didn't say nothing."

Bossman was speaking. "Tally says they're going to clamp down until they get that garnet. Ten chows from now it'll be two stones per..."

"Great Chthon! They'd kill me for sure if they knew I had a piece," Framy whispered, his body tense and shaking. "Somebody must've found the other."

Aton thought, The chimera is the enemy you don't see.

"... Ain't *going* to take it!" Bossman was roaring. "I don't like it no better'n you do. They think they got us by the—" He paused. His voice dropped. "But I got a plan."

The cavern quieted. "We're through trying to talk with those Laza-lovin' weaklings," he continued. "They been lording it over us too long. *We* been the ones doing the work. Now we're going to put the callus on the other foot.

"We're going to take over!"

He paused for the shocked commotion to subside. Revolution! Never before had such a thing been seriously conceived.

"First thing to do is bribe the guard at the hole. Now we got to pool our information, figure what'll move him. Maybe there's a woman, above or below"—his eye fell briefly on the black tresses provocatively draped over one breast of the woman Aton knew—"or maybe we can soften him a little some other way. We got to form a committee, take care of that. Next thing is the plan of attack. I figure we got to get five, six good men up there first, to hold off the softies in case they get wind before we're ready. Once they're stationed, quiet-like, we'll haul up the rest in the basket fast as we can. No one stays below. When we move out, first thing we got to take is their 'denser. They'll fall in pretty quick without water. Next objective is the 'vator; they might try to bust it and make us all starve. We don't worry about them freaks in the private cells; just leave 'em be and they won't notice the difference. Once we got control, we ship all the softies down here and let *them* mine the garnets—and if they can find any blue ones..."

Bossman went on, detailing plans in an atmosphere of growing excitement. He showed the qualities that made him a leader: no mere physical strength, but organization, practicality, enthusiasm, and ruthlessness. "But remember—this revolt is dan-

gerous. If we try it and don't make it, they'll starve us out.
Every one of us. It'll mean the Hard Trek. . . ."

                    •   •   •

"After the revolt," Framy said, again almost dancing with
excitement, "after we take over, know what I'm going to do?"
The others gave him their attention, enjoying the discussion
of grandiose plans. There were a dozen or so gathered at the
mine, unable to concentrate on the work. Revolt day was coming; the decisive variable lay in the assignment of the Bribe
Committee.

"I'm going to catch ol' man Chessy by his white goat's
beard and I'm going to twist his head off until he learns me
how to play that game."

"You might have better luck with that li'l Prenty," someone
joked. "Bet she'd teach you a game."

"No." Framy was firm. "It's got to be Chessy himself.
Nobody else. We're going to lay out the pieces and play in
front of the whole Chthon, and when I beat him a game the
whole Chthon'll know I'm a brain and never did nothing
wrong."

They had the courtesy not to laugh. Each man had his secret
desire, and many would look foolish in the open.

Hastings took his turn. "I don't think I'll fit through that
hole any more," he burbled, and the others smiled with him.
The hole was a yard in diameter. "But if the rope doesn't break
when they haul me up, and the floor above doesn't sink, why
then—"

"I know!" someone put in. "He's going to get himself
'pointed grinder on the 'denser!"

"To reduce."

"Ma Skinflint'll love that."

"Love *what?*"

Hastings patiently waited for these to subside. "Why then
I'll go to Laza's cave. I'm quick with my hands, you know"—
they knew—"and when she comes at me with that stone knife,
why I'll just pluck it out of her hand, and then . . ."

The others leaned forward.

"Then . . ."

"Get *on* with it, Hasty!"

"Then I'll give her what she's been craving so long, so she won't ever forget!"

"What's that, Hasty?"

"I'll pay admission to see that, Hasty!"

"Don't worry—you will," another person said. "One garnet per throw." More laughter.

Framy turned to Aton. "How about you, Fiver? What's your piece?"

Aton looked around. He had been expecting a surprise twist from Hastings, and wondered what had become of it. The man had let them down with an unclever climax.

Garnet was standing quietly at the fringe. She too, it appeared, had misgivings about the future of the revolt. He felt the need to hurt her.

"Tally's got a girl, Silly Selene," he said. "Know her? She made a play for me once, but I had other business. This time I think it will be different." They gathered in for the telling. "Pretty, yes. You never saw such beauty. A creature of perfection. Her hair takes life when she loves; her eyes become black and green as the deep oceans. As with the hvee, she blooms only when—" He saw their glances of puzzlement. What was wrong? Did they find this fantasy of a simple cavern girl so confusing? He shrugged it off, not caring what they thought. The revolt would never come to pass. "I found her at last. She had been masquerading as human, but once I unveiled her she had to hide from man. I took her to an asteroid cabin—"

"Not human?" Framy asked, puzzle-lines between his eyes. "Silly?"

"I suppose her kind evolved from human stock. Genetic modification—but she looked human, divinely so. The legends attribute strange powers, and some...are true. She can't be immortal, but I think she is semitelepathic."

"She can read minds?"

"I don't know. That would explain a lot of things. But it also makes her actions more paradoxical. She made me do terrible things. I loved her when I searched for her, but I hated her when I found her. She was destroying me. I did not dare to give her the hvee—"

"Ain't that the little green flower them people wear? I never seen one."

"Finally I left her and went home. I told Aurelius that I would marry his daughter of Four if only I could be cured of—of Malice. He was so happy he nearly expired. He was nearly dead from the blight, only holding on until I should return. He shipped me to a famous retreat planet."

Aton looked up and saw Garnet listening intently. He had forgotten her entirely. For a moment he had self-doubt. Do I have any right to torture this woman? Don't I owe her a warning, at least? Malice, Malice—you have made me a monster. You make me implement your name, and there is no escape.

Yet Garnet did not look disturbed as much as thoughtful, and there was not a sound from any of the others. What had happened?

A clamor rose above the sound of the wind. Men came running. "It's time! It's time! They've softened the guard! We got to gather for the revolt! It's time! The revolt is on. It's on!"

·   ·   ·

The passages adjoining the transfer cavern were packed with suppressed excitement. All eyes were fixed on the tiny hole in the ceiling thirty feet above. This was the only known connection between the two worlds. Everywhere else the stone was firm and deep, impossible to attack without heavy tools.

The upper caverns were sealed off, but the seal had one weak spot, and that was the guard on the "night" shift. Aton didn't know what they had had to promise him, but Bossman's given word was good, and the man would be secure for life. He had only to let down the rope and stand aside.

Slowly, slowly, the heavy slab crunched over. The dark hole lightened invitingly, a green glow from the far side, the doorway to success. No face appeared. No sound came from above except for the too-loud scraping of the stone.

A pause; then the rope appeared, spinning out from its coil, swinging free of its basket and undulating as it came. The ragged end dropped just clear of the floor and hung in limp invitation.

Bossman gave a grunt of satisfaction. The selected invasion

squad moved to the center, Aton second in the line. The most important thing here was the ability to climb swiftly and silently, with strength left over for immediate combat, if necessary.

The first man, short and game in the legs but with arms of immense power, stepped up and jerked the rope. It gave slightly, but held; it was anchored. Like a tug on a teen-age braid, Aton thought.

The man took hold and skillfully hauled himself into the air. Aton saw Bossman watching the operation closely, shaking his head. Are you worried, Krell farmer? he thought. You also remember Tally's intelligence?

The man climbed swiftly to the top, hoisting himself with both hands and hooking a leg in a bend of rope for occasional pauses. He caught the edge of the hole with his hands and flexed the muscles, raising head and shoulders above it. Aton held the rope, making no motion to follow yet.

A muffled cry came from above. The high legs kicked; the man struggled and lost his grip just as he seemed about to complete his climb. He slid down, back through the hole, and fell heavily to the floor below.

Bossman lifted him immediately, but it did not matter. His throat had been neatly slit.

The rope slackened. A second body fell.

It was the softened guard. The rope had been knotted around his neck. He had served as the anchor, and the climbing weight of the first invader had throttled the traitor.

The revolt had come as no surprise to Tally.

You should have known, Aton thought, that Tally would anticipate such a move. That he is neither sadistic nor a fool, and that he had sufficient reason for his pressure and was prepared for any consequence. You will know, at last, that there had to be a traitor, and you will assume that one of your own crew had been softened. You will suspect, now that you know that Tally's mind is after all as sharp as ever, that there really *is* evidence of a blue garnet. You will search and question relentlessly, every man and every woman—and in the bottom of Framy's water-skin you will find the blue fragment.

Framy will scream out the entire story of the discovery and loss of the garnet. He will appeal to me for verification, but

I will admit only to an affair with Garnet during the time in question. She will agree, telling herself that she will be suspect otherwise, and wanting the black-haired one to be jealous. Framy is known as a great liar, but you will let him take you to the place he says he found it, and there will be nothing there, and he will not know that his proof lies very near at hand.

"I never done it," he will cry at last. "I was framed! I was framed!" And you have heard this before.

The upper cavern people will not relent. They must discover for themselves where that first fragment came from, and learn whether there is indeed a mine for it. Because you refused to deal with Tally honestly, he will now starve you out and make the lower caverns safe for exploration from above. And we shall take the Hard Trek.

Oh, yes, we will!

Seven

Idyllia: sunny planet of retreat. Palms and firs grew side by side as the discreet touch of genetic modification brushed nature and made her smile. Blue water sparkled beside gray mountains; soft white clouds traced their shadows over rustic villages.

Aton performed the registration routine mechanically, his thoughts on the woman he had come to forget. He ignored the indoctrination program. The conceits of a self-styled paradise were no concern of his. Thus he came to find himself ensconced in a beautiful villa, a cabin surrounded by flower gardens and labyrinthine hedge, with no clear idea of how it had come about.

Lovely planet, he thought bitterly. But never as lovely as Malice. Malice—I should have been warned by your name. But I blinded myself to everything but your beauty; I deafened myself to my father's words. I obsessed myself with a childhood longing. And when I found you . . .

He surveyed the gardens. Never strong on the merits of cultivation, aside from the special art of hvee, Aton felt he was off to a poor start. It did not matter; even best of starts would have had little effect on his destructive passion for the minionette.

Minionette. When I found you at last, after the games with the Captain, with the Xests . . . no wonder those amiable aliens were confused. They saw that you *were* the minionette, that strange offshoot of man, no imitation, while I tried to fix my ignorance on them. And they showed me what they could, and I took you away, to a hidden spotel, and there divined the monstrous evil of your nature.

Left to his own devices at this resort, he discovered that life did go on. Idly he explored the gardens, solving the simple riddle of the shrubbery, and turning finally to the bright cottage. The descending sun was a raised outline on the floating cloudlets, too round to be natural. The smell of cooking was in the air.

Then, broken, I listened to you, Aurelius. But you told me nothing, only sent me here to Idyllia, to rest, to forget. To forget Malice.

Entering the cabin at last, Aton found ancient-type botanic prints along the hall, a floor of psuedopine, and antique turn-type knobs on hinged doors. Such a house must Wordsworth keep! he thought. Cheerful fire blazing in the main-room hearth; shadows from ornamental andirons flickering against the rough stone segment of the floor. Wholesome noises from what he took to be the kitchen. Another person was in the house.

He stepped through the arch. Arch? This was not, then, intended to be any historic replica. And he saw her: petite, blonde, efficient. "What are you doing here?" he said. What do you care, Aton?

She turned, sparkling. "I belong."

"But they told me this was *my* house," he said querulously.

"Yes." She came to him and held up her left wrist, showing the silver band on it. "It is the custom of Idyllia to provide slaves for the service of patrons. For the duration of your stay

I belong to you, and in the name of the planet, I welcome you." She made a little curtsy.

Aton was not convinced. "Something was mentioned. But I thought it was to be a caretaker. A—a manservant."

"They are reserved for our female patrons."

"Oh." Too blatant, Idyllia.

She took his arm and guided him back to the fireplace with that gentle command that is the prerogative of the slave, and settled him for the afternoon meal. Aton accepted the situation with equivocal pleasure. No woman had ever taken care of him in quite this way before, and his attitude was ambiguous before becoming positive. It was, after all, a worthwhile adjustment to make.

"What would one call a female slave?" he inquired.

"By her name," she said pertly. "Coquina."

Aton researched in the sturdy intellectual files implanted by his childhood tutor. "The coral building stone? Is that your theme—the hardness and sharpness of—?"

"On Earth," she said, "there once were tiny clams with shells so colorful that they became collector's items. They were called—"

"I see. And what would the pretty shell recommend for a troubled heart tonight?" he said. And he thought, She is trying to oblige—why fence with her, Aton?

"There is a country dance this evening," she said, apparently missing the implication in his question. "If it pleases you—"

"Nothing pleases me, Coquina." But he smiled.

·   ·   ·

The dance was colorful. It happened in a warm brown barn, the smell of hay in the corners, the nests of swallows in the rafters. Tissue banners festooned the hewn beams; soft cider flowed from the central press. People wandered in and out, shepherded by their knowledgeable slaves, smiling desperately. Too often, Aton felt, the striving inner torment shone through the glad masks.

But he drank of the cider and found it potent. It was not soft, despite the evident freshness; it was turning, pungent—

and perhaps the natural fermentation had been artfully augmented. Or the apple-stock itself had been modified. He conjured a picture of tiny trees birthing megalocarpous fruit, each huge apple bearing the legend "80 Proof." His mind became uncommonly clear and he saw that there was laughter even in sadness.

"Sets in order!" Two whiskered stereotypes struck up the music, one playing fiddle, the other a magnificent three-deckered accordion. The room was filled with merriment. Couples formed from the fringe melee and eddied toward the main floor and formed into crude squares. Women flounced their full-circle skirts and took the proud elbows of solemn gentlemen.

Aton spoke aside to Coquina. "How may one obtain a partner for this affair?" The music ascended as busy fingers leaped over white and black accordion keys, strutted against the chord panel, pumped the bellows harder.

"One crosses the room toward one of the seated ladies, bows gallantly, requests the pleasure of her company for the dance."

"How does one make a choice?" he asked, gesturing at the array. White petticoats fluttered above crossed thighs, making interesting shadows.

Coquina arched an eyebrow. "Unaccustomed as I am to judging the tastes of male clientele . . . however, I understand that the third damsel from the right is attractive to certain types, and is an excellent dancer—"

Aton studied the woman as she chatted gaily with a neighbor and leaned to tap one elevated slipper and laugh at some private joke. Her décolletage showed fine cleavage and her feet were small. Her hair was long and loose.

"No!" he said, more forcefully than he meant. "Red hair is out."

Coquina obligingly pointed out an alternate. This time the hair was brown and not too long. She was standing to the side with a cup of cider in her hand, bouncing gently to the music. At the end of the refrain she came down on both heels firmly, breasts and buttocks jumping in sudden sex appeal.

"No—she has green eyes." It was a bleak reminder; sorrow struck him heavily, his emotion amplified by the liquor.

Coquina looked at him, uncertain whether he were serious. Her eyes were blue. "Come," he said, unable to explain his mood. "I prefer my slave."

And so they danced, the girl light on her feet and easy to hold, and for a time the weight upon his mind lightened, retreated half a step. They danced, they swung, they spun, her skirts rising alluringly; but the weight danced with them. The living lines parted and re-formed; men marched to meet their partners in the center, bowed, retreated, marched again, and swung into shuffle-step and grand right-and-left. Right hand to right hand, left to left, meeting each girl with music and a flair of the hip and passing her on to the rear, smiling. Oh, brightening glance! What a miracle such movement makes of the routine figure! What capricious delight, sharpened by irony—for these are smiles and motions only, in the absence of love, intriguing but empty.

Malice, oh Malice, oh Malice, why did you betray me?

·   ·   ·

It was midnight at the cottage when Aton, subdued, prepared to retire. The vision had grown, and now it pounded in the shell of his head, tearing his mind apart, dominant in his fatigue. It was the face and form of Malice, smiling, devastating, at once more lovely and more terrible than any spectral phantasm. The flame rippled through her hair, and he wanted her.

"Coquina!" he called, and she came, clad in nightgown, demure. "I cannot sleep tonight. Will you talk to me?"

"I understand," she said.

"I wonder..." He studied her innocence. But the awful vision was fading as he talked. "Have you ever been in love, Coquina?"

"No."

"People think of love as something romantic, as delight, wonder. It is supposed to uplift a man, make him strong, make him good. Have you seen this *LOE* text?" She nodded slightly. "But, oh, they're wrong. Love is the most awful weapon known to the human race. It can twist a man, wring him up into a tight wad until his blood spills out upon the stone reality, until he shrivels, and is a dry husk. If you ever search for evil, begin with love.... I shouldn't talk this way to a woman."

"I am a slave," she said.

He studied her once more, speculatively. "You say you are a slave. But how much of a slave? Is there not a little bit of

woman in you, too? When you move in the dance, pretty
shell. . . . If I were to tell you to strip naked before me here . . ."

"Idyllia must protect its property," she said. "I will not
strip."

Aton smiled. "It was only an example, a case in point. You
are not so much a slave. But tell me, Coquina, are you for
sale? Could I purchase you and carry you away with me wher-
ever I wished to roam?"

"The slaves are not for sale. They are loaned to the patrons,
to serve within certain limits."

"Certain limits. I see the shell is closed," said Aton. "Too
bad—but only fair. I wish more women were slaves, more
slaves were women. . . ."

Eight

Aton went to parties, danced, saw wholesome theatrical pro-
ductions, and flirted with meaningless women. By day he
swam, participated in antique group sports, took picnics in the
sunshine; at night Coquina took care of him and rubbed his
back with oil. He talked to her at such times, easing his mind
and finding, to his surprise, surcease from the memory of
Malice by talking about—Malice. He told Coquina as much
as he could remember, more than he had told any human being
before, because he had come to regard her not as human but
as slave.

It was not enough. Malice came back to his mind at every
unguarded moment, arousing unquenchable desire, measureless pain. He could hide from her for an hour, but he could not
escape.

"This is getting me frankly nowhere," he said at last. "I've
got to find something that will take up my whole attention for
more than a tiny span."

And Coquina, as always, had a suggestion. "Have you tried
mountain climbing?" she asked. "It is a vigorous sport that
takes many days and uses a great deal of energy. It is not
dangerous, here, and it has special merits."

"You are telling me, gentle shell, that the answer to doubt is work," Aton said. "This is the very finest Victorian sentiment from *LOE*. But if you recommend it, I'll try it. You've been taking good care of me so far."

"I will arrange for a guide," she said.

"You will arrange to *be* the guide," he replied. "Do you think I mean to have you corrupted by some other patron in my absence?"

She smiled, and the following afternoon saw the two of them tramping along the intermittently wooded base of a local mountain. Curling bracken rose on either side, tall as a man already; scented pink lady's-slipper flowers could have been worn by a lady with an evanescent tread. Volcano-like, the giant puffballs spouted smoky haze at the slightest touch. Farther along, milkweed mixed with dwarf sequoia. Great and small, blooming and fruiting, natural and modified, the plants of Idyllia presented themselves for approval.

Aton stopped to look at a lizard, slim and red, perched on a boulder. It eyed him with seeming intelligence. "We will meet again, your kind and mine," it seemed to say, and Aton laughed and slapped at it, making it scramble for safety.

Coquina, delicate though she might appear, carried a full pack and sleeping bag and kept a man's pace. Aton was amazed at her stamina.

They camped early, before the mountainside obscured itself in shadow, and she fixed a meal. Aton stared into the somber water of the stream they washed in, and saw huge red salmon. He moved to flick a twig off his arm, stopped just in time: it was an insect, a three-inch walking stick, so still it might be dead. He was tempted to drop it in the water to see if the fish would take it; but he saw Coquina glance at him, and felt ashamed. Why did he have this urge to hurt, to torture, an innocent insect? He transferred it to a leaf and watched it tread carefully away.

No biting creatures infested the night air. They slept side by side in twin bags on an aromatic bed of fern. Aton half-awoke, briefly, to the call of an owl, and saw his slave in slumber, a light strand of hair over her face. The beauty of her features was classic, even so. It struck him that he could ap-

preciate it without untoward thought, and this was new, for
him.

Daylight, sunny and bright in sections as they tramped
among mixed fir and palm and hardwood. This was a forest
to enjoy at leisure; but Aton drove himself hard, trying to
banish his problems by sheer physical effort. Coquina kept
pace without complaint as the way grew steeper.

Great mossy roots tied down the twisting trail. He doubled
his effort, pushing up the mountain, an energumen, until the
muscles of his legs were weary and his head grew faint. The
slave followed, saying nothing but never falling back.

Aton became genuinely curious. His youth on Hvee, in
gravity possibly fifteen per cent greater than Earth-normal, had
guaranteed his strength. Genetics in the laboratory had strengthened his body generations before he was born. In ordinary
gravity he could perform feats that would astound the uninitiate,
and the years in space had only slightly impaired his stamina.
For this was where it showed: no normal man could match the
endurance of the modified, and among the women only the
strange minionette had shown comparable power. Certainly a
soft pleasure-world such as this was not the place to find a
really durable woman.

That second evening, far up the slope where the gusting
wind was cold, he feigned a greater weariness than he felt. He
threw himself down and pretended to sleep. He watched Coquina.

She went about the preparation of the meal without sign of
undue fatigue, though the bounce was gone. A glance in his
direction apparently convinced her that he was sleeping
soundly; she came and rolled him into a more comfortable
position and placed a pad of moss under his head. She did not
try to wake him.

What made the girl so strong? She should have dropped
from exhaustion long ago. But not only did she stay with him,
she handled the routine chores as well. Did she also stem from
modified stock? Did a slave on Idyllia really conform to the
ancient virtue of the species: having the advantages of wife and
workhorse combined, without the liabilities?

No, she could not completely be equated to a wife, though

she would make a good one. Aton gave up the game, sat up, stretched, rubbed away imaginary fog. There was no point in missing supper. Tomorrow he would discover just how tough she was.

•   •   •

The path became steep and quite irregular. Aton paid no attention to the expanding view below the mountain or to the fleeting wildlife—a beaver, mountain goats, tortoise—that surveyed his passing. He chose the most difficult ascent and climbed with utmost speed. Coquina had become a challenge; he was determined to discover her breaking point. He did not stop to wonder just what it was he was competing with, or to marvel at his rivalry with a woman who was bound only to do his will.

As the day wore on, drenching him in perspiration, it began to seem that his own breaking point was likely to be the one measured. The girl made no comment, no suggestions. She was versed in the art of climbing; her motions were economical, conserving of energy, and she expended far less of it than he. She must, he thought, have escorted many a prior gentleman up these same slopes. That bothered him.

At length they came to an overhanging ledge, where the outcropping rock ascended jaggedly for the better part of fifty feet before retreating beneath its cover of shrubbery. The area was not wide and would have been easy to circle—but Aton had no such intention. This was ideal. His years as a Navy enlistee had familiarized him with the rigors of rope handling; such a hoist would be difficult enough, but within his means. For a woman, however, necessarily lacking the sheer musculature and practice required, it would be the supreme test.

He lassoed a low rock that stood twenty feet above the base. It would be large enough to stand on, and to serve as a take-off for the major portion of the climb. He hauled himself up quickly, his feet walking the almost vertical cliff face. The familiar exertion was good to feel.

He cleared the top, checked the rope, and waited for Coquina to climb. And climb she did, coming hand over hand and walking up the side of the mountain as he had done. The pack on her back obviously threw her off-balance and made it hard, but she said nothing.

He hooked the cord around the uppermost projection and pulled it tight. This would be a longer haul—twenty-five feet at least, with the rock angling out so that the rope hung free. There would be no wall-walking this time.

Aton went up. The climb this time was not so simple. He realized belatedly that there was a difference between swinging on a line at half-gravity in spacecraft, and facing full gravity with a pack on. The strength he had expended so generously for the prior climb was in demand now; he had been wasteful. He should have towed the packs up separately—and he should have secured a safety line, to prevent an accidental fall. His spare rope was coiled at his belt, useless.

But the girl was watching below, and he was strong. He achieved the higher projection and clambered over, very glad for the release. This ledge was secure, and there was space for a second line. He uncoiled his extra and made a loop.

Coquina had already begun her climb. Lying flat with his head and one shoulder over the edge, he could see that he had guessed correctly. She was not used to this particular type of exercise, and did not know the little tricks of rope facility. This was not a woman's sport. She swung out against a backdrop of brush and trees falling precipitously away, and swung in almost to strike the concavity of stone. She was tiring rapidly, but she kept coming.

About fifteen feet up she slowed and stopped. She had come to her limit at last. Aton, obscurely gratified, was about to shout to her, to tell her to let herself down and choose another route.

Then he saw how really tired she was. Her small hands, hanging numbly to the rope, began to slip. The view of distant and rocky terrain spun slowly behind her dropping form; the landing below was death.

Without thinking, Aton flipped his loop over the outcropping and flung himself over. It was the spaceman's reflex: immediate action, thoughtless of personal danger. He dropped, the pack he still wore tugging upward against his armpits. Halfway down the sheer face the taut rope he gripped yanked him to a halt with a violence that smashed skin from fingers and palms and almost tore loose his grip. There were muscles in arms and shoulders that would cause him severe regret on the morrow.

He was dangling a little below the girl. As her hold finally gave way he spread one arm and caught her around the waist, pulling her body clumsily to him. She clung to him weakly, nearly unconscious with her own fatigue.

Preoccupied as he was, trying to handle a double load augmented by the weight of the packs, with a single straining hand on his rope, he nevertheless noted with nightmare irrelevance how lithe and sweet her body was against his. Except for the time that first evening at the country dance, he had never held her; it came somehow as a surprise now that she was very much a woman.

Meanwhile reflex took over again. His hand loosened, permitting a controlled slide down the rope, burning fearfully. But he landed roughly on the lower ledge and let Coquina down on the widest portion, where she could lie safely. As he kneeled beside her, her arm came around his neck, hugging him.

"You are strong, strong," she whispered, eyes closed. "Stronger than I." Then her hand fell away and she was unconscious.

Her words left him elated. He knew they were sincere. Whatever had passed before, she saw him now as a man and not as a pampered patron. That, perhaps, had been the thing he was warring against. With profound pleasure he set about doing the things that she had done before, for him. He made her comfortable, foraged in the packs for food, and brought it to her. Later he wrapped gauze around and around his clotted hand and lowered the packs to the foot of the cliff, and climbed down himself to arrange a nearby campsite.

Only after they were both down did he allow her to put salve on his hand and rebandage it. She was taking over again, and he liked it still—and he realized with a pleasant shock that Malice had been driven completely out of his mind for some time, and that there were far more immediate things for his concern.

Nine

Coquina's first words that evening, as a solitary cricket chir-ruped from somewhere, were of apology. "I'm sorry I couldn't stay with you, Mr. Five. I did not mean to—"

"Never call me that again," he said, cutting her off. "I am a man, not a title—a foolish man who almost killed you."

"Yes, Aton," she said. "But no one dies on Idyllia." She got up. "I have work to do."

Aton grabbed her by the ankle and brought her down again. "Do it tomorrow. Right now you are going to rest quietly if I have to sit on you. Why didn't you tell me how tired you were getting?"

Her smile was rueful. "A slave does not consider personal problems. The patrons usually have more than enough of their own."

Aton blanched inwardly at the reference to patrons. Things had not really changed between them. "Have you been a slave here all your life?"

Another wan smile. "Of course not. No one is born to slavery. There are conventions . . . I came here the only way anyone can: I volunteered."

"Volunteered!"

"It is a good situation. There's a long waiting list. The standards are high."

"So I noticed," Aton said, appraising her figure.

She put her hands in front of her, unconsciously defensive. "I'm not that kind of slave, and I wouldn't care to be judged on such terms."

"Forgive me," Aton said contritely, "for being male. I value you very much on whatever terms you consider to be appli-cable. But surely you sometimes have trouble with men in lonely places like this?"

"Sometimes," she admitted. "But we are trained to protect ourselves."

Aton thought of some of the tricks he knew. "Even against spacemen?"

"Especially against spacemen."

He laughed. "My pride will not let me believe that, but I like you very well as you are." She laughed with him, and he felt a warm glow. But the Malice image hovered in the background, undead.

He banished that thought. "You are suprisingly strong for a woman, Coquina. Where are you from?"

"I shouldn't tell you. . . ."

Suddenly she didn't need to. "Hvee" he exclaimed. "They don't grow women like you anywhere else in the galaxy. Only on my home world." With this discovery his interest in her blossomed. His interest was no longer idle—if idle it had been. "Name your Family."

"Please don't."

Aton snapped his fingers. "Four?" he demanded, and she had to nod. "I should have known. Aurelius' judgment was always impeccable. He swore he had arranged the finest match—and he had, oh, he certainly had. I would have loved you."

Her expression did not change, but he sensed the hurt in her immediately. "I was speaking of the past," he said lamely, but the damage had been done. "It was the song, the broken song. It was driving me, and I could not turn aside. Now I am suspended, a fish on a hook; I can only acknowledge what might have been."

"You have mentioned this before."

Yes, of course—I have been telling her everything, not knowing to whom I spoke. Not knowing!

"How did you come here?" he asked, trying to hide his embarrassment.

"I never saw the man I was to marry, or knew his name," she said, almost inaudibly. "But I—I hated him, when he brought the shame upon my Family. To be refused sight unseen . . . and the Families would not annul the liaison. I couldn't stay."

Aton tried to take her hands, but she eluded him. "I did not know. 'Third daughter of Eldest Four'—it was only a designation, not a person."

"Slaves, too, have pasts," she said. "But they do not matter."

"But you must have known. We were not thrown together by coincidence."

"No. You were my assignment. Your face and your name were not familiar. Until you talked about your past, and I began to understand. The Families could not introduce us formally—"

"And you never said a word. Never a word!" He was not hungry, but he nervously took one of the self-heating food canisters from his pack and began to eat from it. She followed his example, except that hers was a refrigerant package. He knew the symbolism was accidental, but it spurred him to another effort.

"Let's forget what has happened between us," he said. "It—there is too much to overcome. Too much of shame. Let's wipe the slate clean and begin from this point. I want to know about *you*." She did not respond. "Please."

She demurred. "A slave may not—"

"Damn slavery! You're the woman I should have married, and I want to *know*."

She was shaking her head mutely.

Aton looked at her with embarrassed exasperation. She had never seemed recalcitrant before—but of course he had not questioned her about herself before. Surely the circumstances negated any token convention. Unless—

"I have it," he said. "You told me that no one dies on Idyllia. That's not rhetorical, is it? That must mean that the clients are watched all the time—and not only by their faithful slaves. Are we under observation now?"

She lowered her eyes.

"And if I had not caught you, there at the cliff, some contraption would have popped out of the stone, thumbed its mechanical nose at me, and whisked you away. . . . Answer me!"

"Something like that."

"And you'll be demoted to dog-walking detail if you say a word."

"Some of them are very nice dogs."

"Well, if you persist in this foolishness, I'll just have to clamber up that cliff again, jump off, and force that thing to nab *me* in midair before I splatter. *Then* where would your precious job be?"

"Please," she whispered.

"I should have brought *LOE*," he remonstrated dolefully. "'Had we but world enough, and time'—"

"I may be coy," Coquina said, this time with some spirit, "but I'm not your..."

She was lying in the leaves, her hair matted in them. Aton lay down beside her, propped on one elbow. He picked away the bits in her hair. "I was too quick to set aside convention. I did not appreciate the enormous wisdom of the elders' choice."

"No," she said. "That shame is forgotten now."

"I will redeem it. I promised to marry the daughter of Four—"

"No!" The shell was closed.

·   ·   ·

The pace was more leisurely after that. Magnificent vistas spread out below as they toiled near the summit. Aton had to admit that he felt better than he had in some time. Coquina's cheerful mien and quiet strength of character collaborated with the beauty of the scenery to make life once more a worthwhile experience.

He was almost sorry when they reached the top. He would have preferred to go on climbing as they had been, never stopping, never thinking, never facing the complex problems of life beyond this mountain; just breathing the scented breeze and listening to the crackle of dry debris underfoot. Malice, for the moment, was little more than a sinister shadow. So much stronger, now, was the living vision of Coquina—pert without affectation, asking nothing, her short curls bobbing as she walked.

On impulse, Aton put his arm around her. She frowned but did not withdraw. Together they mounted the final incline to the summit.

Aton had been expecting a special view, but the scene that met his eyes here exceeded his anticipation. The mountain turned out to be not single but double; a massive split separated the halves, plunging down half a mile to become a narrow crevice between them. The walls on either side were sheer. He retreated a step, repelled by his own attraction to the chasm.

"This," Coquina said, poised alarmingly near the brink, "was once a field and rill—"

"Rill?"

"Stream. And a field is a flat clearing."

"I won't interrupt again," he agreed.

"Long ago the mountain rose out of the ground. But the rill was older, and it would not move aside. It cut through the rising mass. After a little while—an eon or two—the mountain became annoyed. It ascended more rapidly, until the river could not keep up. The water gave up and went around the mountain after all. Now we have the river bed a mile above the river, and the mountain has two peaks."

"If I had been that river," Aton said, "I would have tunneled *through* that upstart hillock."

"You would have been sorry. The river did try that, and there is a hole at the edge of a pond, leading into the base of the mountain. But the water that goes in one side never comes out the other. So most of the river backs up and stays away from that area."

"I don't blame it. It's a good thing you warned me; you may have kept me out of bad trouble." He stood behind her, watching the wind from the cleft fluff back her hair and catch at her hiking skirt.

"The song is gone," he said.

Coquina turned slowly to face him. "Aton."

The shell is open, he thought. All it takes is the touch of genuine love.

Gravely he removed the hvee from his hair and tucked it in hers. She smiled quizzically, her eyes shining. They stood at arm's length, gazing at each other in silence, waiting for the hvee.

Then she was in his arms, sobbing against his shoulder. "Aton, Aton, hold me. You are the first. . . ."

He pressed her close, savoring an emotion that was real, that had not been contaminated.

She stepped back from him, once more silhouetted against the midmorning sky. She was radiant. "So new," she said. "So beautiful. Kiss me, Aton, so I can believe. . . ."

He put his two hands on her shoulders, bringing her close slowly. As her face approached a cloud seemed to pass before it. A shimmering, a fading . . .

. . . And it was the face of the minionette. Hair the color of the living flame surrounded it, twining in serpentine splendor, in and out. Black-green eyes stared into his. The red lips parted. "Kiss me, Aton..."

"No!" he cried, his dream of freedom blasted. He put his hand against the specter, covering the liquid eyes. He shoved it away with a convulsion of horror.

And stood alone on the mountain, wrapped in the melody....

> "But Love has pitched his mansion in
>   The place of excrement."

WILLIAM BUTLER YEATS, *"Crazy Jane Talks
With the Bishop"*

Interlog:

These are not our people.
The universe was clean in its conception:
Bright pure suns swept up the swirling dust,
Nebulae drifted eternally—until one fell from grace.
Our galaxy is ill:
It rots at the core, dissolves into decay, festers with putrid stench,
Diseased by the ultimate horror:
Life.

From this morass rises an unthinkable caricature of intellect,
Dedicating itself to the greater decimation of order,
Contaminating every particle.
Its guises are several, but our concern is with the nearest:
Man.

These are not our people.
The enemy is man.
This evil must be expunged, our galaxy sterilized.
No vestige of slime may remain.
Yet—the malady is far advanced;
The infection has greater resource than we.
Prematurity is defeat.
We control our revulsion; we study and are subtle.
We recruit the envoys of man's doom from his own ranks.
We select an individual and tame him to fit our purpose.
This creature is less than sane
(His culture says),
He is ideal:
Aton.
Aton has a dream of union
Aton longs to embrace beauty
Aton seeks to murder evil . . .
Aton, Aton, child of illusion,
"Fair and foul are near of kin."
Your strength rises from evil.
Look to your excrement;
Smear your face in truth
Forget ambition;
Return.

For these are not your people—
And we are not their god.

IV. MINION

Ten

It was bright, blindingly bright, even in the heavy shade. Aton had forgotten how much natural incandescence was wasted in the open. The smell of the outdoors was everywhere, rich and ecstatic. It was day and it was warm, not with the arid blast of the caverns, but with sweetness, with splendor.

Freedom! Nightmare was behind him now, his long trial over. The insane evil of the caverns could fade into the past, leaving only the Aton who had won free——the purged Aton, the clean Aton.

There were trees and grasses and open ground. The man who had conquered Chthon and kept his sanity dropped to his knees, not in any prayer of thanks, but to grasp physically at the renewed wonder of it all. His pale fingers dug into the soft turf, pleasure running up his arms; he brought a handful to his mouth, tasting the torn green of it and the fresh decay.

There is no filth in nature, he thought. There is no horror that does not originate in man's own mind.

He rolled on the ground, transported by the joys of familiarity. He knew this planet—it was as though there had been no dark interlude between his murder of Coquina's love and the present wonder, as though all of Chthon had not intervened to avenge that crime.

I loved you, pretty shell. But it was my second love, smaller than the first. And so I freed you.

A noise in the afternoon brought him out of his reverie. It had been morning when he emerged. His attention focused: the sound had been the report from the activation of an ancient projectile mechanism. A—shot. As a boy, he had once heard . . . someone was—hunting.

The associations were promising. A man who could indulge such antique tastes could also afford a private ship. He was likely to be eccentric, a loner.

But if this were a private game preserve, as seemed likely now, Aton himself could be in immediate danger. A number of exotic predators could have been stocked. He had been very foolish to let down his guard merely because he was free.

It would be best to overpower the hunter immediately and take his ship. That would solve his problem of transportation, since he could take off without having to conceal his identity from local officials.

He made his way toward the original sound, moving as quietly as possible. He was used to the rigid rock floor of the caverns, and his feet were calloused and insensitive from the eternal twilight marches. Brittle twigs seemed to project themselves magically under his toes, breaking vociferously. Surely his approach was audible for a mile or more!

He would have to wait for the man instead, hoping that his wanderings brought him within range.

In range of what? Aton had no weapon, and chance would scarcely bring the man within arm's reach. He was still thinking in cavern terms.

Quietly he felt for fragments of stone, collecting them in a little pile at his ankles. He stood behind a slender red tree, sidewise: it would appear to be too small to conceal a man, and his position for throwing was good. There had been only one shot—the man must have fired for practice, or at a mistaken target. Nervous, perhaps. Good.

Aton threw his largest stone in a high arc that intercepted no branches during its ascent. It came down noisily fifty yards from his tree—away from the hunter. The man should pass very near, on his way to investigate. The first stone would have to be accurate, even so; a projectile weapon, properly used, could be as deadly as a knife.

The quarry began to whistle tunelessly, approaching. Did the fool expect to stalk an animal that way? There would be no point in reasoning with such an idiot. Best simply to kill him and backtrack to the ship. Aton could handle any conventional model.

The whistling grew louder. Aton raised his arm, flexing his wrist comfortably. He would have to expose himself momentarily; it was too risky to aim by the sound alone.

The whistling stopped. "I should advise you," a scratchy voice said, "that my old-fashioned rifle has an old-fashioned heat perceptor. If you are sapient, act accordingly."

The tree would protect him somewhat. The hunter would not dare to approach too close, and could not gain anything by circling. But neither could Aton hope to overcome him, since he had lost the advantage of surprise. He would have to parley.

"Sapient," he called. "Truce."

"I'll hold my fire," the voice agreed, "as long as I think it wise. I'm not a very good shot, anyway—more likely to hit the stomach than the heart." The warning was plain enough: this man would shoot to maim rather than to kill.

Aton accepted the warning and put down his stones before stepping into view. He had no desire to experience the niceties of "poor" marksmanship. The hunter was less foolish than anticipated.

The hunter was short, slightly built, and middle-aged. Small, very bright eyes peered out from a deeply creased and sallow face. The hands, too, were yellow, the flesh sunken between tendons, the nails coarse and too long. But the vintage rifle those hands held was absolutely steady, and it bore unwaveringly upon Aton's midsection. This was no pampered sportsman.

The hunter was giving Aton a similar perusal. "When you

return to nature, you certainly go all out," he said at last. Aton suddenly remembered: they wore *clothing* outside, and he was naked from being in the caverns. His hair was filthy and inches long on every side; his beard was matted over chin and chest, tangled with bits of grass. His own skin was deathly pale, except where the dirt encrusted it.

"You have the look of a fugitive," the man continued. "I wondered why it never occurred to you to parley honestly, instead of foolishly trying to ambush an armed man. Perhaps I should immolate you now, before you reverse the opportunity."

The man was toying with his quarry. He could not suspect Aton's true situation, since no one outside the prison knew its location. No one except Aton himself. If this man had suspected it, he would have shot Aton immediately.

Or would he? He was watching Aton now, those frighteningly capable hands caressing the polished stock of his rifle. Did he suspect that Chthon had an outlet here? Did he know the nature of the innocent cave that led into the bowels of the planet, but lack the ultimate proof—proof that would kill him long before he could return to the surface? Did he search now not for stocked animals, but for the one creature that could tell him the secret of that unimaginable wealth, and lead him safely into Chthon?

With what interminable patience had he prowled this forest, year after year, searching for—Aton?

This man would have to die.

"Yes, I see you understand," the hunter said. "You and I will go to the cave, and you will prove your origin there—or die. Will it be necessary to demonstrate my ability to make you perform?"

"You have no ability," Aton said, not bothering to deny what the man seemed to know. "You cannot trust me, and you would be at my mercy—there."

The man smiled, and even Aton felt cold. "You do not know me well enough."

Only once had Aton met defeat in combat, and seldom had he known fear, but he was afraid of this man now. He put a hand to his mouth and spat out a garnet.

The other person's eyes narrowed appreciatively. "I might reconsider, in the face of your argument. You have more?"

Aton nodded.

"Hidden in the forest?"

Another nod.

"Your stones may bring me down after all, since those are what I came for. Do you know what a coded ship is?"

Aton knew. It meant that no one could handle the ship except the registered owner. All mechanisms locked automatically unless manipulated by the touch of the coded individual. He could not take the ship.

"I want more than the few garnets you may have brought," the man said. "I want the *mines*. All I needed immediately was the proof that you can lead me to them, and you have given it. You and I will be partners—rather wealthy ones, in time."

"What shall I call you, partner?" Aton asked. The little ship was spaceborne, the clouded ball of Chthon's planet diminishing gently behind. Seeing it in the screen, Aton was reminded of the seeming incongruity of accelerating to escape velocity, only to decelerate to galactic norm once free of the planet. But this was necessary in order to phase in the § drive. Three hours ago they had traveled at a single mile per hour, relative to the normal motion of this portion of the galaxy, and actually appeared to be falling back into the independently orbiting planet. Now their speed was a thousand times that, and soon would surpass anything possible through chemical means. The § drive could not be used on the surface of a planet, of course, since the initial motion was erratic and wrong.

The man's eyes clouded at Aton's question, betraying polarized contact lenses. "That will do nicely," he said.

"'Partner'? As you wish. I am Aton Five. You must understand that no power can send me back to Chthon until my business outside is finished. Show me that you can help me in that, before you trust me to cooperate with your designs." What a pompous snot I seem—but this principle of mutual distrust is unreliable, he thought.

"Understood. By the time you know what I offer, you will be eager to join me. There is time, and I am at your service."

But the grim mystery of the man remained. Aton had no interest in the wealth of Chthon, and had no intention of returning, but could risk neither killing nor deserting Partner until he learned more of the man's capabilities. Meanwhile, business should be conducted on an innocuous level.

"I'll buy a planet from you," Aton said, meaning that he would turn over another garnet for information about its location, and transportation there.

Partner reached for the Sector Index, a volume about the size and texture of Aton's lost *LOE*. "This covers most of the human sector—two million stars or so. I never charge for public information."

Aton took the book but did not open it. "I can't use this."

"You don't know Galactic Coordinates? I thought you were a spaceman. That system is pre-§. Centuries old. But there are always the maps."

"I know the system. But I don't think the planet I want is listed here."

"Of course not. These are stars. You have to use the subsector ephemerides for the planetary orbits. But why bother? They'll message the information to you when you pull into the system."

"This is a proscribed planet," Aton said sourly.

Partner looked at him again, pupils momentarily colorless as the lenses shifted. "You do have a problem. You know where we'll have to go first."

Aton knew.

Eleven

Earth: home of humanity and of its legends for ten thousand times the time that race had been in space, and more; whose population thrust forth a hundred million human bodies to space in each sidereal year, and did not diminish—until the catastrophic chill imposed *de faco* quarantine upon the mother world. One month—to wipe out forty percent of all its inhabitants, to bring the fusion bombs necessary to cremate the mountainous offal in the wake of that brief siege. Even so, Earth retained a population more massive than the rest of its empire combined, and still her lands and seas and atomsphere were crowded with carpets of living flesh.

Not even the chill could solve this problem.

But Earth had power. She was the irrevocable queen of a billion cubic parsecs of space, not through military, economic, or moral force, but through her surpassing knowledge. Here was technology beyond the rustic imagination of such detail and range that storage and referencing alone usurped the facilities of a small continent. Here was the Sector Library.

Computors organized and sorted the unthinkable complex, delivering any information known to man, to any party, in moments. A man had only to enter a booth and make known his desire.

Unless it was proscribed.

But there were the "stacks"—comprehensive files of printed documentation, of interest to hardly one seeker in a thousand, but sustained by ancient custom in the face of rising opposition. Some year the renewed pressure of population would abolish this monstrous relic. Meanwhile, it endured. Dedicated ancients maintained the archives in leisurely exactitude, and interest was the sole criterion for admission. Earth was after all free, and upheld the right of every person to search for knowledge and to discover as much as determination and ingenuity could provide. And the information was there, all of it—if the seeker could find it. The very awkwardness of the stacks created this advantage: the archives were far too cumbersome to purge selectively. They could not be expurgated.

The stacks occupied cubic miles of space. Never had Aton encountered an enclosure of such dimension: two hundred tiers of long, low hallways, each lined from floor to ceiling on either side with thick volumes, each extending so far into the distance that the walls seemed to meet. At regular intervals right-angled crosswalks cut off segments, making intermittent alternate passages whose staccato lengths also pressed into distant closure. Aton imagined that he could see the ponderous curve of the planet in the level flooring, and that it was the horizon that terminated the halls.

Chthon itself lost its novelty within these passages. Ever

did the works of nature, he thought, bow before the works of man.

But how to start? Every volume looked the size of *LOE*—forty million words of print. Every shelf was tightly packed, with only occasional blanks: three books to the foot, six shelves to the wall, two walls to the hall. A ten-foot section of one hall would contain 360 books—more than fourteen billion words.

Aton was not a rapid reader in either Galactic or English. A solid day of intensive effort would get him through no more than a tiny fraction of a single volume. He would be here for decades, merely finishing what was in sight, no matter how he rushed. If he skimmed, he would run the risk of missing a vital clue.

He began to understand why these files were not restricted. Only by the wildest of blunders could a person come across dangerous information—if he recognized it when he saw it. Only through the computer could the library be used effectively.

Partner, always at his elbow, had been studying him. "You've never seen a library before?"

"I thought I had." But there had been librarians who listened to the problem and flounced off to generate a collection of books in some undefined manner. Never—this.

"Accept some advice, then. You do not visit the stacks to *read*, any more than you go to space to look at a vacuum. You research. You set up coordinates and adjust your course (I'm talking about space at the moment) and ignore what doesn't concern you. You can't locate your planet by blind reading here any more than you could do it by looking out the port at sublight to find it in space.

"First you need an index, a *library* index. You need to locate the specific section of the library you want, then the specific book. Right now you don't even know where you are, although I thought for a while your wanderings had purpose. Take out a book. Look at it."

Dumbly, Aton obeyed. "This is an analysis of the Oedipus complex," he said. "A collection of essays on it." He paused. "Why, the entire book is filled with alternate interpretations. Forty million—"

"And probably not one of those people really understands it," Partner said, too sharply. "*We* certainly don't. You let your wandering feet lead you to a section and a book that has no possible relevance to the riddle you have to solve. What did you think you were doing?"

"I suppose it *was* futile," Aton said absently. He put the book back, his hand seeming somehow reluctant to let it go.

A melodious chord sounded, surprising him. A colored bulb set between shelves began to flash intermittently. "Pay attention to what you're doing!" Partner snapped. "That's the wrong place."

Aton quickly withdrew the book and found the correct slot. The alarms subsided, but already footsteps beat their heavy tread nearby. Labored breathing paced that sound.

"What's the matter with you now?"

Aton brought himself under control. "Something—something terrible, just then. A memory." His face regained its color. "I don't . . . seem to be myself, right now." His whole body was shaking.

A fat, bearded man turned the corner. He wore the emblematic cap of the Sector Library, numbered 14. "Having a little trouble, gentlemen?" There was a curious quality about his accent. Then Aton realized what it was: native Earth English, spoken by a man born to it.

"A mistake," Partner replied. "Sorry to bother you."

The attendant stayed, obviously not intending to trust any more books to their unsupervised carelessness. He was old, the wrinkles showing through the corpulent mounds of his cheeks, and the backs of his pallid hands were landscapes. "I may help you?"

"Yes," Aton said. "I'm looking for a planet."

"In a library?"

Aton smiled dutifully. "Its name is Minion." Would the man react?

Caretaker 14 lifted his smooth beard thoughtfully. "Mignon. That would be one of the flower planets."

"I don't think so," Aton said, but he looked upon the man with a certain dawning respect. There *was* a planet of Mignon; he had seen it in the ephemerides when he searched for the other. All the planets of that system had been named for flowers.

"Ah—I knew the term was familiar. Did you know that our standard typeface is Minion? Seven point print, about ten lines to the inch—"

Aton shook his head in negation. "This is a planet. An inhabited one. But I don't know the name of its primary."

"We'll find it. The index, the Cyclopaedia, the ephemerides—oh, never fear, we'll find it!" Number 14 spoke with subdued excitement and confidence, as though he had forgotten the origin of the request. It had become his own problem, and he would not be satisfied until he ran it down. Aton smiled at the man's simplicity. "Proscribed, of course?" Aton frowned at the man's insight.

"It may be. Frankly, I had heard about it, but didn't seem to find it in the regular lists—"

"Yes. And you could not afford to use the computer, because it records all dubious requests. We get a number of similar cases. But don't be concerned. Stack personnel are harmless and confidential. Generally."

Was the man requesting a bribe for silence? Or trying to pry additional information to sate his curiosity? What were his terms? They followed him down interminable passages, ill at ease.

They arrived at somewhat wider halls. Lining one wall was a series of booths, each with a central table and bench. Number 14 settled them in one and began rounding up references.

Aton looked at Partner. "Can we trust him?" his glance inquired. "We have to," Partner's expression replied.

Number 14 returned with an armful of books and a small box. He piled them all on the table. "You have to approach a proscribed planet—don't be alarmed, these booths are sealed private—deviously," he said cheerfully. "The primary has to be listed, of course, since you can hardly hide a star by ignoring it, but there may not be much evidence to link it to the planet you want. Now here we have the index of all the stars in the Earth Sector. If the sun we want is in it—and we'll have to assume that it is, because there are a hundred thousand sectors in the galaxy, most of them impossibly alien—we can be

certain that it is listed here. This reference does not indicate
whether there are habitable planets, but they are not hard to
spot: the early explorers named the habitables and let numbers
do for the others. Unless they had a special interest in the
system, in which case they named them all. But the point is
that *all* inhabited planets are named, even though not all named
planets are habitable. Are you with me so far?"

Aton and Partner nodded. Had this man *ever* appeared ignorant or naïve?

"Comes from a lifetime of spot researching," 14 said in
answer to the unspoken comment. "A good library assistant
can locate things even the computer balks at." He smiled, to
show that this was a slight exaggeration, and fiddled with the
box. It glowed, and the end wall lighted. "I'm going to project
a sector map," he said. "You are familiar with the type, of
course—white for the front stars, red shift for the distant ones?
And you've heard the joke about the color-blind navigator?
Too bad. And you understand that only the established navigational beacons can be shown in such a comprehensive illustration. We'll get on to the detail maps in a moment." He
touched a plate, and intricate networks appeared, linking the
stars in curious patterns. Aton was reminded painfully of the
Xest painting. Perhaps that was the origin of Xest art.

"This is an overlay showing the routes of exploration," 14
said. "It does not occur to most people that all inhabited planets
have to be discovered by someone, in order to get that way.
We have records of all the early explorations. Now we can get
a fair idea of the placement of your planet if you will answer
a few questions. Is it settled?"

"Yes," Aton said, fascinated by the dispatch with which the
search was moving at last. "For several centuries, I think."

"Good. That eliminates the recent colonies, which far out-
number the established ones." The overlay changed and the
majority of the threaded patterns disappeared. "This sets the
limit at §100—much less complicated, as you see. By using
this outline, we can reduce our list of prospects to several
thousand. Do you have any navigational data at all?"

"No. It could be anywhere."

"It can only be where it *is*. Are the natives modified?"

"They must be. At least, the women have a reputation—"

"Ah. This reduces the number again. Do you happen to know *why* it is proscribed?"

"Only the legend. The women are reported to be sirens that live forever. It is said to be—to be death to love one."

"Ah," 14 said, uncomfortably alert. "You love one of these sirens. I hope for your sake that the legend is not true. Even a normal woman is bad enough. But we shall assume that genetic engineering has granted the inhabitants longevity. Which certainly could be grounds for proscription. Earth is overpopulated, even now, and she long since decreed that colonization should be by export from the home planet; she deplores natural increase in population through longevity."

"Earth can't dictate—" Partner began. He had been quietly studying the projection.

Number 14 shrugged. "Have it your way. But the planet is out of circulation nevertheless. And this narrows the range further, because longevity is post-§ by about fifty years. It took a score more before it became commercially feasible—bad side effects, you know—and ten years after that the law cracked down. Or whatever unofficial euphemism did, since as you point out, Earth cannot dictate."

"Ten years," Partner said. "§70 to §80."

The overlay changed again, and now the map enlarged and the routes were replaced by bright colony indicators. "Modified colonies for that period are few. A mere hundred or so, as you can see. We could look each of them up in the index now, if we could be certain that it listed all the planets. But planets, unfortunately, are not the navigational hazards that stars are. I think our time would be wasted."

"There is no colony record?"

"Not for proscribed efforts. They simply aren't mentioned, at least not by name, and not in the up-to-date volumes. We simply haven't the space to preserve annual publications; the old books that predate proscription would list your planet, but they were thrown out centuries ago. We could run it down by elimination—but if there is more than one proscribed planet hidden in the list, we could not be certain which one is yours."

Partner was busy with the index. "Get me the sector Cyclopaedia volume covering 'Point,'" he said.

"'Point?' As you say," 14 agreed. "But the Cyclop' doesn't list stars."

In a moment they were poring over the text. "'Point, Jonathan R., stellar scout, §41-154,'" Partner read. "That should be our man."

"The discoverer of Point, one of the stars on our list," 14 said. "Probably his first 'habitable,' since he named it after himself. But what makes you think—"

"I followed your advice," Partner said. "I approached the problem deviously. Your conventional approach can only take you a certain distance, since, as you point out, they could simply number a proscribed planet, as though it were uninhabited, or skip it entirely, leaving you without proof of its identity. But the clue lies in a homonym." He found his place and read aloud again: "'Point: an ancient unit of type measurement . . . seventy-two points to the inch . . .'"

"I don't follow—"

"Get your index and read off the named planets of Point."

Baffled, 14 opened the book. "The first two are unnamed fireballs; then Excelsior, Diamond, Pearl—why, I recognize these! They're type sizes!"

"Go on."

"Pearl, Nonpareil, Brevier, Bourgeois, Elite. That's all."

Partner's gaze was bright. "Sure you aren't missing one?"

"Why, the type we use here—"

"Minion!" Aton exclaimed. "Seven point!"

"The seventh planet," Partner whispered.

"One has to allow for an explorer's sense of identity," Partner said. "And his humor. Jonathan R. Point probably had a private contract signed for settlement of the first few good worlds he found, and anticipated trouble when Earth caught on. He had no intention of letting a little thing like a proscription obliterate one of *his* planets."

Twelve

Minion reminded him of Hvee, with its gentle green mountains, its absence of industry, its innocence. The ship, nestled in an isolated clearing, seemed an imposition on the virginity of the planet.

Aton cut cross-country until he struck a dusty road that brief aerial reconnaissance indicated led to the nearest native village. Partner allowed him to travel alone, here—there was no way he could escape a proscribed planet, except the way he came. Minion was backward, of course: the inhabitants would certainly know *of* galactic technology, but be unable to partake of it themselves. The penalty was cruel.

The first primitive huts came into view. They were fashioned of rustic thatch and clay, but looked comfortable, and the odor characteristic of bucolic habitation was not strong. That meant the natives were clean. People walked about, human rather than humanoid, paying the stranger no attention. Modification, at least, had taken no objectionable turns—not visible ones, at any rate. The men were small, garbed in short cloths and deep frowns; the women were tall, veiled, clad in all-concealing togas.

A couple came toward him, up the road. The man was a full six inches shorter than his companion, but seemed comfortable enough in his loincloth and neatly rounded beard. The woman stumbled under the weight of an enormous parcel that, combined with the meshes of her toga, threatened at any moment to bring her to the ground.

Aton stepped aside to let them pass. It seemed to him that an intolerable heat must be trapped inside the heavy wrappings of the woman, and indeed, she swayed as she walked. Her foot caught on a projecting stone in the rough road and she stumbled and almost fell. The heavy package in her arms brushed the man as she struggled for balance.

The little man spoke sharply in a dialect incomprehensible

to Aton, but it was easy for him to identify well-turned invective. The man wheeled in wrath and struck her full in the veil. The woman fell, the package spinning from her arms and rolling across the road almost to Aton's feet.

As the woman scrambled to get up, the man cursed again and kicked her violently. Aton had never seen so vile a temper. The woman made no sound, but moved quickly on hands and knees to recover the package. Reeling, she stood up, grasping the heavy object once more. From the far side of the road the man spouted a steady stream of monosyllabic vitriol.

They went on, never acknowledging Aton's presence at all.

As he passed through the village he noticed that none of the men were doing work of any kind. Only the women labored— and strenuously.

One old man leaned against a tree at the edge of a central square, alone. Aton addressed himself to this man in Galactic sign language. "Where may a stranger stay?"

The oldster eyed him. He gestured lackadaisically. "Have you a woman?" The symbol actually used was "female chattel."

Aton thought of Malice. "No."

"You have come at a favorable time, then. You may take Pink Rock's house and woman this evening."

Aton hesitated. Customs varied widely in the galaxy, but it was best to understand the situation completely before committing oneself. "Is Pink Rock going somewhere?"

The man gestured at the square. Aton saw what he had overlooked before: a man bound to a great vertical stone, sinister instruments ranged on a platform before him.

"Executed? A criminal?"

"No."

"A sacrifice?"

"No."

"Why is he bound, then?"

"He was careless."

"?" (The signal for perplexity.)

"He fell in love with his woman."

(Perplexity.) "For that he is to be tortured?"

The old man stared him in the eyes. "It is merciful."

Aton did not stay to witness the rites for the careless Pink

Rock. Instead he promised to return after the ceremony, and wandered around the neighborhood, trying to reason out the mystery of these poeple. Monsters they might be branded, officially and in folklore—but where was the terror that held the galaxy at bay? Why the inviolate strictures against commerce and communication? All he had seen so far was an incredibly patriarchal society, with the women reduced to such absolute subjugation that it was a crime for a man even to love one.

But doubt remained. Swathed in their drapes and veils as these women of Minion were—he could not think of them as "minionettes"—it was impossible for him to make out face or feature. Still there was a quality about them that was distressingly familiar.

He shrugged it off. Of course there was familiarity. Malice had been generated here.

At the village well a solitary woman was filling a large leather bucket. She closed it with a cord looped around the top and slung it over her shoulder, staggering with the weight.

Aton stepped into her path, offering to take the bucket. He did not do it from any particular chivalry, but because he saw an opportunity to learn more about her. She shied away.

"But I only wish to help," he signaled. He reached for the bucket, catching the strap, but she arched back so quickly that a corner of her veil was trapped. It slid off her face.

Aton stared. It was Malice.

He let her go. He knew, intellectually, that Malice could not be on the planet. Even if she were, the odds against encountering her in such coincidental fashion were prohibitive—and after the thing he had attempted so long ago, and almost suppressed from memory, she could not again tempt him with a well. He remembered also the seeming change that had come over the face of the daughter of Four, and the picture he had seen later in a huge gas crevasse in Chthon. He could not always trust his vision.

But in case this were not another fevered fragment—

Another woman came down the path. He stepped up to her, offered to assist, and clumsily caught loose her veil. Again the face of Malice. No—the eyes were not so deep, the hair less flamed. This was a faded Malice. What did it mean?

Until this point he had hesitated, careful of native proprieties, but now he had to know. Which was mad—himself or the planet?

Two women walked together down the road, carrying their inevitable burdens. Aton blocked them off and, in an agony of anticipation, tore free both veils.

Identical faces returned his stare. On each the fire hair flowed long, and deep green eyes looked out. Twin reflections of his love.

"Who are you?" he cried, aloud and with the signs.

Twin smiles of devastating beauty answered him. "I am Torment," one signaled. "Horror is my name," signaled the other.

At last Aton understood.

Evening, and the errand of mercy was done. The gutted corpse hung silent now, the stink of burning entrails slowly dissipating. Pink Rock's empty sockets surveyed the gathered friends sitting in the sweet grass of the square, relaxing after their service to him.

Aton stood at the edge, certain without knowing why that no sadism had been involved. Pink Rock had not been censured—it had merely been necessary to cleanse him of his foul emotion. Certainly the last vestige of his love had been torn bloodily out before he had died. Now the lovely minionettes removed their veils and sang in rapturous chorus, more sweetly than any human group could sing, their hymn of accomplishment. Aton thrilled to the sound. Not since his childhood had he felt such enchantment—though there was an uncomfortable alien bitterness close beneath the surface.

The men of Minion sat in a separate group, washing their hands and scowling. I understand, Aton thought. You performed from necessity, angry that your artistry was required, angry with your beautiful women, angry at your society. You are always angry.

At last the minionettes reset their veils and rejoined their masters. Scowls and curses faded into the dusk. Surely these women would be happy to leave this planet, to serve normal men, when the opportunity presented. Yet Malice's motives had hardly been that simple.

One woman stood silently before the corpse in an attitude of prayer. Aton came up behind her and took her arm. This was Pink Rock's widow.

She led him to a hut near the outskirt, and stood aside courteously for him to enter first. She had accepted the change-over without protest or surprise. She had had a man who loved; now she had one who did not. That was all.

The dark interior smelled of fresh hay. Aton's eyes adjusted to a room somewhat larger than anticipated, quite clean and well arranged. There was a mattress of soft grasses across the back, wide enough for two. A low table beside it supported several light fiber pillows, a candle, and a whip.

"I hunger," he gestured peremptorily, and she fetched flat bread and flat water. He spat it out in a show of anger, and she went outside to bring replacements. "I tire," he signaled, and she undressed him gently and led him to the mattress. She lifted his feet into place and propped him with pillows skillfully.

The minionette was dutiful; the minionette was strong.

Aton's mind returned, horribly, to a similar scene. He did not want to remember it, but could not help himself. Once before he had found himself in a confined space with a woman, a minionette. Once before he had undressed.

"Tell me your name." He had to destroy that memory.

"Misery," her signal answered. He heard "Malice." He saw again the bubble confine of the asteroid lodging—the spotel. The two of them had docked the shuttle, passed directly from ship's lock to entrance lock and on into the lush private accommodation. He had doffed his skin-tight protective suit immediately, becoming naked before her in the half-light. Malice had been quiet and mechanical—hardly the sparkling creature he had captured so recently at the Xest outpost. She did not strip.

"Do you want to know my name?" Inane conversation, hardly visible in the coming night. Anything to kill that terrible recollection!

Misery answered: "If it pleases the master to tell it."

"Damn!" he exploded, looking at the veil, seeing the blank

mask of the space suit holding her beauty from him. "You servile husk! Don't you have any will of your own?"

He had spoken out loud, forgetting to signal; he knew no native could understand. But Misery responded with a beatific smile visible even through the dark veil.

Angry and alarmed, he tore off that veil. Had he been trapped into—

Her hair was dull, her eyes gray. She resembled more the Captain than the nymph. She was smiling still, but blankly.

I am a fool, he thought. If she had understood my spoken words, she would not have smiled. This *is* a native girl, trained to react to harshness with a forgiving smile.

Yet the man who loved her had been tortured to death.

"You may think of me as 'Stone Heart,'" he said, adopting the evident custom of the planet. He was still angry, as perhaps the native men were angry—at her, at the system she represented, the enormity of it and its somber mystery. At the awful memories this situation evoked by being unfairly similar.

"Why aren't you beautiful?" Now he was being deliberately unkind, and his anger turned against himself. Must fury beget fury?

She only smiled.

"Take off your clothing," he ordered. He could hardly see her now. "First light the candle. I want to *see* you." She obeyed slowly.

Her body was glorious. The long hair flowed over shoulders and sculptured breasts, and his eye followed the fold of the space suit as it peeled away from her narrow waist and swelling hips and thighs. Alone with her, entirely alone, for the first time . . .

But this is the memory! he thought. *It is Misery I am looking at, not Malice! Not Malice. Not—*

Not, not subject to the laws of any planet, but here, in the inviolate privacy of the spotel, the rented transitory lodging of newlyweds and wealthy travelers of space. A luxurious retreat, a luxurious body, unfettered at last.

Misery!

I love you, Malice, and you are mine.

Misery!

Why don't you respond, Malice?

Memory . . .

Why are you silent?

Malice . . .

Why have you withdrawn? Are you ill? Malice, Malice . . .

But she was in radiant health, hair burning, burning, eyes never so deep; natural, normal, except that she seemed to have no awareness of him.

Speak to me!

She would not. What unseen hand had placed a spell upon her, made her mute, in the hour of triumph? Had some post-hypnotic state been invoked, some command inflicted by an unknown enemy intent on his destruction? Was it now his duty to break her out of it, a sleeping beauty, with a single splendid kiss?

He kissed her, but she did not wake to him. Her lips were mushy, unresponsive.

Or was a greater effort required? Should he make love to her?

When he had not yet given her the hvee?

He took her in his arms, one elbow beneath her shoulders, the other under her knees, carried her limp body to the couch, and spread it out.

Misery! With a terrible shock Aton wrenched himself back to the present. Misery lay on the staw pallet, nude and lovely, open to the caress of his hands. He had thought his Malice to be unique, but here was a duplicate form, one of dozens in this village alone, and hundreds, thousands on the planet. He had mistaken the standard attributes of the species for beauty, duping his emotion all his life.

Misery smiled again, twisting her body in pleasure. How strange that this woman, the one he did not desire, reacted so positively to his careless touch, while Malice . . .

Malice—was it amnesia? Yet she showed no distress, no alarm, no confusion. She saw him, recognized him—but as an article of furniture, not as a man. She was not catatonic, nor did she collide with him when she moved.

Could her love for him have failed? Had it ever existed at all? Her bright hair and measureless eyes denied both. Her love was strong. It had to be for him; the minionette did not glow in the company of the wrong man. She would never have come with him, without love.

She had been a captain in space, enormously capable. Never would she do a thing without excellent reason. There had to be a motive. Did she know something that he did not? Something that she was unable to tell him?

He had a vision of the elemental drama for children: behind the lock there stands a criminal, blaster in hand, about to rob and ravish the heroine. At the entrance is her lover: muscular, handsome, intelligent. But if she makes known her plight, that lover will be the first to die. And so she must be silent, and try to signal to him in some manner that the hidden intruder will not intercept. If she is able to convey the message, however obscurely, the resolution is assured.

Malice lay exposed, arm hanging down, legs gently spread, astonishingly lovely. Her breathing was regular, her eyes closed.

Where was the villain? The airlock had borne the unbroken seal of the proprietor. There could be no third party here, not on an isolated airless asteroid, pressurized only upon their entry. There could be no secret monitoring device, no remote-control threat. Privacy, above all else, was what the proprietors sold. YOU CAN DEPEND ON PRIVACY AT THE SPOTEL, the company advertised, and it had the means to protect its reputation.

Malice lay passive. The mystery was deeper than that . . . and he could not bring himself to perform an act upon a mannequin. He was baffled.

His mental censor balked. Memory would not go further. Relieved, he turned his full attention to Misery.

Her hair, in the candlelight, was brighter now. This woman, if he understood the signs, was learning to love him already— and all he had done was to aggravate her. Suddenly he felt remorse, felt warm respect for her suffering.

Misery recoiled.

This time he had neither signaled nor spoken, yet she had reacted. The minionette was telepathic! He had suspected this before; why had he forgotten? She could read his thoughts, or at least, his emotions, and was responding to these, not his words.

There remained one oddity.

Aton gathered his mental forces and sent a blast of emotional ferocity at her, hate and fury as sheer as he could make them.

Surprised pleasure lighted her features. She bounced up, caught his shoulders, pressed herself against him, kissed him passionately.

Her emotions were inverted! His hate was her love!

Things fell into place: the villainy of the little man on the road, the response to any male irritation. And Malice—she had been most affectionate when he was angry or miserable, and cold when he felt romantic. No wonder she had been impossible to get along with!

Misery was close to him, her hair brightening by the instant. He hit her. She rocked with the force of the blow, smiling dazzlingly. He grasped her flaming tresses and brought her roughly to him, smiting her with hate. She leaped to meet his savage kiss. He bit her soft lip, hard, to bring blood; she moaned with pleasure and did not bleed.

Aton locked an arm over her neck, pinning her securely. Then he brought to mind an image of gentle fields of hvee, the waiting love overflowing, selflessly desiring an object.

Misery twisted and struggled, her face a mask of pain. "Yes," he said, "it hurts you, doesn't it? How much more would it hurt if I were to love you, yourself, not just the hvee?" A strangled cry broke from her.

He held her still, though she was very strong. "Don't you see, Misery—I'm actually being more sadistic than you can imagine. I know it hurts you to be near love—therefore I hurt you most by loving you. And you must return with joy the love of the man who hurts you most."

She ceased her struggles and looked up at his face with confusion. She could not understand his spoken words, but the mood behind them was devastating.

"I will have mercy on you," he continued, not releasing her. "I will spare you, as my darling did not spare me. Because I cannot directly feel your emotion, not in the sense you can feel mine. Because you cannot comprehend the paradox of your make-up. Because I know the sincerity of your intent, and the necessity of your widowhood. Because I want to make you happy in the brief time available to me. I shall reward you by taking out on you all the fury I feel for what your sister has made of me.

"I'm going to kill you, Misery."

He took her head in his powerful hands, hooking his fingers in her ears, and twisted. She smiled. His muscles jumped as he wrenched, trying to break her neck, but slowly. She gave herself up to the luxury of it. She was like a doll, limp, pliable, unbelievably tough underneath. Then the fury took him, and he drove her head against the mattress as though to tear it off and bury it by brute force.

It was a long, long time before, exhausted, he realized that bare hands, no matter how capable, were insufficient to kill the minionette. She was a creature of punishment; she was made for this; she delighted in it.

Aton rested, defeated, her body warm against his, caressing him, loving him. He had not been able to expunge that which was in him.

Would a knife pierce that seemingly fragile flesh? He was afraid to find out. The whip, well worn, had left no sign on her body.

But there were other mysteries. All the minionettes were cast from a single mold; all responded to the sadistic love inversion, while the men appeared to be normal. But he had seen no old women. Could they all be young?

"How long do you live, Misery?" This time the signal.

She tried to answer him. "There is no limit—"

"You are immortal?"

"No."

"How do you die?"

"When there is pain, too much, it kills."

And our love is your pain, he thought. As long as a man hates you, you live and grow more beautiful and your hair flames. But when he is kind to you, when he loves you, you die.

Yet it had been Pink Rock who had died, not his woman.

"Do you know the meaning of love?" he asked her.

"Oh, yes, it is my being. I love—"

"Did you love Pink Rock?"

"Yes—he was good, at first. But we had no son. Then his mind became twisted, and he hurt me. I might have made him love me again, if they had not taken him away."

Of course. The minionette was tough. She would not expire in simple feminine helplessness. If a man began to "hurt" her, she would try to cure the pain by recapturing his original attitude. She would, in fact, do everything in her considerable power to make him, by male definition, hate her. The men of Minion could hardly allow that. The line between love and hate might seem narrow to some, but it could also be appallingly wide—wide as the chasm of Chthon. For who could say in what manner that terrible emotion might manifest itself, before it settled on the intended object?

The men of Minion were wise. They understood the devastation lying stored beneath the careless torch of uncontrolled emotion. They took the necessary and merciful step, and extinguished it before the minionette acted. They were kind, in their fashion—they tried to give the man back his natural hate before he died, to take with him to his spirit world.

The civilization of the greater galaxy was not so wise. It envisioned mercy as abstinence from death. It recognized the inherent danger of the love of the minionette, but preferred to ship the victim to the eternal prison of Chthon, rather than perform the execution directly.

But even Chthon could not contain the evil of that love. How many there had died?

Why had Malice come into the galaxy? How? What had made her seek him out? Why had she enticed his young love, love that must have tortured her from the beginning? She would have been better off without him, secure in her position in the Merchant Service. Or on her home world, where men understood.

His brain knew the answer, but would not yield it to consciousness. She had told him, there at the—

"Misery—was Pink Rock's love stronger than mine, before he changed?"

"No, Stone Heart. Your love is the strongest. More than any man."

Because I am of the galaxy. Because I am a member of a species not conditioned to the minionette. What a rare treat, when a woman of this planet escapes into the galaxy, where every man feels his feelings with naïve strength. Where, unaware of the telepathic linkage, his every confused nuance of anger and pain sears his imagination.

Yes, my emotion is strong. The sensitive hvee responded to it and grew for me in my childhood, and Malice understood that potential—and something else—when she encountered that little boy on that pastoral world. She made her sacrifice and cast her fine net over that boy, and sent him away before the burgeoning sensation became too much for her. She knew that my love was not for her, not then, though it tempted her sorely. I was then a harmless dalliance, a moment of anticipation, not ready for harvest.

Not until I sought her out, torn by such frustration and such doubt from the fruitless search that she was unable to resist. She tried to savor me secretly, close but disguised. Until the Xest picture penetrated the Captain and revealed the minionette...

...And doomed us both.

"Come, Misery," he said. "I will inflict on you a love you've never dared dream of before."

10

Ninety-nine men and a hundred and forty-two women began the terrors of the Hard Trek. Not with courage and boldness, not seeking destiny with consummate determination; but frightened, desperate, driven—driven by the certain knowledge of hunger and pain behind.

The revolution of the lower caverns had been betrayed, and every one of them had to pay the price of failure. No food came down from the upper caverns any more. Tally's people had ample reserves, many stones hoarded for just such an emergency: they would not relent.

The fragment of Framy's blue garnet might have purchased time, had it been known to exist before. Instead, it was proof of doom, showing that they had denied what the upper cavern leaders had known to be truth. The revolt had never had a chance, in the face of that; it had been no more than a convenient pretext to abolish the entire nether population.

The trek began with fatalism. No one could doubt that the majority would soon be dead, and not cleanly.

The legend of Doc Bedside guided them. He had set off five years before, downwind, homemade pack and kit bound to his wiry body, a sharp stone in his hand. He had disappeared into the land of the chimera and never been heard from again—until Aton brought the confirmation that he had won through. Bedside had emerged the other side of sanity—but could such madness take two hundred and forty-one experienced and fore-warned travelers? They followed his route, searching for the tokens of his passing, if they existed; it would be easier, this second time.

They were wrong, of course.

Aton marched in the vanguard for ten hours, or what he thought of as that length of time, following the spacious caverns and passages up a gentle but steady incline. The walls spread farther apart, the ceiling grew higher; as the space increased, the wind diminished and cooled. The journey became almost pleasant. But for the total lack of food, the outer caverns were far better for human residence than the ones they had known.

They rested for an estimated six hours, hungry bellies growling. No one stood guard. Everyone had to travel together, and the fearsome pit creatures never approached so large a party. Almost, they hoped for an attack—because concerted action might trap and bring down even the chimera, and there was sure to be meat on its body. Starvation would halt the journey as its beginning unless something edible was located soon. Bedside must have eaten from the caverns.

On the third march the first people collapsed from exhaustion and hunger. They were methodically butchered and eaten.

Aton stood in the faltering circle as Bossman showed the way: he severed the warm limbs with his axe as other men pulled them away from the trunk of the first corpse. The blood spattered and covered the blade, poured over the stone floor, thickened as it flowed morbidly back down the trail they had taken. Hastings made fire, burning a few of the old, dry, useless water-skins; the smoke and stench were nauseating, and the meat scorched and dropped and did not cook well. Future preparations would have to be raw.

Bossman's axe did further duty, reducing the limbs to

smaller sections and breaking up the trunk. Individual knives and stones were pressed into service to finish the job. "Whoever is hungry, eat," he said.

Not many did, that first time. Usable portions were wrapped in the remaining skins and assigned to surly porters, since Bossman didn't believe in waste. The bones and other refuse were left for the chimera. During later marches more and more people broke down and ate, gagging over the rawness of it but finding it preferable to starvation.

In time, every surviving member of the party was eating— by definition. Those who had been unable to surmount their scruples, starved.

Scruples were not for the Hard Trek.

During the fourth march the attacks began. Stragglers screamed and were found with their innards strewn. A clean-up crew was organized to salvage usable portions. But the main party was not approached, and the chimera remained unseen by any eyes not inside it.

For the fourth sleep Bossman found a use for their traitor. He bound Framy to a projection a little beyond the camping area. "Sing out if you see the chimera," he advised. "Sleep if you want to."

.   .   .

Aton listened.

". . . I know I done wrong. I lied all the time. Aton, he was smart, he only lied when it counted. Must've figured we'd both get canned if they knew. I wonder who found that other chunk of blue? Somebody picked it up and smuggled it up the hole. But I guess I'm paying for all them little lies now. 'Cause I can't make up for the real ones, they're part of me. But I know I got to pay, and the only way I can do it is that way he showed me, by taking it out on something else, like Garnet did. I got to be punished for the lie I didn't tell, and maybe that makes good the ones I did tell and can't take back.

"Who's that? I hear you, you can't hide from me, I hear good. Don't try to fool me. I hear the—the tread of your foot, and—and the bellow of your breath and the swish of your tail and . . ."

The choking screams brought the men running from the main group, to stand sickened at the sight of what remained. Blood dripped from empty sockets and from a mouth where a tongue had been and down between scratched legs.

Bossman studied the living body and hefted his axe. One blow severed the cords of the neck. "I made him feel a little easier," he said, apologizing for his weakness.

Another man cut the corpse free from the projection. "Maybe that's what separates the men from the chimera," he said. "We kill *before* we take the delicacies."

Do we? Aton wondered. Do we really?

·   ·   ·

Early in the sixth march they encountered the river, perhaps a hundred miles from their starting point. Narrow, but deep and swift, the clear water cut across the wind cavern, forming a small chasm of its own. It was the first flowing water they had seen in Chthon, and the sight was miraculous.

"The lots," Bossman said. "If we can drink this—"

The collected garnets were produced and shuffled. Hastings handled the routine. He plunged both hands into the skin of stones and withdrew two closed fists while Bossman shaped the others into a rough line. Hastings put his fists under the nose of the first person, a dour woman. She slapped the left one; it opened to reveal an ordinary red garnet. She took it and flipped it disdainfully back into the cache and drifted away unchallenged.

Hastings returned the empty hand to the bag and brought it out again, closed. The next person in line selected the same fist: a second red garnet. He also left, relieved.

Aton was third in line. He chose the same hand—and the fatal blue fragment was his.

"One," Bossman said. "Better take one more, to be sure."

A woman stepped out of line and came up. It was Garnet. "I'll do it," she said. "Might as well move up my turn." Bossman frowned, but let it stand.

The line disbanded. It would reform at the next crisis, with the man following Aton at the head, in fixed order, until every person in the party had drawn. After that it would begin again. The garnets were put away.

Bossman pointed to the stream. "Drink," he said. "Good and deep. Fill your skins, too." He spoke to the others. "Stay on the 'denser. We ain't sure yet."

The others needed no warning. The water could be poisonous, or there could be minute marine creatures deadly to living flesh. Or larger ones, waiting for the first unwary entry into the water. Chthon was never innocent.

Aton and Garnet drank. The water was not cold, but it tasted fresh and sweet compared to that extracted from the air. If the two of them lived, the others would know that this source was safe.

"If we traveled the river," Hastings pointed out, "we might not need the 'denser at all. Or the skins."

Bossman looked at him. "Which way do we go—up or down?"

Hastings spread his hands. "I see your point."

"*I* don't see it," Aton's friend with the black hair cut in. "We go upriver, we have water, and we're heading for the top. What's the matter with that?"

"We go upriver," Hastings said calmly, "and we may find nothing but a layer of porous rock with the moisture percolating through and dripping down until it collects enough to make the river."

"Follow it down, then," she said with affected indifference.

"How fast do you think we'll reach the surface if we travel *down?*"

She looked at him suspiciously. "You fat tub. We got to go one way or the other."

"We follow the caverns," Bossman said, cutting off the argument. "They go up, and the wind proves they go *somewhere.*"

The party, not as large as it once had been, forded the river carefully and moved on. The tunnels continued to rise and expand. The glow from the walls diminished, bringing shadow; the front and rear of the column were attacked more persistently by unseen predators. Aton and Garnet walked together near the center, a little apart from the others, who gave them leeway

on either side. Their position was not coincidental: the water
test would be invalid if they were to fall prey to the chimera
instead. They were protected by their position, but until sufficient time elapsed, close association was not desired by the
others. An illness spawned by the water would find these prisoners with very little natural defense.

"You don't curse me much, any more, Garnet," Aton remarked.

"There's no point, Aton. I lost."

"Why did you cover for me?" he asked, needling her.

She closed her eyes, navigating by the sound of massed
footsteps, as everyone could do now. The question needed no
answer, but she spoke to the intent behind it. "Because you
are like *him.*" This was her first reference to her life before
Chthon. "Not in appearance, but in your rocklike heart. Such
men, such demons as you, there is no pity in you, only purpose."

"And you loved him, and you killed him, because he
wouldn't love you," Aton said. "And now you love me."

"I tried to fight it. I knew what you were the first time I
saw you."

Oh, Malice, Malice, do you taunt me as I do this lonely
woman? Why must I hurt her?

"Don't you know that I will never be yours? I will never
kiss you. I will never love you."

"I know," she said.

"Are you going to kill me, too?"

She marched on, unable to speak.

"Or yourself, this time?"

Revenge was bitter; he no longer cared for it. Garnet had
been a pawn in his game, no more. She had alibied him from
association with the blue garnet by agreeing that they had been
making love at the critical time. It was a more pleasant memory
than the truth: that he had raped her once and found her wanting.
Now she shared the blame for Framy's death, and knew it.

"There is no escape," he said, talking as much to himself
as to her. "I tried to break her hold, but she reached across the
light-years to strike me down." Why did he tell his secrets to
this woman? he wondered. Had he really captured Garnet for
revenge, or merely because he needed a foil, a property, even
in Chthon? Did he understand any part of his own motives?

11

Two more marches brought them to really spacious caverns. The ceiling towered into a lofty gloom, and passages were a hundred feet across. The wind was no more than a fading whisper, and it was cool: distinctly disconcerting, in Chthon. There was a feeling, an expectation; the caverns could not continue much longer. The steady rise must already have brought them very near the surface.

The walls peeled back abruptly. They stood on the brink of the passage termination: an enormous chasm, so wide that the farther shore was lost in dark obscurity, so deep that toppling pebbles never returned the sound of their landing.

They gathered apprehensively, two hundred men and women milling at the brink. On either side the floor ended; there was no way around.

"Fire a torch," Bossman snapped.

One of the rare brands was lighted, sputtering its yellow light with unfamiliar brilliance. Holding it aloft, Bossman stood at the edge and looked down.

"They ain't supposed to burn that way," someone muttered. "That's too fierce."

"How would you know?" another said. "Three years since you saw real light, ain't it?"

The ceiling of the chasm became visible as the light flared up. It was nearer than Aton had thought, within fifty feet, a mass of depending porous formations like an undersea landscape, from which streamers of opaque vapor drifted down. There was something ominous about it. What vapor was heavier than air? But the far side was still out of sight, and the depths into which the mist descended were murky.

Bossman shouted, and the echo took ten seconds.

"There's one way to find out how deep this thing is," a man suggested.

Bossman smiled.

"No!" Hastings exclaimed, jumping ponderously to stop

him. But he was too late. Bossman had flung the torch into the gulf.

Hastings stared in horror. "That's gas, you fool," he said. "It'll burn."

Fascinated, the group watched the glowing stick go down. As it fell it grew brighter, illuminating the sharply slanting canyon wall beneath their feet. The brilliance was extraordinary; the light became a minor nova. Now it was reflected from below, from a whitish cloud filling the foot of the crevasse. The near wall was featureless.

The torch struck the nether cloud, and suddenly there was light, flashing silently, like sheet lightning, and then vanishing. Again the flash, revealing the splendor of Chthon in neon radiation.

Aton peered down, and saw the face of Malice, in the fire and the depth, flickering on and off, on and off, in a beckoning smile. "Kiss me," the silent image said. "Here is the other side of the song."

Strong hands pulled him back. "You don't want to die that bad," Garnet said.

At last the glowing failed, and the abyss was dark again.

"Not dense enough," Hastings said, the cold sweat running off his body. "Praise Chthon you didn't blow us all to hell. Can't you see what this is?"

Bossman accepted the reprimand. "What is it?"

"The fire cycle," Hastings said. Faces stared blankly at him. "Look, the vapor drops from the ceiling there, some kind of natural gas. It settles in a pool at the bottom. Probably there are many crevices and rifts that suck the mixture through to the flames. Miles of tubing, similar to what we have been traveling through, only much farther down. The whole thing is a gigantic blowtorch (if you remember the primitive term), spewing fire and superheated air out the other end, heating the caverns. As that air travels and expands, it cools, until it arrives back here and brushes those saturated formations above, picking up more fuel."

"What do you know," Bossman said in amazement.

This meant, Aton realized, that this was a closed cycle. Water vapor, oxygen, combustibles—all seeped through porous rock, allowing no physical exit. There could be no escape

this way, even if they found a way to cross the main chasm.
The draft went nowhere, and they were still trapped.

•   •   •

The party slept: men and women sprawled in all attitudes
across the floor, gathering strength and courage for the march
back to the river. In the "morning" those unable or unwilling
to continue would be slaughtered and prepared; this was already
routine, and no lots had been necessary so far for the performance of this ultimate service. Some few volunteers kept guard
upwind, though in the overriding fatalism the chimera had lost
much of its terror. If it came, the first scream would precipitate
a savage chase—for the meat on its body.

Garnet did not sleep. She stood overlooking the sheer drop,
silent and still. Her hefty body had slimmed with the lean
marching. Soon it would be too slim—but right now she was
a handsome figure.

Aton came up behind her. "I could push you over, now."
Would it never end?

"I guess the water's safe," she said.

"Turn around."

Garnet turned with a sullen half-smile. Aton put a hand on
her collarbone, fingers touching her neck, the heel of it just
above and between her breasts. He exerted slow pressure.
"Your body will tumble into that mist," he said. "Over and
over until it thuds against the bottom with no sound for human
ears, and lies there, mistress to the rock and gas until it rots
and sublimates into food for the sacrificial flame. A pyre for
Garnet. You'll like that, won't you?"

"We both drank, and nothing happened. Must be good
water."

"Perhaps I will make love to you first," he mused. "Then
you would have to die. Everything I touch has to die."

"Yes."

He nudged her, but Garnet did not flinch. "It is deep behind
you," he said. "Deep as a well."

"I never knew quite how she traveled," Aton continued, his
hand sliding down to press against her breasts, but keeping her
poised at the brink. "I left her on the asteroid, locked in the

spotel, and I took the shuttle myself, so that she had either to remain or reveal her identity and location to outsiders. I went home, and then to Idyllia, but somehow she never left me . . . and I found her again on Hvee. She was in the forest with her song—the song she never finished. I knew then that I had to kill her."

Garnet's bare heels rested on the verge.

"But there was no cliff, no mountain, there near the farm. It had to be that special way, you see. I took her to the forest well, so narrow, so deep. Let the fall kill her as it killed my second love, as it broke the shell."

He stepped close, bending his elbows, placing a hand on each of Garnet's shoulders. "Because death made love an illusion. 'Kiss me, Aton,' she said, there on the mountain, there at the well. And then the song came up." He shook her. "Say it."

Garnet's eyes were closed. "Kiss me, Aton." Death was as close to her as his lips.

"The crime that budded in effigy had to blossom in reality. I touched her lips." He kissed her, carefully. "And I hurled her—"

Garnet's feet left the edge as Aton's brutal strength lifted her out. She swung beyond the drop, and sank, and fell, and came to rest beside him, lying on the floor.

He stroked her hair. "And she said, 'I knew you could not do it, Aton—not when it was real.' And I could not. And love made death an illusion."

He held her there, still and mute. "There is no song about you, Garnet," he said. "But if I were to love you, the song would come, and you would perish, for only the minionette rules me."

"The minionette," Garnet whispered.

He held her, feeling her terror. "And my planet, my home, my Hvee world, it sold me to Chthon, because I loved her. Now I return."

"We'll all die, Aton."

"I have no choice, you see," he said, and kissed her again on face and breast and left her.

12

The Hard Trek, Aton thought, the Trek has taken us from the world of the rushing winds where we tarried so long in what we did not know was comfort. It has shown us the world of the furnace heart, where the generative gasses fling their essence into the wider system, as Earth herself flings hers, without abatement and without compassion, to flame briefly and flicker out and return at last, tired, only to be blasted forth again. And now it shows us the last of its mighty elements, the world of water.

He stood at the edge of the river, looking into it and dreaming. It had been spurned before; would it now, like a woman, show them its vengeance?

Miles below, downstream, the party had gathered and was resting while two men reconnoitered, one upstream, the other downstream. Each would leave tokens behind, marking his trail; the rest would follow the one who did not return. This was logical: what man, finding freedom, would venture again into the caverns? What man would risk the loss of a hopeful path by turning back? Only defeat would make him welcome his fellows.

Thus Aton found himself alone, tracing the source, because his urge to escape was the strongest. He was armed, and he had a pack with rich red meat, and he had a vision. Bedside had come this way, perhaps, and Bedside had escaped. Somewhere there would be a sign.

The glow was brighter, here by the water. Aton stooped to dip his fingers in the clear liquid and touch the shining fringe at his feet. The surface of the path was smooth and a trifle slimy. His passing contact left patches of darker stone, as though he had crushed the vegetable beacons eating at the rock. The green luminescence came up through the water, casting its energies into his face with surrealistic beauty.

There was a narrow channel along one side of the stream, a kind of raised pathway about eighteen inches deep that clung to the upright wall. Aton followed it, since it was uncommonly convenient. The alternative was to wade waistdeep through the swift flow, trusting his naked feet to whatever lurked beneath.

He took the path, but did not trust it. Never yet had Chthon offered a gambit that was safe to accept. The walkway had to be used by something, and that thing was bound to be inimical. He moved quickly, not so much because time was short—though this might easily be the case, if the distance to the surface were far—as to confound any stalking creature behind him. Or surprise anything lurking ahead.

A mile passed, and more, but there was nothing. No vicious pit animal barred the way. No sudden precipice appeared. The path continued firm and level, and the water flowed beside it passively. At length the walls began to spread, allowing the river to slip over its marble banks to decorate a tumbling landscape. The path remained, winding steadily over and around rivers of stone, and occasional debris.

The caverns began to show their variety. Stalactites came into view, great stone icicles aiming at the floor, stalagmite columns rising like monster teeth to meet them. The river shaped itself into brief rapids and quiet pools, and all about it the stone was polished in restful hues. The gentle light, refracted from both the water and shining stone, lent an eerie loveliness to all of it.

Aton went on slowly, struck by the unfamiliar surroundings in much the way he would have been affected by a beautiful but unknown woman. These caverns were still; there was no wind here, and its absence was subtly disquieting. The flexible chambers widened and narrowed and widened again in serpentine rhythm, carpeted with slippery flowstones and walled with mineral tapestries. The columns dropped commandingly, forests of them, parting only for the winding river channels and for the even path he followed.

It was suspicious. This was not the deadly underworld he knew. Where were the salamanders, the chimeras? Where was the owner of the path? Where the red tooth, the claw?

Movement! Aton gripped his fragment of stone and stalked it, for if it did not flee, it would soon be stalking him. Behind the curtains of stone he saw it fleetingly: a huge hairy body, gray.

Hairy? In the caves?

Was this the sign that the exit was near?

He brought the thing into sight. It was not hairy after all.
It was an enormous lizard, rapping at the wall with strong buck
teeth: a stone chipper, not a carnivore, eating the green glow.
Probably harmless after all. Surely the chimera had preyed on
something before it had discovered man.

Aton came at it from behind, studying for a vital spot beneath the leathery scales. The creature was large, the size of
a man, standing on its two hind feet and bracing its front
members against the wall. It did not turn; either it could not
hear him, or did not consider him dangerous.

He plunged the makeshift blade in under the right foreleg,
where the scales were thin. It went in easily, ripping through
soft flesh. The chipper fell to the floor soundlessly, not understanding, clutching at the wound with the opposite claw.
Dumbly it tore itself open, trying to stop the pain, as Aton
stood and watched, breathing heavily. After a while he cut out
its eyes and left it, struggling yet, stirring its own gore into the
green stone.

The walls closed in again, and the river and the path resumed. This time he saw shapes in the water: eyeless, rubbery
fins, flexing about from side to side along the bottom. Marine
life, at last.

The miles passed uneventfully. Abruptly the passage ended.
The water plunged from a tall vertical tunnel, bubbling in a
circular pool and flowing on into the bed he had been tracing.
The path circled this small pool and diverged. Through the
rock it bored, a round passage.

Aton looked down that sharply cut passage and saw nothing.
He put his ear to the wall and heard a distant tapping, a heartbeat. Something was at the other end. Something large.

He looked into the pool and saw a strange globular jellyfish
deep below, perhaps a yard in diameter, balanced in a pothole
just out of the striking falls. He craned upward and saw—light.
Daylight.

The wall of the shaft was rough. The severed strata defended
themselves in concentric circles, some reaching an inch or more
in toward the glassy column of plummeting water. One side
was comparatively smooth, as though the water had eroded it

clean during some capricious housekeeping effort; but now there was a foot or more of space on every side, between wall and water.

Aton removed his water-skin—a ludicrous impediment in the circumstances—parked it with his other supplies, and prepared for the most difficult climb of his life.

The diameter of the shaft was about a yard at the bottom, and it appeared to expand slightly at the top. Aton braced his back against the smooth side, spread his arms in a semicircle against the wall at shoulder level, and lifted one foot around the devastating center column to find a purchase against the opposite side. He brought the other foot into play and began to climb, letting the river plunge harmlessly between his spread thighs. With his arms he lifted his back away and up; then took two baby steps up the far side. Again and again, advancing two or three inches at a time.

The climb was not hard, at first, but there was a long way to go.

He decided not to conserve his strength, since even the act of resting in such a position would fatigue him. If he could achieve the top quickly, there should be ample opportunity to rest. If he did *not* get there promptly, fatigue might prevent him from reaching it at all.

He accelerated his pace, humping up in a rocking pattern, sometimes painfully, the muscles of his legs bunching and relaxing and bunching again. His arms grew tired first, and he turned them down at the elbows, wriggling just enough to make progress, scraping his elbows but not caring.

Fatigue rose about him, but he kept on. His eyes stared fixedly into the still center of the column so close at hand, letting those depths mesmerize him. He wanted to let go of the wall for just a moment and embrace that perfect shape, and ride it down smoothly to the base, kissing its clean surface. Suddenly he was thirsty, more thirsty than ever before in his life, excruciatingly so—and the cool spray on his face tantalized tongue and throat.

One drink, he knew, and it would be over. It was the cup of death he sought, denied him by air and fire but never so deliciously close as this.

Death. Why had he killed that chipper? It had been an act of pure sadism, an act he had enjoyed. Why? Why did he want to die? What was the matter with him?

In the glass before him the liquid eyes of Malice shone, hinting at an answer he dared not grasp. She was in the fire; she was in the water. The prisoners of Chthon were right to fear him. He was in love with evil.

But the power of that image bore him up. He had been unable, before, to kill the object of his terror. The ties of childhood had been too strong. But after the rigors of Chthon he would have the strength, and he would do what had to be done.

First he would unravel the mystery of the minionette, traveling to the home world that Hastings, for a private garnet, had discussed. Minion—a proscribed planet whose location was as secret as that of Chthon, because of its deadly inhabitants. No—they were human, but genetic engineering could do strange things within the shell of the human body, and leave it less compatible to the mainstream of the species than many an alien shape. No, Hastings had not actually known what it was about the inhabitants, he had claimed, and had left suddenly, as though repulsed by Aton's inquiry. Hastings no longer talked to Aton; no one did, any more, except Bossman, curtly, and Garnet.

Yet—*he* was not of Minion. He only wanted to know. What did these rough prisoners see in him, that drove them back?

Why had he killed the chipper? It was Malice that needed killing. He was the enemy of the minionette, not of others. Except for that need, he was a free agent.

"And each in the cell of himself is almost convinced of his freedom," the ancient poet Auden had said in the remembered depths of *LOE,* now boarded by Garnet. Almost convinced!

His straining body had hoisted him very near the tip. The endless tunnels waited eighty feet below, and well might wait in vain. Five feet above, daylight spilled over the lip; light mixed with the pouring water. The green glow was gone, unable to face the sun; and it was bright, far brighter than he could remember any day ever being—on a habitable world.

Was he to be helpless against the brilliance of freedom? He

waited, staring into it, forcing his eyes to adjust, before going on.

His head came up above the turn and he saw the surface of the planet, just feet away. The mouth of the cave was open to a level sheen of water, sucking it down. Reflected from the distance was a tree—a palm tree. The smell of the outdoors wafted in luxuriantly.

Rising out of the water to meet the upper dome were the stalagmites of man: steel bars. A perfect prison: the sound of the falls would override any effort to call for help, assuming that such an ear did not belong to a prison guard. The bars, of course, would be proof against tampering. Any effort to break or dislodge them would sound the alarm. Set inside the cave, they prevented visible signaling; the water, coming *in*, would carry no messages out.

Almost convinced.

This was not the escape from Chthon. This was the ration of Tantalus.

Aton never remembered the descent. He found himself lying on the narrow footpath, aching in shoulders, back, and thighs, abrasions stinging the length of his backside and the soles of his feet. A word was ringing the length of his mind and through the echoing tunnels of his brain. He concentrated and it came: rill.

And suddenly he knew with a faith that denied coincidence the true identity of the surface of Chthon, saw the poetic allegory of it and the irony of his denied redemption. What would there be above hell, except heaven? It was right, it was right, he told himself, that he be refused from below that which he had cast down from above. The cell of himself was not ready for freedom.

He dipped a hand in the cool water and splashed his tight brow. He knew this water, this river, this rill that went in one side of the mountain—and never came out again.

V. MINIONETTE

Thirteen

The minionette did not ask how he came to be free. It was natural that his methods, like her own, were sufficient. They walked together in the forest of Hvee, ever their meeting place, and the great-barked trees stood over them, accepting so gladly the play of their emotions.

The nymph of the wood moved in splendor, hair flaming against a dress of pastel green. Light feet trod the sere debris of ancient years, and fingers of ecstasy clasped his. She had said, and he had accepted, long ago, that there could be no woman to match her. The echo of the broken song surrounded her, tantalizing, rapturous, the essence, the quintessence—

"And did you have a woman, in Chthon?" she asked him, playful in the knowledge that any mortal woman was a figurine.

Aton tried to think back, tried to imagine another woman, any other; but in the presence of Malice it was not possible. "I don't remember."

"You have changed," she said. "You have changed, Aton, and it is the handiwork of the distaff. Tell me."

"I had a minionette."

Her fingers tightened. Never before had he felt her surprise. She did not speak.

"Yes," he said, "I know. But she did not have the song." That was all; no explanation, no soliloquy was necessary. Misery had been forgotten, after a single night of strange romance. Neither the appearance nor the nature of the minionette served as the basis of his love—only the person of his childhood vision, bearing the music and the magic of his youth. O joy that . . .

The forest diminished, laid open by an asphalt highway, hot black waves bouncing into awareness. Above it a distant spaceshuttle lifted, intent on some rendezvous with an orbiting visitor. This was the realm of exploration and commerce, of navies and merchant fleets. And beside him the minionette seemed to walk in uniform: handsome, competent, severe, ruthless, female.

"No more for space, Captain?"

"No more, Machinist."

"You could have returned, when I went to Chthon."

She shook her head, precisely. "The guileless Xests knew, and word spreads quickly in space. It is death for the minionette to wander openly among men. And . . ."

"And . . . ?"

She was silent, and it was answer enough. The spotel—

They crossed over the black heat, into a field of hvee, his father's field, and walked among the young plants reaching for an object for their love, so like himself. Above, the sky retreated before ascending cumuli; a summer storm was in the making.

From the forest to the spaceship: Aton remembered his first journey—he and his hvee, searching for love. He, as with the hvee, had found it to be something horrendous in its full formation—a dragon whose tail, once grasped, could not lightly be relinquished.

Why had she come to him, on that first day of his new year, when all the men of space were within her range? Could it have been coincidence, that artful meeting, wherein she had shown him the melody, given him the hvee, kissed him, and forever bound his heart to hers?

Why had she hidden from him, once his love was captive? Why had she flaunted the image of the Captain, knowing the torture within him? He understood the answer, now, after the experience with Misery. But even that did not wholly account for the incident at the spotel—the incident that had exposed to him the basic evil in her nature and sent him fleeing from her so ruinously. Evil not of the emotion, no.

There had been that silent treatment, then—

Then—

A lock on his memory fell open, and he understood at last what horror had denied him for almost three years. If—if the minionette was evil, so was he.

"You tried to defend that native girl—the one who deserted my father!" he exclaimed, now and in the spotel-past.

Now and in the past, the minionette failed to speak.

"When did you go to space?" he demanded. They had left the hvee behind and were sitting beneath the old garden shed. It was a peaked roof supported by four stout, weathered posts. The breath of the building storm came down and through the absent walls, bringing chill tingles to the skin.

The emotional chill had been closer, then, as Aton advanced by rugged steps toward the truth his intellect rejected. The two of them, in an enclosure very like this, subjectively, struggled for comprehension in the face of peculiar resistance. Aton had never before appreciated the full force of cultural conflict.

"I know the answer," Aton continued. "I know when you went to space. I read it in the lay roster of the *Jocasta*. You joined the merchant fleet as an on-deck cleric, early in §375. You transferred to the *Jocasta* despite many more favorable opportunities on other ships, five years later as a member of the business advisory staff, and arranged to have it dock over Hvee the year following.

"But the vital point is that you went to space just months after I was born. Why you wanted that particular ship and that schedule, long before you rose to command it, is less important than your earlier history. Where were you before §375? What did you call yourself? The roster didn't say."

Malice did not move at all, in either shed or spotel.

"You were on Hvee," Aton said, and she did not deny it.
"You knew Aurelius, after his wife of Ten perished. You knew
of me. And—you knew the native girl he married. The girl
from Minion. You knew her well."

She sat still, looking intently at him.

"In fact," he said with the supreme effort, "you *were* that
girl."

They sat together, in sight of the thing they both had known
and never spoken.

The one who deserted my father. The stepmother I have
sworn to kill.

Oh, Malice, I could have forgiven you that, after I learned
your nature. But that is not the evil for which I searched. That
is not the horror that drove me from your side.

"The woman of Ten died two years before I was born,"
Aton said, admitting the truth for the first—and second—time
in his life. "Her baby was stillborn. I had no stepmother."

"Yes," she said, breaking her silence at last. "Yes, Aton—
I am your mother."

•   •   •

In the cooling shade of the open shed, they looked across
the field of hvee. No person labored there at the moment, but
the plants were healthy. Someone with great love was caring
for them, as Aurelius could do no longer, and in his heart Aton
recognized that touch.

"Why didn't you tell me, that first time?" Aton asked her.
"Before the—spotel." And knew the answer as he spoke: a
single answer then, doubled now. She was his mother. How
could she tell the man who thought he was her lover, that—
what could she say to him, who had mistaken her love so
shockingly? Yet how could she give him up, her son?

But he was dissembling. She could have tried, during the
early meeting in the forest—and he, too young to grasp the
complexities of it, would have gone to Aurelius and destroyed
everything. His father was anxious yet to have her back, and

he was not without power. The moment he knew—

And the second time in the forest, Aton had been old enough to see in this miraculous woman some little part of what his father had seen. Aton too was not without power, as events had shown.

Thus had he reasoned, spuriously, at the spotel, driven by forced hiding behind the façade of reason. He had not then really understood, and had suspected that he did not, and been measurelessly discommoded by his seeming satisfaction.

Now he understood the second reason, more basic, and lacking the trappings of social convention. For to the minionette, pleasure was pain, pain was pleasure. She had responded to a visitor of her world who had been torn by sorrow and self-hate—Aurelius—because his child, in living and dying, had murdered his beloved. The minionette had loved Aurelius because she found his tremendous guilt and sense of betrayal irresistible. He was in mourning for the daughter of Ten, yet found Malice attractive, and fiercely condemned himself for this, and thus conquered her and defeated himself, unknowingly.

She had accepted the ceremony of his culture, which meant little to one who was emotionally telepathic, but without the exchange of the hvee, because his guilt could not permit that honest token. She had gone with him, delighted also by the joy of his alarm over the proscription that he was violating. Neither one of them had known, then, the reason for proscription.

On Hvee she had conceived his child. As they came to know each other more thoroughly, his agony diminished, and gradually he came to love her without guilt. Then she understood their peril—too late. She birthed his child and deserted him, because a longer stay could only have entailed far greater agony for them both. Her continued love would have destroyed him, simply because she was what she was. Because she did love him in her fashion, she could not bring herself to hurt him in the ways her culture demanded. A man of Minion would have understood, but not Aurelius.

Her son had grown up with such hate for the memory of the wayward mother that he had rejected his knowledge of the facts and had chosen to remember only the mother he wished he had had. No one could have told Aton the truth prematurely. He had been blind.

More: the very hurt and rage he nurtured became her own delight, for she *was* the minionette. She could read the hate in him, even as a child who did not know her, and it was the ideal emotion for her species. Oh, yes, she kissed him, enraptured by his confusion, and sent him home before that wonderful emotion faded. When she met him at fourteen she had done it again; his guilt and frustration at what he suspected was wrong were sufficient.

When he had searched her out aboard the carefully chosen *Jocasta*—which only now did he comprehend as the signal it was, intended to guide him to her when he was mature enough to understand—her dilemma intensified. He had come too soon; but he had been raging with the compellingly appealing frustrations, and she could not hold herself away. The game had gone on, bringing her further into his orbit: his horror of the Taphid cargo, his cold anger at the leverage her exposure of his lay roster provided her, his grief over the woman he thought he had lost. Until the crafty Xests, themselves semitelepathic, had penetrated her ruse and left her helpless against the naïve love of her son.

She had gone with him, since he was not to be resisted, and her position with the merchant service was already forfeit. She had gone with him although she still did not know how to handle the coming crisis. She could not tell him the truth, since that would have sent him away forever—but neither could she submit to the passionate embrace he had in mind. She could not stay and she could not leave.

Thus, at the point of no return, the silence. Only in this way could she keep him close yet distant, until some more permanent alternative offered itself.

Thus Aton rationalized, now but not in the past—and found that even this was not enough. His imagination was fighting desperately to protect him from full realization. His mind had blanked the entire episode from memory as long as it could, and now gave ground unwillingly. He had to search out the evil, knowing it was there, knowing that he was not yet mature enough to face it.

The spotel episode had not been concluded. The two of them had to play it out, past and present, until the full reason for his torment lay exposed.

The secret was out: Aton was in love with his mother. Start with that, and go back. Relive it—if you can.

Back—as she had known he would, he reacted to the news with anguished indecision. The thing he had dreamed of could not be. Sweet as his emotion might be to her perception, brightening her lovely hair, it was a hollow luxury. He would go and never meet her again. He would spare her.

How little he understood the minionette!

Nude, as she remained after he had doffed the space suit, she beckoned him. "Aton," she said. She was absolutely beautiful.

He came to her, as he always had, embarrassed for his thoughts as much as for the situation. It hurt him terribly to lose her, for she had lived—as a woman—in his fond imagination since the first forest encounter.

"Aton," she repeated. "On Minion"—this, at the spotel, had been the first time he had heard the name of her home planet, and the name alone had stayed with him—"on Minion our culture is not like yours. I was wrong to go away with the outworlder, but I was young then and did not understand." She took his hands in the familiar gesture. "Aton—on Minion the women live a long time, many times the life span of the men. The minionette outlives her first mate, if he is not soon executed, and then belongs to her closest of kin. By him she will bear another kin, and later yet another, from one generation to the next, until at last she is too old and has to birth a daughter. This is our way."

Aton kneeled dumbly before her, his two hands prisoners to hers. What was she trying to tell him?

"Aton, you are half minion, and you are my kin."

The horror of it began to force itself upon him, then. "You are my mother—"

"Yes. That is why this must be. That is the reason I came to you so early in the forest and gave you the melody and the hvee—so that you would know in your spirit what you could not know from your book. That you are minion, born to possess the minionette. You must do this, and your son after you, because it is in your culture and in your blood—your minion nature."

Fighting what he knew now was the truth, Aton suffered a greater shock. For though the culture *he* understood forbade this thing utterly, he had, in an inversion that paralleled her emotional one—that he had not known about, then—grown up to believe her to be the most desirable of women. Because she had been, according to his incomplete knowledge, no relationship to himself.

Now he knew that she, by beliefs of his own that were fundamental, was forbidden. And he found her—

Found her still the most compellingly desirable woman he could imagine. She had offered herself to him—and he wanted her, physically, more than ever before. That was what upset him most.

"Until this moment," she said, "you were not ready, Aton. I had to wait a very long time to win you." She relaxed on the couch, splendid in repose, pulling him with her. The living flame of her hair spread in and out, over face and shoulders and perfect breast, highlighting her body. Black-green eyes, so near to his, opened in deep vistas.

"So long a time," she said. "So lovely, Kiss me, Aton, and come to me. Now, Aton—now!"

Fourteen

The day was turbulent. They rose together and left the garden shed, walking in the wind.

"Why did you let me discover your identity, at the spotel?" Aton asked her now. "The thing you wanted—it might easily have been, if I had not known."

"Aton," she said, shaking her head in gentle reproach. "Have you, have you not been to Minion? Have you not seen what love, your love, will do to the minionette?"

He had allowed himself to forget.

"Your love would have killed me, as that of your father would have killed me, had it been as you imagined when you courted me," she explained. "Only your knowledge of the truth could make you condemn. Only through that—to you, negative—emotion could you approach me physically. You had to know."

Aton could not reply immediately. She had waited a long time—but their meeting *had* been too soon. "Death and love were always linked, for us," he said, not looking at her. "The death of illusion, the love of pain. I had to think that you were evil, and you had to let me believe that. But my resistance was stronger than desire. I left you, after all."

"Did you, Aton?"

The path became steep, though the wind had dropped. He helped her climb, though she did not need it. Their discussion died as she seemed to metamorphose again, to fit his lonely parade of memories. Now she wore a pack and her blonde hair fluttered in an idle gust. On her wrist the silver circlet glittered.

Aton felt a qualm, suddenly wondering whether there had ever been an interlude with a pretty slave girl, a second love hoping pitifully to combat the first—a love that would have saved him from Chthon, had he been able to accept it. Had she been a genuine person at all? Or only another translation of his imagination? Had he ever really left the side of the minionette?

Theme of the shell! Were you part of the broken song? Was my dream vain, even then?

Even then . . .

Nothing dies on Idyllia—except hope.

They were at the tip of a hillock representing a mountain. Aton forgot his doubt. Under the massing clouds the view was beautiful, bright with that special color of early dusk. The shell, the song—no use to understand.

"I love you!" he shouted, his voice distant in his own ears. "I love you—" and once again his emotion was honest and strong.

Her hair was red; it was black; it was writhing in pain and she fell, as she had to fall, stricken cruelly. Thunder blasted sky and forest and field and love, and the rain fell, drenching, soiling all of it. And the melody he loved was washing away and soaking its blood into the ground.

He tumbled after, rolling, bumping, down the hillside,

shocked with the blow he had dealt unwittingly, grasping at the song and finding only mud and torn weeds. Love was forbidden. He had never taken a woman for love, only for morbid purpose. Always the song had severed love—and now he was beyond the song; he had lost it, broken it forever . . . and the cold water sheeting into his upturned face was drowning him.

The rain stopped, in an hour or an instant, and Aton was in the swamp at the foot of the hill, beside the foul pond that bred the vicious annual larvae and spawned the deadly blight. On the far side lay the body, naked, lovely, but not dead, not dead. From the dark surface of the pool came a green glow, a Chthon-glow, casting back the slimed shadows and betraying the ominous ripple at the rim.

Suppressed memories stirred in him, intimations of horror and terrible slaughter. He had been here before. He had—

The undead body rose, and the hair was neither blonde nor fire but a soggy in-between. The form of it was not divinity but merely female. She came at him, circling the dark pool, treading on a narrow ledge.

Aton stood on that ledge too, unable to retreat from the noisome brink. There would be no way to avoid her, except to run around that nightmare track in helpless flight, unable to understand his panic. He did not yield to it; he stood and watched her slow march toward him, her small heavy steps. He watched her second body march in step behind the first, and the third behind that: many bodies, horrible bodies.

Terror triumphed. He spun away from the pool—but the choking rain was up in walls he could not penetrate, arching unbroken into an opaque dome overhead. He could not break out.

He looked into the pool, and it seemed to him that the shapes in it were not tall weeds, but tongues. One was larger than the rest, nearer; it was a gross tubular tongue that came up blindly casting for flesh. It would sense him soon, and slap its way in his direction.

He fled, feet skidding. But from the opposite direction some other thing was coming, something dense and lateral, a massive spike, and there was no escape.

Aton spread himself with his back to the slippery wall,

raised his eyes to the arching bowl above, and forced himself to think. He thought not lucidly and not well, the appetite of his intellect gagging on the sickening stuff before it, but digesting enough to save his waning strength and make his world stand still for just a moment.

This impasse, this horror is somehow of my own making. It cannot be real, in a physical sense. Only in Chthon are such things literal.

My mind has clothed its tumult in some frightening allegory, as it has done before. It has dramatized my mental conflict, forcing me to solve it now, or give up the pretense of sanity. I am standing on the bank of the swamp pond, and there is no monster in it, no wall around it; there is only the incipient, blight and the steady rain. There are no reduplicating figures closing in on me, no terrible spike from the other side; only the woman I love and must hate, the alluring minionette.

But the *conflict*, he knew, was real, and his moment of decision had come—whatever the elements of it might be, and whatever its resolution might mean. He was trapped by a web spun long ago, when he had followed the half-heard melody into the wood and became its slave. Throughout his life he had been unable either to complete it or to escape it. Chthon itself had not resolved that dilemma. Now he had to face the ghastly alternatives himself, and embrace the rigors of that choice.

The marching column of women represented Malice, in all her forms: ubiquitous, but unable to accept direct love. His normal emotion was a sword, wielded against the minionette. Should he slay her with that love?

Or should he wait for the dread spike closing from the other side: the obscene inversion of their relationship? Impaled on it, he would became a creature of perpetual hate, a minion, his self-identity and integrity buried in sadism. *She* would flourish; her song would be complete. But he—

He stared into the rank water and saw huge movements there, and heard the limber tongue slap nearer. He could escape his choice by flinging himself into the maw of that personified muck. The septic threads of slime would foul his skin and imprint in it the malodorous blight that had taken his father. It would not be merciful.

Did Aurelius still live? Aton did not know.

There had to be some other alternative. Some outlet that would free him, or at least postpone the choice. A drain, an exit from the pool—some rushing aperture leading into the unknown, but an escape, a relief. Could he find it?

When he recognized his need for it, it was there: an opening into the unknown. It might lead to death, or to choices more appalling even than those he fled from. Once taken, this step could never be withdrawn, as a plunge into a waterfall cannot be reversed. He hesitated.

"Aurelius is dead," the minionette said, very close. She would have felt the old man go, vanquished at last by the genuine pool-monster, the blight. Aton had felt the loss himself, had felt the cessation of an emotional compartment, in that half-telepathy he had never before admitted he possessed. That same sense hinted darkly that he had had some part in the death of his father, however unintentionally. Had the decision he was making been so wide-ranging? Was this the price of his escape?

Committed now, by obscure circumstance, he took the step, refusing to examine whatever hideous price was being exacted. He would skirt the verge of insanity itself, for the sake of the fainting hope it offered. The swirling vortex sucked him in, and the dark smothering wave closed over him, carrying him after all to—

Fifteen

Aton found himself on the surface of the spotel asteroid, naked between its bulk and the immensity of space. Naked because this rock was featureless and night was close; no gravity comforted him with her embrace, no atmosphere caressed his clinging suit. Only the static action of his boots maintained his tenuous contact with the little planet, linking them firmly enough so long as he did not deliberately wrench both feet away at once. So long as he did not jump.

He looked about, awed in his blood by this singular and not unpleasant confrontation with inanimate nature. Behind him was the lock of the spotel, leading to the shuttle he meant to pilot away from here, leading also to the plush interior and an offering he could not accept. No matter what she said, what she was, she was forbidden. He had to get away from her. But first, this walk on the surface, to calm himself.

Ahead was almost total isolation, and he needed that. Easily was the contrast made between the facets of man, with his measurable accomplishment and immeasurable loneliness, who thus traversed a rock on which he could not live.

This asteroid was flat, a fragment from some larger body; it reminded one of the ancient days of the Earthhome and the fearful, foot-loose ancestors who thought their world was flat. They would have been right, had they lived here.

This featureless tableau was as barren as the landscape of his life. The bright stars were all about, this nightside, promising excitement and adventure and comfort in their great numbers, if only it were possible to step to their population. Yet he had *been* in those far systems already, and had suffered through their evanescent promise and found his heart alone.

Long strides carried his body across the plateau as he ran, one foot always touching, throwing himself toward the edge of a plain that the vacuum's clarity claimed was miles away. Its end was precipice, the brink of the tiny planet limned against the starlight in a thin vice-versa silhouette. He would throw himself off, into oblivion, to fall forever through the open reaches of his wasted intellect, inchoate at last.

Too soon he reached that fringe. His mind balked at the attempt. My flesh, he thought with bitter humor, is willing; it is my spirit that is weak.

Momentum, deceptive in the absence of gravity, carried him on. He spun around the broken edge, boots clinging as tenaciously to land as his spirit clung to a barren life. The asteroid was thin, this far side, scarcely a hundred feet in depth. Mountainously jagged strata exposed the wound that had torn it from its mother-lode and flung it into limbo an eternity ago. With what terrible pain had it begun its journey, alone, so much alone?

He bent and found a fossil: a great leaf-shape imprinted in the stone, larger than his hand. It was the skeletal remnant of a living thing, more lovely in its demise than ever it had been in life. For never would its beauty fade; never would its essence die.

His gloved fingers caressed the fixed serrations in honor of a lingering camaraderie. Would the fossil of Aton ride through space with such indifferent éclat?

Death, where is now thy—

He tried to shake off the mood by climbing toward the bright sunside of the asteroid. The leaf must have grown in sun-shine, once. If one could only enter the heaven of the fossil's past, see the waving foliage, touch the mighty tree. Turn back the metronome of matter, allow all doubts to be resolved in the soft embrace of life's origins.

The sharp horizon brightened as he appraoched sun-side. One heave, around the second corner—

He was bathed in the warm brilliance of that sun; light, light everywhere, banishing all dark and all doubt.

The mechanism of the suit compensated immediately, protecting him, allowing him to look out upon the land, to see the air on it, the shining mists in the air, the growing things in the soil, the great green leaves.

To me this land is lush and lovely, convex hills so high and fine, matching mounds so softly rounded, waiting for—

Aton shook himself, the sealed suit shifting with him like a second skin. What was happening to him? Why was he thinking in metric feet? There was no atmosphere; there could be no trees, no poetry. This was a bare slab of rock hurtling in orbit around a numbered star. There could be no security in hallucination. If he ever really forgot where he was, death would be a blunt reminder.

Yet down beyond those yearning mountains, where the passive waters shine, the source of life is waiting for me, waiting while I—

Shocked, Aton turned again, resuming his progress toward the fossil at the planet's edge. Somehow, unconsciously, he had traveled farther down the valley, lulled by the hint of some fierce ecstasy—to which he dared not yield. Something was speaking to him, luring him, drawing him onward to some unimaginable rendezvous.

Beyond the mountains are the waters, thick and warm as fresh-let blood.

"Jill!" he cried. "Stay out of my fantasy." I fled from your cruelty ten years ago; I hardly remember you; you don't belong here; I am afraid of the thing you stand for: the feel of blood upon my hand, the sound of laughter at my ear. Not blood, you say—not blood, but bliss, offered to my fourteenth year.

Aton turned once more, breathing hard, trying to achieve the objectivity of the stone leaf. That had been the turning point. Until then he had been in control of himself.

Reality came back, showing the conical outcroppings he had walked between, the glaring shadows they cast in the beam of the distant sun. As he watched, those shadows softened, became misty. The hills turned green and more than green, breathing with luxury.

Before him was a curving field leading down to a valley sheltered between gently rolling bluffs. The secret lake was there, more exciting, more inviting than any isolated mirage. The bliss it offered within its depths no longer wholly repelled him. His blood sang with the need to enjoy that liquid, to plunge himself totally into it. He had come from it; he would return to it.

No! But the vision reached inside his resistance and turned it off, leaving a faint muted protest tingling far behind. Fourteen steps he took to reach that lake, and hesitated, afraid to pass beyond the nameless barrier within himself. The water called, it called, but that tiny castrate conscience, damned somewhere behind the frozen leaf, pleaded with him not to sacrifice the thing he had been for the thing he would become. The shaking sweat mottled his face as he fought, knowing that the outcome had already been determined, but fighting still to preserve the forms of a bygone innocence.

Slowly a hand came up to unfasten the helmet of his suit. Could it be his own? The clasps came open, the seals were broken, the helmet came away from his head. He did not die. The air of the valley came to him then, musky and sweet, exhilarating in its freshness. He tasted the bloom of it and felt strong. Soon the remainder of his impeding suit was off; naked, he ran into the water.

Once more the fading doubt held him back, a doubt permitted now because the usurper felt secure. Resistance had become mere titillation, adding luster to the act. The dominant emotion toyed felinely with his timorous conscience and gave it the freedom of thinking it was free.

He was suffused with the sense of impending accomplishment. The touch of the water at his bare toes electrified his body. He could not see the liquid any more. Only his flesh was aware of it sliding voluptuously over his ankles, enfolding them in a closure of incipient pleasure, tantalizing at its commencement, luxurious in its completion.

A fundamental meaning was rising in him, a meaning whose only expression had to be calamitously powerful, a thrusting-forth of such magnitude as to remove mountains and impregnate the entire lake with animation.

The warm pressure ascended, circling calves, knees, thighs. It washed against him rhythmically, drawing forth the deepest force in him with delicate strokes. The tide of it increased, suddenly, compellingly, throwing him into a second vision of a young hand traveling up younger skirts, touching the forbidden junction. But this time the stickiness did not alarm; it drew him on and in with tempestuous passion.

The two scales of flesh and liquid merged under a superimposed image of the vernier, jumping into focus before his closed eyes. Unable to hold back full expression any longer, he plunged in all the way.

The water, the landscape, the universe rang with the tumescence of his urge, and from the depths of his most intimate ambition the fluid essence surged, climbing, swirling, subject to enormous pressure, bursting into a hurricane of force, exploding at last in a tortured pleasuration rending flesh and dissolving bone and satiating spirit beyond endurance. In Heaven you have heard . . . Love has pitched his . . . O joy! O joy! O joy!

Some power outside himself buoyed him up, lifted him through surging currents of excruciation far, far to a light above. It was her hand, warm on his arm, bringing him away from the obliteration his equivocal passion had led him to. A dark god waited at the terminus, a thing to whom passion and guilt were simple tools, a god whom a sane man could not serve.

A god that Aton *would* serve when the full implication of the asteroid allegory reached his conscious mind.

The rain had stopped, though he was soaking; monsters and confining walls were gone. Sunlight played down, not on the broken column he half expected, but on a glistening countryside, high and green in the dusk and wondrously attractive.

"You have—won," she said, selecting an imprecise word. She was the woman of the forest, nymph of love. "I cannot, I cannot let you go that way. Not to so great an evil." *She* spoke of evil: not the thing they had done at the spotel, but the god he was to serve. The god who had offered him sanctuary.

The phantasmagoria was over. The specters were gone, whatever they had been, and Malice was once again the unspoiled luster of his dreams. The lovely lady of his childhood had returned, the object of all his love, never to be distorted again.

15

After that it was easier. Nineteen men and nineteen women survived, the fittest, by nature's definition, of all the nether caverns. The size of the party was manageable and efficient, and game was increasingly plentiful and less vicious. The air was sweet, the water clear, the temperature cool.

Bedside's signs appeared at regular intervals, always pointing down. How he had come this far alone they never expected to know; but he obviously had, with his wits still about him, and that was enough.

"What was he like?" Aton asked Garnet, as they climbed over damp stone sculptures.

"Highbrow," she said. "Small and smart. Weak eyes, but underneath, a mind like a scalpel. He had this thing for escape—"

"But if he got this far, what could have driven him mad?"

"Maybe he saw the chimera." Men were still disappearing—not women—without a trace. It was assumed that the chimera still stalked the party (how had it gotten past the dome?)

and brought down the unwary. The steady sound of the river would drown out a distant scream.

The days of marching continued. The river grew, fed by tributaries that no longer interested them, and with it grew the surrounding caverns. The wind tunnels ceased. Instead, the party traveled through carved formations, water deposits and erosions, treelike stalagmites, and caves of white crystal. At times the river split into several branches, winding through linked vaults with obscure ceilings and indefinite boundaries, only to regroup below.

At last it widened into a mighty, slow-moving lake. They paced the left bank. Fifty feet across, the water was terminated by a sheer cliff, arching into a three-dimensional labyrinth overhead. Their side was level, however, and by the shore was a beach of white sand. The lake itself was clear and cool, a swimmer's delight—but one of Bedside's signs labeled it with skull and crossbones. They took his word for it.

Once again the caverns of Chthon were showing their beauty and peace. But this time no one believed in paradise.

The open walkway gradually narrowed, as the wall closed in against the lake. The wall on the far side withdrew equivalently, making space for the beach on that side. The shores were exchanging characteristics—or, more properly, the river was simply shifting its channel to the near side.

At last they came to the sign that pointed to the water. It was time to cross.

But in the center they could see the white wake of a large marine creature. A wake that had paced them for several marches. Bedside, with his ingenuity, might have prepared chemicals to repulse the thing. This party had to find other means.

Bossman did not take long to make up his mind. "The lots."

Garnet approached. "I know what you want," she said dully. "I'll do it. I can swim good."

Bossman brushed her aside. "I didn't tell you to do nothing! The lots."

She refused to move. "You can't spare any more men. I can swim good. I want it."

Bossman studied her for a long time. He turned away. "You

stay here," he told her over his shoulder. "Five—come with me."

Aton accompanied him to a place away from the group, where the wall curved back briefly to make an open room bounded on one side by the river.

"I been meaning to talk to you, Five," Bossman said, laying his axe down near the water and divesting himself of all other armament. Aton, knowing what was coming, discarded his own stone weapons.

"We're all of us down here for our own reasons," Bossman continued. "Ain't none of us good enough to talk about none of the others. But we got to have a settlement, now." He stood with hands on hips. The muscles, firmer now than they had been before the trek, shone with light sweat. "I don't know what you done to get shipped down here, and I ain't asking." This was standard courtesy only; the word about Aton's min-ionette had long since circulated. "But you been more trouble than any ten men since the mines were started. You're slick, you're tough—but I know you. I saw the sign long time ago.

"If I'd had my way, you'd've been tied decoy to that stone for the chimera, 'stead of that scared little man who never had the guts to make real trouble. You'd've been the one stuck in that hole, waiting for the axe, 'stead of the only man with brains enough to get us through. You'd be the one to take that lonely swim coming up."

Bossman was not quite as ignorant as Aton had thought. How much did he suspect? "Are you accusing me of Framy's crime?"

"I ain't smart," Bossman said. "I don't know what goes on in people's minds, and I take a long time to figure things out. But I know that Framy wouldn't've fingered his only friend. He didn't work that way. He'd've named his worst enemy, to save a guilty friend.

"But he didn't *know* who got the other half of that garnet. He figured you were innocent, because *he* was. He expected you to alibi him. but you didn't, and that was the end of him. You only had one reason to frame him like that, and that was because you knew we wouldn't get no one else to confess, because no one else had done it—because *you* were the one who picked up the other half-garnet and slipped it into the basket for Tally. You were the traitor."

And Bossman, slow to catch on, had executed Framy before figuring out the truth—and now had to stand by that mistake.

"Too bad," Aton said sympathetically. "You also hold me responsible for Hastings' death?"

"You're smart." Bossman had missed the ironic note. "You knew we'd wind up on the Hard Trek, and that's what you wanted all the time. So other people would die instead of you. You couldn't chance it alone. Everyone that's died here, is dead because of you."

"Even the victims of the chimera?"

"I looked when we heard Framy scream, and I didn't see you. That's when I began thinking. You came up from the other side of the tunnel. The chimera had to go right past you to get away. But you said nothing. You wanted Framy dead, so he couldn't talk any more and maybe have someone believe him—"

"Sure. I have the hysterical strength vested in me by the sorcery of the minionette. I can kill instantly with my bare hands. I can take hold of the mass of cords in the front of a man's neck and rip it out, or jab my fingertips in under his ribs and tear loose the entire rib cage. I can use my unkempt human nails in the feline trick of hooking the nose of my prey and breaking its neck by pulling the head around. I can neatly duplicate the cut and tear marks, the parallel lines left by animal claws, and the distinctive half-chewed, half-slashed look of the fang attack. I can do this because I have a secret cache of specialized appliances designed for the specific purpose of imitating the marks of the phantom chimera, and accomplishing this in a matter of seconds. I made these tools, since I forgot to smuggle them in, in my hidden laboratory in Chthon, where I have a serviceable metal press and a small blast furnace to smelt my crude iron. Stone is too awkward, you see. I had to cut a hole to the surface of the planet for the smoke and fumes to escape through unnoticed. Every so often I have to go up there and shoo the tourists away from my chimney, because this is very private business and I don't want any interference. My lab is soundproofed so that no one can overhear the noise of its operation, and I have a private railway paralleling our course on the Hard Trek, so that I can fetch my implements every time I feel the need for another execution. I have special equipment to erase my bloody tracks, and of course I wear an all-enveloping covering, a form-fitting suit similar to those used in space, that takes the brunt of the spattering blood, and that I can peel out of and hide immediately so that my person retains no more than its natural grime, and no one can tell what I've been doing. For, you see, I have to be ready to rejoin the group at once, so that no one realizes that I'm missing when the sound of the first scream comes. I was a little slow with Framy, I must admit; but I've been practicing diligently. Oh, it takes the finest split-second timing. A real challenge. I can't tell you how much fun it has been—"

Bossman continued, unmoved by Aton's too-elaborate sarcasm. "I seen what you done to Garnet, too. She's a rough gal—but she don't deserve what you give her. I can't do nothing about the rest of it. But I'm telling you now, you're going to make it up to her."

Yes—the time for a settlement had come. "You quite sure of that?"

"I'm sure," Bossman asserted. "That's one thing this farmer can do. She's got to die, but she'll die happy. You're going to ask her real nice, and bring her in here where nobody can see you, and tell her those lies you know the gals go for, and make up to her like you meant it. She deserves that much, and she's going to get it. The rest of them'll take a break and get ready for the crossing."

Aton studied him. The man was serious. "You expect her to believe it?" He shifted position slightly.

"She'll believe what she wants to believe. I know her well enough for that. And you're going to make it easy for her. You're a good enough talker when you want to be." Here Bossman permitted himself a slight smile. "Why she fixed on you I can't figure. But she's ready for anything you put on the line. You make it good, and you carry it all the way through— or *you'll* be decoy this time, not her. If you don't believe *that*—"

Aton didn't. Trained to give no warning, he twisted over,

a bare foot lashing out with all the deadly skill of his fighting art. The krell farmer was overdue for a lesson.

The edge of an iron hand brushed the kick aside. So fast he hardly seemed to move, Bossman was inside the thrust of the leg. His calloused foot kicked Aton's other leg from under him. The bruising slam of his body against the stone floor was doubled by that of Bossman's weight on top of him. Under what little fat was left, the farmer was hard as a cavern wall. An unyielding arm clamped Aton's head; a powerful hand locked his own arm in an unbreakable grip. Fingers probed under his jawline.

Aton thrashed wildly. He screamed. An explosion of intolerable agony in the throat, an involuntary and useless recoil against the restraining arms, a howling darkness on the world.

The world came back, oddly unreal except for the light touch of those steely fingertips on a buried nerve center. A voice said softly, "Baby wants to play?"

Bossman let him up, on guard. "Tell her we fought for her, and you won," he advised. "I don't want you to look roughed up, spaceman—yet." Bossman had made his point.

And so they played it out, the three of them, setting the scene for Garnet's sacrifice—

—while Bossman waited with corded fist, knowing the sounds of love were false, when his compassion would willingly have made them true.

—while Aton found, obscurely, that the knowledge of death brought the melody, and the melody brought a passion astonishingly real.

—while Garnet accepted a willing death as the only way to bring that passion, and perhaps a hidden moment of genuine love, to end her misery.

... And the white wake waited....

VI.   CHTHON

Sixteen

Aton recovered slowly. The calendar on the wall across the room opened on the face of Second Month, §403—almost a year after the horror he remembered. He had kissed the minionette, and . . . almost a year!

Where have I been? What have I done, in that vanished interim?

He looked about. The first substantial feature of the comfortable room that his attention fixed upon was the hard-backed wooden chair: the mighty chair of Aurelius, guarding the exit. Across the floor was the plush couch, also too familiar—the couch he had always thought of as his mother's. Above it still was the framed picture of the daughter of Ten, evoking no guilt now. Beside that—

Beside that was the webwork of Xest artistry: mother and son.

He blotted the room from his mind and studied himself. He was wearing a light shirt and clean farming overalls and the soft heavy footwear of the hvee farmer; whoever had dressed him had known how. Could he have done it himself, in some amnesiac state?

There was a stirring in the adjacent room. Aurelius? No, he was dead, as the nymph of the wood was dead, as everyone who had cared for him was dead. Who occupied this house of Five? The tread was light, familiar.

"Theme of the shell!" he exclaimed, suddenly glad, very glad. He had thought of her, too, as dead, if she had existed at all outside his dreams. He had killed her—but it had been a symbolic execution, a denial of his second love, and now the symbolism was gone.

She stepped into view, her hair longer than that of his four-year memory, glowing silver against the green hvee in the afternoon sunlight. Her fair features were set; her wrist was bare.

There was no physical death on Idyllia, and they both had known it. Yet he had pushed her off the mountain at the moment of rapture. She had no telepathy; she could not have known that his action represented denial, not of her, but of the minionette. To Coquina it was his second rejection . . . and the vibrant hvee she still wore showed that her love for him had never faltered.

To be worthy of such a woman—

"Daughter of Four," he said, "I love you."

She looked up. "Aton?"

Nonplussed, he stood up. His body felt strong—he had not spent the past year in bed. "Coquina—don't you know me?"

She studied him carefully. "Aton," she repeated, smiling at last.

He strode toward her. She retreated. "Please do not touch me, Aton."

"Coquina—what *is* it?"

She stood behind the large-boned chair of Aurelius. "Things may not be as you remember them, Aton."

He returned to his own chair and sat down. "Were my dreams mistaken, pretty shell? *Did* something die on Idyllia?"

"No, Aton, no—not that. But you have been—gone—a long time. I must be sure."

"Sure of *what?*" he demanded. "The minionette is dead and I love you. I loved you from the first, but until I conquered the minionette—"

"Aton, please let me talk. Things will be hard for you, and there is not much time." Her formality amazed him.

"Coquina!"

She ignored his cry and began talking, a trifle rapidly, as though reading a lecture. "I went to the forest before you were released from Chthon and I talked with the minionette. I talked with Malice. I showed her the hvee I wore, and she took it and showed me that she loved you, even as I."

"She did, in her way," Aton said.

"She was lovely. I could see the family resemblance. She told me those things about you that I had to know, so that I could care for you during your recovery, and she warned me about the evil one that would come from Chthon, so that I could protect you from him. She said—she said that she would be gone, soon, and so she left me the song."

"The song!"

"She wanted you to be happy, Aton, and she saw that your minion blood was destroying you, while the evil one waited for the remainder. She gave you to me. You did not conquer her, Aton. Not that magnificent woman."

Comprehension appalled him. "All this—*before* I escaped from Chthon?"

"We loved you, Aton."

"Malice *knew* she was going to die?"

"Yes. Her name, by the terms of her culture, means 'Compassion,' and she loved your father enough to leave him, and you enough to die for you. When Aurelius saw you pass the fields, with her, he understood, and he gave up his long fight against the swamp blight. She died soon after. The cousin of Five came, and we buried Aurelius beside her in the forest."

"The song," Aton said, unable to concentrate.

Coquina glanced at him. "I had to wake you . . . early," she said. "The song—" She came to a decision. "This is the song."

She sang, then, and it was the melody of his childhood. Her

voice lacked the splendor of that of the minionette; but no voice, he realized, could compete on such a level. It *was* the song.

She followed it through to its conclusion, but the magic was gone. "It isn't broken any more," he said, understanding only now that the true appeal of it had not been the melody itself, but the fact that it was incomplete—as had been his whole relationship with the minionette. Not the song, but the *break* had been his compulsion. Why had he never seen this before?

Coquina watched him closely. "It means nothing to you, now, Aton?"

"I'm sorry," he said, finding the expression inept. "You might as well have spared yourself the trouble."

"No, no," she said, smiling more warmly. "That is good. It means that the minion in you is gone. You will be well again, if only—"

The repeated references to mysterious things irritated him. "If only *what?* What is all this about my 'recovery,' and the 'evil one'? Where have I been; what have I been doing, this past year? Why won't you let me near you? Why did you have to 'wake' me at all, early or not? Have I been asleep?"

"I can tell you now." She came around the chair and sat down, keeping her distance from him. "Half minion, half man, you could not live on either world. She warned me about the terrible consequences, if you went free before that conflict was resolved. But after she sacrificed herself you were a madman, roaming the forest in a terrible, blind rage. Your cousin of Five—Benjamin—roped you from the aircar and brought you to me. We put you on drugs. We could not notify the authorities because they would have extradited you to Chthon. We kept your mind blank while it healed. The minionette warned me that it might take two years before the shock of her death purged your mind and set you free, a normal man. We knew we would have to keep you passive all that time. But—"

"Drugs! A whole year?"

"It was the only way. In your food. Benjamin ran the farm, and I helped him with the hvee and took care of you. You have been a vegetable, Aton—that is why I'm not used to you now. I took you for walks outside, for exercise—"

"An animal on a leash."

"The dog-walking detail!" she snapped. "Please let me finish. We kept your presence a secret, but there was one who seemed to know: the evil one of Chthon. His god is telepathic, more even than the minionette. This man came for you, claiming that you belonged to Chthon, now. He knew—a great deal. He said that only in Chthon could you live safely, that only that god of Chthon could make your mind whole. He tried to take you away from me."

"An emissary from Chthon?" Aton was perplexed.

"The hvee did not like him," she said, as though that finished the matter—as perhaps it did. "I—I hurt him, and he went away. Now he sits in his spaceship, waiting for you to wake. He says you will come to him, when you have the choice. I'm afraid of him. And now you must face him before you are ready, because I had to stop the drugs too soon."

"Your supply ran out?" Aton was not wholly pleased with any part of this strange situation.

"No." She would not say more, but instead led him to the door. He obeyed her gesture.

Night was falling, and the floating clouds were carded across the dim horizon, embers in the sky. He had never seen his home more beautiful.

"O joy!" he thought, "that in our—"

"You must go to him," she said, her voice urgent. "You have to do battle tonight, while there is time. Please go."

Aton stared, absently noting her lovely pallor. "Do battle? Why? I don't know anything about this, this 'evil one.' What's the hurry? Why won't you explain?"

"Please," she said, and there were tiny tears on her cheeks.

"Let me touch my hvee," he said, bargaining for time to comprehend the mystery. Coquina stood still, a frozen doll, while he lifted the little plant from her hair: the token of love that he would reclaim permanently when they married. She loved him, strange as her actions might be; the hvee attested to that. Now she was acting as inexplicably as had the minionette, so long ago at the spotel. Were her reasons as valid?

In his cupped hands, the hvee withered and died.

"The hour of the waning of love has beset us," he thought,

astounded. But lost *LOE* was no comfort now.

Whom the hvee cannot love—

He stared at the limp green strand. It had condemned him as unfit to be loved, and there could be no appeal. Had all his aspirations come to no more than this?

The clouds were dull and gray in the fading light: ashes in the sky.

Seventeen

Cold Coquina had not told him where to find the evil foe, but Aton strode over the fields in a familiar and purposeful direction. Three miles into the dusk he came across the black silhoutette: the ship from Chthon.

For almost a year this man had waited for him, not as an arm of the law, but as the emissary of a god. Coquina's vigor had repulsed him. She had not been bluffing when she had spoken—so long ago, when love was rising—of her ability to subdue agressive men. But she had not been able to defeat the power of Chthon which backed this man. That was for Aton himself to do.

He did not mean to return to prison on any basis.

The lock was open. Foolish man, to forget your defenses! Aton found the inset rungs and climbed.

His head came level with the port, reminding him of a prior climb and a prior hope. Something pricked his nose. He held himself rigid while his eyes probed the shadows.

It was a tiny, thin-bladed knife, held with a surgeon's precision. The squatting figure's slightly luminescent eyes bore intently on him, and Aton knew that the potent contact lenses rendered the gloom—vincible. The lips below were pursed in a silent whistle, part of a tuneless distraction. "Hello, Partner," he said.

"Partners we shall be," the man replied. "But not as we have been. You know me now." The knife did not waver.

"Yes," Aton said, bracing his legs more comfortably beneath him. "The minion of Chthon, come to take me back. It was no coincidence that brought you to the hinterland of Idyllia, Chthon-planet, to find me and shepherd me through discoveries that betrayed my fitness for your master. How well it has been said: no one escapes."

"No one," the man agreed, unimpressed by Aton's rhetoric. The blade did not retreat.

Aton knew better than to back down, either verbally or physically. If he had not been obsessed with other matters, he would have seen through Partner's façade long ago. The man had been too patient, giving him time on Earth, on Minion, on Hvee, fading into the background while Aton explored his own nature. Partner had not been interested in garnets *or* the mines from which they came; that had been a convenient pretext to lull suspicion. Partner already had the key to the mines, to all of Chthon.

Aton paused before making his next statement, not certain whether it could cause the knife to withdraw or to slice forward. He plunged. "No coincidence. Indeed, we are very much alike—Doc Bedside!"

The blade disappeared. "Come in," Doc said.

Aton clambered into the chamber. The tight residential compartment was much as he remembered it from their several journeys together: water and food-supply vents along one short wall, descending bunks along the other. This was a sport ship, intended for wilderness camping and/or private parties. The space that should ordinarily have been allocated to cargo was retained simply as space. The floor area was a generous eight feet square.

Bedside gestured, and soft green light radiated from the walls: the light of the caverns of Chthon. Aton made no comment. "Partner" had suffered through conventional illumination, to conceal his identity, but now the mask was off. What was the real connection between this man and Chthon, and why had he chosen to hide his history before?

"What is 'Myxo'?" Aton asked him.

"Mucus. That wasn't obvious?"

"Not at the time," Aton said, thinking of Chthon and the horrors therein. The Hard Trek had saved its worst until last. What sort of man could like it well enough to post academic riddles for those who might follow? "Do you know how many died, trying to make the escape? How did you manage it, alone?"

Bedside settled back against the wall, squatting as though he were in the bare caverns he evidently longed for. His scalpel was out of sight, but ready, Aton was certain. No careless man survived the perils of the trek. No normal man. No sane man.

"Insanity, of course, is a legal fiction these days," Bedside said, choosing to tackle the implied question first. "Biopsychic techniques have eradicated the problem, officially. Just as other medicine has conquered physical illness, with a chilling exception or two." Aton could not miss the ironic reference to the worst illness of all, the chill. "Nevertheless, it becomes necessary for society to incarcerate certain, ah, nonconformists. When I found myself in Chthon as a prisoner, my—oh, let's call it my escape complex—my escape complex was activated. I had purpose. In that circumstance I became in effect sane. Do you follow me?"

"No."

Bedside frowned. "A man who is adjusted to an abnormal situation, while living in a 'normal' society, has a tendency toward nonsurvival. But place that man in a situation conforming to his particular bias, and his traits become those necessary *for* survival, while the normal man perishes. This is the reason it is said that no sane man may escape from Chthon. Chthon is not oriented toward sanity. Of course, the odds against a compatible juxtaposition of anamorphoses—"

Aton was shaking his head. He was not paying much attention to the words; he knew that this was only a conversational prelude to the desperate contest to come. He was confronted with as deadly a foe, here, as he had ever met in his life—one that he had to kill. On this battle hinged his future, though the issues were devious. A loss would mean a return to Chthon and neosanity; victory, a return to the blasted prospects of a dead hvee. Perhaps, after all, he was only fighting to preserve his right to blot himself in suicide.

"Put a fish in water and it swims," Bedside rapped. "Put that fish on land—"

Aton nodded, not wishing to carry the subject farther.

"Chthon was my element," Bedside continued remorse-lessly. "I made my way out. I swam. The monsters there were as nothing to the monsters in my mind. But once I returned to society, I found myself drowning in air, as I had drowned before. My aberration quickly signaled my position, and I was arrested again. They could not ship me to Chthon a second time, because they thought I might lead the entire complement out. They could neither ignore me nor let me go. They preferred to apply a little medicinal insanity to their own intellects, and assume that there *was* no escape from Chthon, and that I was therefore merely a demented creature who identified with the notorious Dr. Bedecker. All of which was true enough, in its way.

"At any rate, they put me in a 'hospital' for 'observation.' This imprisonment reactivated my escape syndrome, and I was able to function effectively again. Their walls and guards were child's play, after the Hard Trek."

Aton watched him cynically. "If you knew that freedom would cost you your sanity, why did you strive for it?"

Bedside smiled with his teeth. "Another romantic lunacy. We assume that a personality problem can be liquidated merely through an understanding of it—as though a man could lift a mountain once he admitted it was heavy. No: recognition is *not* synonymous with solution. I fly toward freedom as a moth toward the candle, and nothing so insubstantial as Reason will turn me aside."

Aton thought of his own headlong drive to unite with the minionette, her hair red for passion, black for death. Reason—how could it hope to bridge the cold, bleak void gaping open, the loss of a song that was healed, a shell that was broken? The moth hurt because its wings were ashes, but had not yet grasped the fact that it could no longer fly. With what mixture of metaphor could he analyze himself? Caterpillar to the in-ferno?

"But you are sane and free now." Unlikely.

"Neither one is natural," Bedside said. "But yes: I have more sanity and more freedom now than ever in my life before, and this is the offer I bring to you."

"Freedom and sanity—in *Chthon?* You offer garbage,"

Aton said, and positioned himself for action.

"Did you imagine," Bedside said, curiously quiet, "that you could brave the lungs and the stomach of Chthon, and not be accountable to the brain?"

"I'm not accountable to your god. I won my freedom."

"Not yet," Bedside said. "Chthon granted you a reprieve. You did not conquer it." The words had a familiar ring. How many forces fancied they were manipulating his life? Or *were* they fancies?

"As you remarked," Bedside continued, "we are very much alike. By normal standards, I am mad. Only my mission for Chthon preserves my balance. Chthon takes care of me in a way you will soon understand. But you—"

"I was judged to be criminally insane," Aton admitted. "On Hvee, that term is still in vogue. But that was before the death of the minionette. I am well, now." The falsity of that statement stung him as he made it. The hvee did not love him any more, which meant that he was totally depraved, whether he comprehended the reason or not. Had Coquina suspected? Was this the reason she had kept her distance? Then why had she cared for his body, all this time? Why had she sent him forth to defeat this "evil one"? Too much was unresolved.

But he would do this one thing, for her, for the sake of the love he thought he felt, though he knew it now to be a shallow, selfish thing, a love unworthy of her. He would make this offering, since she seemed to want it: the lifeless body of Bedside.

"Your particular madness stems from a biological basis," Bedside said. "There is no cure for it. You cannot undo your parentage. You will go on killing sadistically because the minion in you craves the telepathic pleasure of innocent pain. You will go on forgetting your crimes because the man in you cannot accept the guilty pleasures your other self demands. You will go on vindicating the judgment of those who proscribed Minion, hating yourself far more than any other thing—and not without justice.

"Oh, yes—you know your madness now, don't you, minion?"

"I did kill," Aton said, "but not sadistically. There was justice and mercy in my action. I was not the chimera."

Bedside did not relent. "I am not talking of honest murders, minion. I know there are times in Chthon when killing is necessary. Nor do I mean your failures: your Idyllia girl, your vengeance on the minionette, the cavern woman. You tried to kill them all, but you were so much at war with yourself that you could neither love nor hate effectively.

"No, not these actions. But think back to one specific case: your little friend, Framy. (Yes, my god tells me everything.) You protest your innocence there because you did not technically spill his blood. But you betrayed the nether caverns, and pinned the blame on him, and had him posted for execution. And you were there, listening, when the chimera came. Your minion sensitivity responded to the savage little mind of the chimera as it stalked, and you knew it was coming for Framy. You could have alerted the others, and saved him—but you did not. You were there, savoring his agony, as that chimera struck, and still you gave no alarm. Only his dying scream alerted the others—too late.

"This is what you did in Chthon, not once but many times. You used the chimera to gratify your brutal passion. Was this your justice? Your—sanity?"

Aton remembered. Chthon, where his lust for pain had been intensified by confinement. The men whose dying he had savored, the macabre tortures inflicted upon them by a creature he could have stopped, but didn't, as their lifeblood dwindled. The unholy ecstasy that had thrilled him, the almost religious joy culminating in transported spasms of pleasure as those death agonies came.

He remembered, too, the trial, on Hvee: the experts testifying that his aberration was after all biological, not emotional, and that there could be no cure. That he had not murdered, yet, but could not be set loose again, for the safety of mankind. That even a complete personality-wash would not remove his proscribed urges. He remembered the sentence: Chthon.

The minion traits had come upon him with maturity, but for a time had been wholly directed to the search for his minionette. When her influence diminished, the horror began. His love of Coquina had been the last struggle of the human qualities within him—a losing struggle.

The hvee had known. It had not been with him during his

madness. It had loved what he once was; but when, after Chthon, it touched his macabre hand . . .

"This is the reason," Bedside said, "that you will return to Chthon. There you will be safe—from your fellow man, since you are an outlaw, and from yourself. Chthon will support your sanity more perfectly than you can ever do yourself. Chthon will be your god, and you and I will be brothers—forever secure, forever free."

It was tempting. Aton saw that his entire adult life had been a destructive nightmare of passion and pain, contaminating everything it touched. The minionette had been part of it, naturally and knowingly. But Coquina—it would be kindest for her if he had the same courage of the minionette before him, and simply stepped out of her life. She would be better off with her own kind. The love he bore her could achieve its finest expression in deprivation.

But the minionette had died to give him human semblance. She had known him well, known of his link with Chthon, and had cried out against it. Malice and Coquina, minionette and human, his first and second loves—these two had come together not as rivals but as sincere collaborators for his benefit. They had agreed that he had a chance, and both had staked their lives upon it. Could he betray them now?

Perhaps both were mistaken—but they believed in his recovery, and he owed it to both to make the ultimate effort, to resist the easy way. He could not abolish his crimes by running away from life. He had to live, to atone, to make some effort to balance the scales. He had to face what he was and what he had done—and search for a way to make amends. This, perhaps, was the real battle he had come to participate in: that against the capitulation rendered so attractive by Doc Bedside.

"No," Aton said.

Bedside's aspect changed. "I will show you what you are," he said, his voice sharp, his mouth gaping, teeth exposed like those of the cavern salamander. "You rationalize, you delude yourself with hopes of future goodness. But your true wish is still to kill yourself, because you know you are the partner in a crime against your culture. You tried to blame the minionette, but *you* are the one that forced the act. Yes, you know what I mean, minion."

Aton's attitude also changed subtly as he listened. It was coming now, and he could neither stop it nor tolerate it. Bedside's blade was on guard. His space training had prepared him for action against a knife—but not one wielded by the hand of a mad surgeon. Normal reflexes would not be sufficient.

Bedside continued: "You have so conveniently forgotten your incestuous passions. Careful!" he rapped as Aton moved. "I would not kill you so long as Chthon needs you, but you would not find my surgery entirely painless."

This was Bedside's final effort. Could he nullify it? The man was infernally clever.

"There in your spotel," Bedside whispered intently. "That's when you did it. Chthon knows. That's when you had the minionette alone, knowing what she was." The bright eye-lenses glittered in the green glow, just above the pointing blade. *"That's when you raped your moth——"*

The knife clattered to the floor as minion struck with the strength and speed of telepathy. Bedside stared at the thing he had loosed, a living chimera. "Pray to your god for help!" it whispered, hot teeth poised, talon fingers barely touching the bulging eyeballs, ready to nudge them redly out of their sockets. "Perhaps it will help you die."

They remained in frozen tableau, the young warrior and the old. Then the chimera faded. Aton let the man fall, unharmed. "I am not what I was," he said, "and I was never the *physical* chimera. I will not kill you for distorting what you do not understand."

Bedside lay where he had fallen, at Aton's feet. The menace in him was gone; he was a tired old man. "You have slain your chimera."

"I have slain it."

"I return to Chthon in the morning. You are free."

Aton went to the port and swung out, feet searching for the ladder.

"Let me speak for a moment as a man," Bedside said, halting Aton's descent. "Chthon desires your service, not your demise. There is no resentment. Chthon will help you to win your other battle."

"No."

"Listen, then. Had I had a woman like your Coquina to love

me, I would never have needed Chthon. She broke my arm,
eleven months ago—I had not thought she knew your fighting
art—but she is a woman you cannot replace. You will lose
her, unless—"

Aton dropped down to the ground and began to move away.
"Think, think of the date!" Bedside cried after him. "And of
the hvee! Otherwise . . ." But his voice was lost in the rapid
distance.

Eighteen

Aton had escaped in body only; but the sacrifice of the minionette and the care of the daughter of Four had swung the
was the refuge of those who were dominated by such impulses.
Doc Bedside, now the agent of Chthon, had almost proved that
Aton had escaped in body only; but the sacrifice of the minionette and the care of the daughter of Four had swung the
balance and brought the civilized man in him to victory. He
had been roused too soon; with more time he would have come
to understand and accept the painful truths he had blinded
himself against. Blindness had not solved the problems of Oedipus, nor had the ritualistic physical blinding of victims solved
the problems of the men of Minion. Aton had been obsessed
with blindness, physical and emotional.

More time, and Bedside could not have roused the dying
chimera at all. It had been close—unnecessarily close. Why
had he been thrust into battle prematurely? Could Coquina have
wanted him to lose?

No, it was not possible to doubt her motives. Coquina was
good, and she loved him far more than he had ever deserved.
He had been the one to fall short, every time. He had denied
their betrothal, even before he had met her. He had thrown her
off the mountain. He had killed the hvee.

Think of the hvee, and of the date. What cryptic message
had Bedside intended?

How little he knew Coquina, after all. His brief time with
her on Idyllia, in retrospect, had been the happiest of his life.

If he had only been able to stay with her then, instead of chasing his own obsessions. He had, he knew, a great deal in common with the daughter of Four. Her background was naturally similar to that of a son of Five. She was intellectual, upper-class Hvee, on a planet that made no presumption of democracy; she was a far cry from the low-caste girls of the latter Families. Lovely shell! Why had he never looked inside? How well Aurelius had chosen!

Think of the hvee....

But the hvee had died. All his life had been nightmare, except for Coquina—and the hvee had condemned that too. Had he won the battle of his future, only to endure it alone?

Think of the date....

The date was Second Month, §403: no more distinctive than any other month or year, on the even-tempered, nonseasonal planet of Hvee. This appeared to be an extraneous riddle.

The hvee—there was something meaningful. Bedside could not have known about the recent episode, since it had happened less than an hour prior to their conflict. But he had known that it *would* happen, whenever Aton actually touched his plant. He had warned that Coquina would be lost, unless—

Aton began to regret his contemptuous sloughing off of Chthon's emissary. What was there about the hvee that could save Coquina for a man it had deemed unworthy? A quality that a knowledgeable third party could predict?

Think ...

Aton thought. His steady jog carried him across the countryside, familiar from his childhood. He could smell the light perfume of the scratched tree barks, of scuffled earth and crushed weeds and wild forest flowers. He could see the black outlines of the taller trees against the starry sky, and hear the nocturnal scufflings of minor foragers. Memories stirred in him, small poignant recollections of detail that became important only because it was unimportant. The feel of a dry leaf, the whiff of an idle breeze—all the wonderful things set aside by adulthood. Soon, now, he would pass near the spot where he had met the minionette, where he had acquired the wild-growing hvee.

The minionette had plucked it from the ground, and he, too

knowledgeable at seven, had prevented her from keeping it. "Hvee is only for men!" he had asserted, and so she had made him a present of it, and it had been his until his betrothal. It had been his after that, too, for it would not live in the possession of a woman who did not love him. The hvee loved its master, and tolerated the lover of that master, so long as that love endured, and so long as that person was worthy.

The minionette had plucked it.

The minionette!

The hvee had fixed on her! *She* was its mistress!

Suddenly it fell into place. He had loved her sufficiently, or perhaps his minion blood had loved her, to preserve the plant. And she had after all been worthy, not evil. The hvee responded to true emotion, and did not notice inversions. The hate Aton had thought he felt for her, later, had been false hate. The hvee had not been misled.

The death of the minionette had taken with it not only the evil chimera, but also the good hvee—except that the hvee, in the possession of the lover of the lover, had not known that its original object of affection was gone. Coquina had seen the dead minionette, but she had not understood that this was the mistress of the hvee—and the hvee had taken her innocent faith for its own. Love, not reason, was its essence. Even its apparent judgment of worthiness was illusory. It loved the man who, basically, loved himself, and rejected the one who genuinely hated himself.

Had the hvee really belonged to Aton, it might have died anyway.

But he had not actually been condemned. It had died because *he* knew the fate of its mistress, and knew her link with it, though never consciously aware of it. When the hvee came back to him and his knowledge, it had to wither.

He could take a second hvee and offer it to Coquina. This one would not die.

He came into sight of the house. A dim light burned in the window.

Doubt continued to nag him. Why had she sent him out prematurely? Why had she refused to touch him? After she had devoted three years of her life to the care of a dying father and a terribly living son, with the end of torture so near—why had she been crying?

Think of the date....

Yes, the date had been premature. But *why?* Bedside must have intended something.

He reached the house and pushed open the door without a pause. A man turned to meet him—a stranger. He was husky, perhaps fifty, at the prime of life, with a solemn visage and work-soiled hands. There was power in his bearing, unobtrusive but immovable. This was Benjamin Five, the uncle he had almost forgotten.

"Where have you been, Aton?" Benjamin inquired gravely, his tone disconcertingly like that of Aurelius. Behind him a woman's form was lying on the couch.

"Coquina!" Aton exclaimed, passing Benjamin with disrespectful haste. She did not stir. Her pale hair fell limply over the edge of the couch and almost touched the floor. "Coquina— I will give you another hvee—"

"Young man, it is too late for that," Benjamin said.

Aton ignored him. "Coquina, Coquina—I won the battle! The evil one is gone." Her eyelids flickered, but she did not speak. "Coquina." He put his hand on hers.

Her hand was cold.

Think of the date.... This was the year and the month of the chill. The chill! She was dying, far past the point of return.

"Did you think her love was less, young cousin," Benjamin murmured, "because it did run smoothly?"

Aton understood at last. The chill had struck Hvee in the first month of §305, and was due again in the second month of §403. Coquina knew this well, as every resident of Hvee knew it, and could have left the planet—if she had not had a virtual invalid to care for. There had been no place off the planet where she could hide Aton—not from the scrutiny that quarantine officials still gave every ship leaving a planet under siege. And so she had stayed, and had risked the chill with him, and had lost. Instead of leaving the moment she contracted it, Coquina had remained, caring for him—and had finally roused him so that he would not wake alone, confused and helpless, or die from neglect under the drugs.

No—her love had not been less.

She had wanted him to win his freedom while she lived, while her support was with him.

The chill. He would have known the moment he touched

her, for she had been far gone when she had talked to him.
She must have sustained consciousness only with great effort,
while trying to prepare him for a contest she only partly understood herself. Now that contest was over, her part was done,
and she had stopped fighting.

Unless she had stopped fighting when she had seen the hvee
die.

Aton kneeled for interminable moments beside her, his hand
on hers, looking upon her quiet face. Was she never to know
that he had not betrayed her that third time? The tears came
to his own eyes as the cold crept from her hand to his, crept
on into his spirit.

My love, he thought to her, my love for you is not less
either. All of what you shared with the minionette before,
belongs to you alone, now. My second love is greater than the
first.

She lay still.

Aton bowed his head, defeated. "The price for freedom is
too great," he said.

There was an imperative knock on the door. "That's
Chthon," Aton said to Benjamin, no longer caring whether his
semitelepathy showed.

Bedside entered. He went immediately to the dying girl.
"Terminal," he said.

Aton nodded. The last of Bedside's riddles was becoming
clear. It was Aton's turn to make a sacrifice.

"I will pray to your god," he said to Bedside, "if only she
lives."

Bedside nodded acceptance. "We must go immediately."

Aton got up and slid his arms under Coquina's numb form,
lifting her into the air. He carried her to the door.

Benjamin did not move. "I think you have sold your soul,"
he said.

Aton stepped into the night. The clear stars shone overhead—stars that he would not see again. "'Hide, hide your
golden light!'" he quoted softly. "'She sleeps! My lady sleeps!
Sleeps . . .'"

16

The caverns were quiet. There was no wind at all, and even the current in the water had disappeared. Some liquid hung in stagnant pools, too shallow to swim in. The rock formations had taken on a peculiar cast, an unnatural gray, and the grotesque shape of diverging passages repelled the eye.

Foreboding grew. This had the smell of a dead end. The once-mighty river had gradually seeped away, and the plentiful game had become scarce. Once more the party traveled hungry. Soon the lots would come into use again, unless someone volunteered by collapsing. The last of Bedside's markers had been spotted two marches ago. If another were not found by the end of this march, they would have to retrace the trail.

Fourteen women and six men had survived the thirty-march journey of the Hard Trek—so far. Accident and fatigue still took their toll, and the chimera still stalked the group, though it seldom had a chance to strike any more. They were farther away from the surface than ever—and between them and final escape still waited the nemesis that had driven Bedside mad.

The march ended. They camped huddled together, trying to protect themselves from the ominous gathering of unknown forces. These caverns were menacing.

"How much more?" a woman demanded, her voice too sharp, addressing herself to the sinister passages. Aton agreed: what other pressures would be brought to bear before Chthon let them go?

A shout. It was the voice of one of the women on scout duty. Teams always went out on prowl, now, while the main group rested. The chimera never attacked an alert formation.

The others gathered around. It was one of Bedside's cairns, with a message scratched on the floor. The rock was soft, here, and could be decorated readily.

"What does it mean?"

It was the typical skull illustration of danger, but without the crossbones. A single word was underneath.

Aton spelled out the crude letters: MYXO. "Must be a medical term," he said.

"Myxo," Bossman muttered. "Don't mean anything to me. Ain't like him to leave his picture unfinished."

"Either something drove him off—" a woman suggested.

"Or there's a Myxo 'round here that don't quite kill," another finished.

They stood in a circle, looking at each other. No one knew. But one thing experience had made plain: Doc Bedside's humor was scant, and his warnings were not to be ignored.

"We better move on fast," Bossman decided. They were tired, but there was no dissent. There *was* danger here.

Fifteen minutes later a woman fell, clutching at her throat and head. No animal had attacked her, and nothing was wrong—visibly.

They halted for a brief consultation. Life was more precious at this juncture. If many more were lost, the party would be too small to win through the remaining challenges. There had to be scouting parties, guards, and reliefs for these, as well as individuals for special assignments for unpleasant work. Once the disciplined system broke down, the demise of the remainder would accelerate. Concern for the laggards was something new—but necessary.

They camped and made the woman comfortable. She was examined closely. What was the matter with her?

Her breathing was labored, rasping. Gradually her skin whitened. A slimy mucus was exuded all along her body, and a stomach-twisting odor arose from it. She had fallen prey to a disease—the first disease known in Chthon.

"We better kill her now," a woman urged, "before it spreads."

Bossman considered the matter.

"Why bother?" Aton said. "We've all been exposed by this time."

"How did *she* catch it?"

"I ain't seen nothing like *this* before."

"Leave her here and get out," a man cried, the contagious tinge of panic coming out.

A second woman fell. "Too late," Bossman said. It was always too late by the time they understood the manner of the next danger. "Better stick together and fight."

"Fight what?" the man wanted to know. But the question was academic: a third woman was toppling.

In quick succession the women fell, to lie with skins smeared white. They did not appear to be in pain, after the initial spasm: but the acrid exudation grew steadily worse. It re-formed the moment the skin was wiped clean, and it was everywhere.

Aton, Bossman and the other four men stood by helplessly. During the trek the men had taken more risks and died more readily, and the chimera seemed to prefer them. Now the tally was being reversed, as the mysterious malady mummified the females. Bossman did what he could. Taking a woman by the foot, he dragged her to the nearest pool and tried to wash the slime away. This seemed to help; she sat up and began to splash herself, slowly, but with some effectiveness.

They did the same for the others, dumping them into the water and holding up their heads by the hair until they revived. The crisis seemed to be over.

Then it started on the men.

The masculine attacks, as though to make up for lost time,

were far more violent. Almost as one, the men went into con-
vulsions. Their skin reacted, sending out the calcifying sweat.
It was the women's turn to play nurse. Soon everyone was in
the pool, and the water took on a milky hue. If this were to
be a fatal disease, all would die.

But Bedside had omitted the bones.

Aton was the first of the men to recover. He had experienced
no pain, aside from the extreme tightness of throat that had
restricted breathing. Instead there had been a lassitude, a desire
to let go, to drift—a desire shocked away by the cold water.
Now, in reaction, he was disgusted. Not at the ludicrous com-
munal bath, but at his failure to resist the disease.

"The Myxo!" he exclaimed. "This must be what Bedside
was warning us about. Some kind of virus."

The nearest woman looked at him. The black-haired one,
no longer as pretty as she had been before the trek, but still
interesting. She had always steered clear when Garnet was
about; but Garnet had fed the creature with the white wake
while the others were swimming safely across the river, and
now the field was clear.

If things ever eased up enough to permit a relaxed disburse-
ment . . . "Must be in the air," she said. "We *better* get out."
And he had never learned her name.

Bossman revived. "Yeah," he agreed.

They moved on, trying to escape the malady they knew they
carried with them. They did not get far.

The women were first, again. This time it was fever, rising
unbelievably. There were no gauges, no thermometers here,
but the simple touch of the skin served notice that there were
several degrees between the sick and the well. The fever rose
to the limit of human endurance. Then it increased.

They no longer tried to march. It was obvious that they
could not outrun it, or hide from it. The passage ahead expanded
into a bubble-dome, another relic of Chthon's formation, out
of place in this section of the caverns, but welcome. The base
was filled with clear, shallow water. This was convenient and
relatively safe. They settled down, in and beside the pool,
waiting for what might come.

At what point, Aton wondered, did brain damage occur?
Surely this fever was already cooking the neural tissues of the

present victims. There was no specific limit to the temperature a living body could endure, despite the attitude of the medics— but such fever *was* dangerous. Was this the actual course of the Bedside madness? If so, was it possible to circumvent it?

Was there some way to hold the fever down until the illness ran its course?

He gazed into the water. It was cold; they were far below the fire cycle. Fully immersed—

The fever came. Aton slipped into the pool and lay down, propping himself in such a way that his face alone was exposed to the air. The relief was a blessed thing. But the juices in him were boiling, the tissues curling. The inferno of the blue garnet itself had hardly been as hot as this.

Vaguely he heard scuffling and splashing around him. Something was going on, but he was afraid to sit up and look, afraid to leave the water because of an irrational fear that he would burst into flame the moment he did so.

But he had to. He was finding it difficult to breathe for some reason. There was an obstruction.

Aton sat up and put his hand to his mouth, to find it slimed with a thick layer of putrid paste. Inside, this time, obscuring nasal and glottal passages, instead of external skin. His nose was already entirely blocked. He hooked one finger into his mouth and scraped out a wad of yellow mucus, rank and rotten, which hardened immediately upon exposure to the air. No wonder his breathing was difficult. The stuff clogged the breathing passages by solidifying around them.

He looked around, or tried to, and discovered that a similar pus rimmed his eyes, almost closing them. It was the same for the others, male and female alike; the illness no longer seemed to distinguish between the sexes. Some were already retching, nauseated by the deposits. One man yanked out a huge solid chunk, and there was blood on it from the adhering membrane. No one dared to let it collect, or the choice would be between mutilation and suffocation. And still the fever raged.

Aton buried his face in the water, trying to wash the matter away. This helped; the lumps dissolved. He spat out a thick stew, gagging anew at the stench, and rinsed again. Water had saved him a second time.

The others followed his example. For three it was already

too late. Several more were in doubt and would probably suffocate shortly. No one had time to assist his neighbor. There seemed to be no defense against the attack—only a temporary abridgment of the symptoms by continuous rinsing.

The pool had been fouled. "Move on—a little," Bossman said.

They moved on, just far enough to locate a clear pool. The short walk was immensely tiring. The illness had sapped the strength of all of them drastically.

It continued for an interminable time. Toward the end most were crawling from one pool to the next between sieges, unable to walk upright. Judging by the state of his hunger, Aton estimated that the actual time elapsed since the onset was less than two marches—but subjectively, it was many times that.

The first recoveries came. The women, earliest to succumb, led the way to equilibrium. Gradually the symptoms abated for all of them.

Eleven women and three men survived. Of these, three continued in distress: Aton, Bossman, and the black-haired woman. Aton saw this, realized something, then lost the thought as he fought back another surge of dizziness and nausea.

17

Recovery: but those who had recovered completely, at least so far as the visible symptoms went, were not helping the others. They merely stood there, lethargic, waiting—for something. They did not speak.

At length the remaining three relaxed and sat up, free of the fever. The standing eleven looked on, blank-faced.

"All right," Bossman called, his voice of command a shadow of its past. "We got to move on nex' pool."

He set the example, but the larger group did not follow.

"What's the matter with them?" the black-haired one asked.

"Aren't you coming?" Aton called back to them.

No answer.

"You know what?" the woman said. "They act like zombies."

It was the key. The standing people did not appear to have free will at all. All of them were known to Aton, after the rigors of the trek. While they were not noted individualists, they still should—

His previous thought blossomed. Individualism: only the three most independent members of the remaining party were in motion now. The ones who always spoke for themselves, who acted on their own motivation, who habitually demanded explanations.

Further conjecture was cut off by another onset of the disease. All three staggered to the next pool and tumbled in, battling both fever and mucus with the cool water. And the others watched stolidly and did nothing.

In his fevered imagination it seemed to Aton that he was losing control over his own body. His arms responded slowly. Other muscles were sluggish, uncertain. This was an aspect of the illness that was only now beginning to make perverted sense.

But the thought of Malice buoyed him up. Her song was incomplete. He could not rest until he possessed her. Nothing else mattered. The fire in his blood was not more fierce than that in her hair; the pool no more refreshing than her deep eyes. Her love alone—

The siege passed. Aton felt stronger, now. It had been easier to resist, once he remembered his purpose. But the other two had been less fortunate. They gazed at him alertly, but did not try to rise. It was up to him to penetrate the mystery of the zombies.

Ten women and one man had neither fled the last attack nor been affected by it. Aton advanced on them.

They retreated—as a group. They shuffled away, awkward, stiff, in unison. There could be no further doubt: they were possessed and under common control. This time it was no caterpillar, at least not a physical one, but the effect was similar.

"Kill them," Bossman rasped from the pool. "They ain't human no more."

Aton caught up to the lone man, a medium-built, hard-

working, and congenial person, hitherto. "Snap out of it," he
said, yanking him back by the shoulder. But the man fell
backwards at the pressure and crashed stiff-bodied against the
floor. He did not try to get up.

Aton got down and listened for the heartbeat. There was
none. The man was not breathing. He was dead.

The women continued their retreat. He went after them
again—and was stopped by a third assault in this intermittent
series. This one was more strenuous than before. He could
hardly force his legs to cover the distance to the nearest pool.
They wanted to jerk to the same rhythm that ruled the marching
women. The coagulating slime in his mouth increased his distraction.

He got to the water and toppled in headfirst, not caring for
the moment whether or not he drowned, so long as it was at
his own direction. Malice appeared again, a lovely vision, and
his insatiable yearning for her drove back the other fever, reluctantly. That was the only thing that stiffened his will to
resist. The urge of the fever was too strong to endure for long.

It passed, leaving him weak and gasping. Beside him Bossman was rigid and staring, eyeballs caked with blood. Aton
was afraid the leader had been overcome, but a voice came out
of the twisted mouth, clogged and croaking, but Bossman's.

"I . . . can't fight no more," Bossman said. His arm struggled
in the water and brought up the shining axe. "Take it . . . kill
me if I go. . . ."

Aton took it. He stood up and strode toward the group once
more. Again the women shuffled away, some not even facing
him, but moving in automatic steps with the others. And again
the fever struck.

He realized that the fever was under conscious direction.
As he withdrew toward the pool, it eased; as he advanced on
the zombies, it clamped down. The message was clear: leave
them alone.

Aton made his reply clear. He focused his mind on the
dominating picture of his love, his unobtainable minionette,
and continued to advance. He struck with his free hand at the
nearest woman; the coordination required to wield the axe was
beyond him. She fell without a sound, to lie as the man had

lain. The strain of transition must have weakened the zombies so much that any added shock was fatal. He could kill with a single blow.

"Kill—!" he thought. "But these are human beings, the people I have traveled with and lived with through the most terrible adventures of our lives. How can I kill them?"

But he knew the answer to that, and in the disorientation of the mental attack the reasoning made sense: kill, because these people were no longer human. They had given up their minds and wills to some Chthon influence as insidious as the caterpillar, and death was merciful. He knew this intellectually, and he felt it, somehow, emotionally: there was no personality remaining in the zombies. Kill.

The invisible attack against him intensified. His breath was cut off, his sight wavered, but he fought and advanced and struck out almost blindly, again and again, connecting now and then with solid flesh, and all about him the silent females fell. It was carnage; one blow meant death, and there were many blows.

At last the pressure against him became too great, and he fell. Unable to rise, he tried to roll toward the water. But he had pushed himself too far. He succumbed, not to possession but to oblivion.

To—

"Your dream is futile," the voice seemed to say. *"The min- ionette is forbidden; only while you are apart from her is your emotion real. You cannot bring these opposite poles together; they can unite only in disaster."*

He brought it into focus: a mass of green. It formed into whorls and petals: the flower of the hvee. Petal lips spoke again.

"There is no magic in your song. Only because it is broken does it fascinate you. Only because your love is incomplete does it endure."

"No!" But somehow it took hold, fatalism rising like the tide, lapping gently at idealistic castles of sand. For the hvee did not lie to its master.

"You are not my master. You are only—"

Aton blanked the image from his consciousness, afraid of

what it might say. The flower wavered and turned gray. It was a hanging structure on the ceiling, a crystalline stalactite, cracked and hollow like a monster shell.

The women were washing his body in the water. Their motions were unpracticed, clumsy.

Aton recoiled. They were zombies!

The axe was on the floor, where he had passed out. He had not achieved the water himself. Was he a zombie, too?

"No!"

Aton jumped up, clambered out of the water, lumbered to the weapon. He slapped a hand on it as though afraid it would wriggle away. He was armed now; he was no zombie.

The women came after him, mechanically. He backed away, hesitant after their kindness to him. He had been destroying them; why had they spared him?

Something touched him. Whirling, Aton saw a man. It was Bossman, standing outside the water. His skin was clear. His eyes were vacant.

Aton knew what he had to do. He lifted the axe.

The attack began. He clenched his mind against it and swung the suddenly heavy axe. The great blade of it strove overhead, ponderous, too massive for his strength. He forced it onward, slowly, guiding it as gravity took leisurely hold and toppled it down. It came to rest at last in Bossman's skull, and he fell, fell.

I have paid my debt to you, and—I'm sorry.

The force of the attack lay on him like a smothering blanket, but as he staggered back it eased again. The dead women lay all around; only the two who had revived him were animate. He could kill them—

And wander through the endless caverns of Chthon, alone. Was this the way it was to end? And if he succumbed, eventually, to zombi-ism, who would there be to kill *him?*

What had the love of Malice led him into?

"Truce." The cracked voice came from the pool behind him. He had forgotten the black-haired woman, the last holdout.

She was rising from the water. He was not alone!

She approached him, moving with the awkward gait of the possessed. Her eyes stared straight ahead.

The last of the zombie conquests was coming to him, easy prey for axe or fist. What did it mean?

"Truce," it repeated.

It could talk. There was intelligence behind the Myxo half-death! The skull without the crossbones.

Now it was ready to parley.

18

Aton held the axe, unwilling to take the action that would leave him entirely alone and lost in the caverns. Intelligence, even malevolent intelligence, was a more promising opponent than solitude.

"Truce," he agreed.

The woman-thing stopped before him listlessly. "Do not kill," it said.

The zombie-master wanted to save its remaining conquests! He had a bargaining point. His mind explored the possibilities.

"Who are you?" he asked, not really concerned, but needing to gain time for further thought. Could he win his freedom through this thing?

The figure's eyes blinked. She backed away, eyes on the axe. "What happened?" she asked plaintively. "Why are you—"

She had thrown off the possession! "You don't remember?"

She saw the standing zombies. "I—I lost, didn't I?" she said, hesitantly. "I went under. All the hurt and terror were gone—but not quite all the way. I wasn't quite a . . ." she paused, gesturing toward the others.

An incomplete take-over? He did not like the smell of it. Whose agent was she now?

She straightened, becoming rigid again. "I am—Chthon."

Chthon—this time a title, not a place. The Myxo intellect.

It had learned moderation. The true zombies were useless to it, because it could not control their bodies effectively. But by leaving a part of the human will intact it was able to draw on the speech center, and perhaps much of the memory and mind. But what *was* it?

He asked it.

It did not know. But, in halting interchange, a gradual picture of sorts grew. The geologic forces in the subterranean Chthon-planet had carved caverns, hundreds and thousands of cubic miles of them: hot lava tubes, winding waterways, smooth wind tunnels. The subsequent whims of nature heaved and overturned the elaborate structure, crushing the passages, kneading them down, and beginning the process over. Lava flowed again, and again; water cut across the honeycombed strata, riverbeds melted, cool lakes were crushed between molten layers. Crystals formed in the interstices, all types, growing enormously, only to be buried. New pressures on them generated restless currents, for some were semiconductors, and diodes were formed and destroyed, while electrons ran along and through the metallic strands left as residue from prior furnaces, and discharged into the flowing waters, jumped across broken networks, and accelerated through natural coils. The sparks ignited accumulated gas, exploded the volatile bubbles. A perpetual recirculation formed, heating and cracking the cold rock and vaporizing the percolating waters as the fires settled, changing tolerances. And the crystals continued to grow and change in the new environment, and some metamorphosed into forms that were scarcely natural, and the current in them developed circulations and feedback analogous to the fire cycle nearby. At last, in whatever indefinable manner the transition from slime to living slime is made, the transition from current to consciousness was also made, without the interposition of life and the Chthon-intellect was created.

"What do you want with us," Aton asked it, "with human beings? What good are we to you?"

The woman faltered, lapsed into zombie status, then back to human. "It wants me to explain to you that it has no—no moving parts. It is all—electronic, a computer. It can think, but it can't *do* anything, unless it controls mobile units. The local animals aren't very good. They can't follow complex instructions, and Chthon can't adapt readily to their animate nervous systems. It needs units with—intelligence."

"It has two zombies," Aton pointed out. "Three."

"They are not—strong. They have no—it takes great concentration to make their bodies move, because the—circuits are even less familiar than those of the animals. Foreign. It needs—willing units."

Aton's sympathy was small. "What's the going rate for a 'willing unit'?"

"Security. Sanity," she said.

Aton's laugh was harsh. "I'll make it this deal: I'll refrain from killing what's left of these 'sane,' 'secure' people, if it guides me to the surface safely."

"Yes," she said.

"Yes?" Aton did not believe it could be so easy. "Chthon agrees?"

"Yes."

"Now?" He was looking for the catch. Was it planning to spirit away the zombies when his attention wandered, then renew the siege for him? "We travel together—the four of us," he amended, "or I'll kill them now."

"It will take—six marches," she said. "The—others cannot travel that far. They will die."

"Uh-huh. I can shorten their misery."

"You will die—if Chthon summons an—animal—and releases its mind."

Power politics. The thing was learning rapidly. Could it bring the chimera, or was this a bluff? But this gave him an idea.

"If Chthon can summon animals, our problem is solved. Have it bring something to ride."

There were further negotiations; but before long Aton found himself mounted on the back of an enormous rockeater, knees braced against the soft scales of its sides, hands gripping the great loose folds of its neck. His weight required it to travel on all fours, but the creature was sturdy enough to carry him easily. The others were similarly steeded. The long trip began, calculated at only two marches this way.

This was the Easy Trek.

The pace was swift. The huge pseudoreptiles, released from Chthon's direct control after being given the message, hunkered

along at a good ten miles per hour. The gray caverns passed
as they picked their way through the maze. Aton saw that he
could never have found his way out alone. He became drowsy,
but did not dare to sleep. He might wake to discover the zombies
gone. A strange twist of fate that made such onerous half-
people valuable!

Yet common sense told him that there would be no practical
way for him to catch the zombies if their animals deviated from
the course his own steed was taking. They would be lost in
seconds, and Chthon would stun his own mount and prevent
any pursuit. With hostages gone, he would have no bargaining
leverage. He was really much more at the mercy of the cavern
god than it seemed to realize.

He looked around him, aware of the passage of time, his
legs cramped by the constant strain. The surrounding caverns
had changed, and he knew that he had either slept or been very
close to it. But the zombies still paced him. Apparently Chthon
was holding to its word. A surprising, unrealistic development.
Chthon was hardly that stupid. Why was it humoring him?

Obviously it had rather special plans for him. The agreement
had been a ruse to obtain his temporary cooperation. There was
nothing he could do now but play along and wait for it to show
its—hand.

They were traveling along a tunnel, similar to the prelude
to the jelly-whale's parlor, but with a dry stream bed. The
gently ascending path led on and on, meandering but unending.
He was reminded of the trans-system of a spaceship, and wondered fleetingly whether they were likely to encounter any cross
traffic. But of course Chthon would warn away any other animals, particularly caterpillars.

More time passed as the tireless creatures proceeded. Aton's
whole body ached. But his demand for freedom overrode any
bodily discomfort, and he refused to plead for a halt. He wondered just how hard he would have to fight to obtain that
freedom, when the moment of decision came. It would not be
granted easily.

Abruptly, it was raining.

We're on the surface! he thought. We've come out of the
caverns! Stop the march—I want to get off right here!

But the time had not been sufficient. It was the first march, and they were still deep in the planet. In a few minutes they were out of the weather, under an overhang, and Aton understood that this was simply another wonder of Chthon: an opening so great in size that it had a separate meteorology of its own. Or, more likely, there was a steady precipitation from a cold ceiling far above, or a leak from some high river. It had been, neverless, a surprise.

The animals ducked into it again, and Aton clung soggily. There was something about exposure to the rain that bothered him. He had a premonition of death, of terror, and of the end of love. Strange—he had never feared the rain before.

Brief flashes of strange vegetation could be seen as they passed. Luminescent gardens, glowing in green and blue, steamed steadily under the precipitation.

Aton was sorry to leave that section behind.

At length the first march was over. They dismounted stiffly and tried to relax. Aton realized that he was hungry; he had been hungry before the weird ride had begun, and now he reeled from it. The Myxo sieges had not strengthened him, either.

The half-woman spoke: "Build a fire, if you wish, for comfort; an animal will come." And in this manner they were provided for. Aton discovered that there was nothing inferior about zombie-animal meat.

They were camped in wind tunnels, but unfamiliar ones. These might be part of a system opposite the one they had known as prisoners—across the mighty gas-crevasse. He would have been inclined toward exploration, if he had not long since become aware of the futility of it. What could he hope to find, except more caverns?

They slept, Aton with his arm over the half-woman, not from any personal desire for her, but to ensure her securtiy as hostage—for what that was worth. He reasoned that she was the most valuable of the conquests, because her mind was largely intact. Some part of the supposed bargain would be binding as long as he retained power over her. Had there been any other way, he would not have touched her at all; the concept of such alien possession was repulsive to him.

Fresh mounts waited in the "morning," and the four resumed their journey. The wind tunnels were left behind, and they threaded their way through a forest of stalagmites, brown and discolored with concentric rings marking gradations on the outside. Again the surroundings upset him, vaguely; the sight of such treelike columns rising from the floor reminded him of the childhood forests of Hvee, always friendly—now filled with nameless forboding. Almost, at this point, he hesitated to leave the protective caverns, with their all-seeing god-figure. He was afraid of what he might find Outside.

He brushed the feeling away. Probably Chthon was trying to tamper with his mind. But nothing could stand in the way of his love for the minionette.

The mounts slowed early in the second march, moving on their equivalent of tiptoe. Aton, more alert than he had been on the previous march, looked around suspiciously. He saw the heaving hide of some gargantuan creature, sleeping. This was some dragon of the underworld, with the bulk of an elephant, lying astride their path. They were in its burrow—passages hewn recently out of the rock, ten feet in diameter, bore the scars of giant claws. But its sleep was sound, assisted, no doubt, by the influence of Chthon.

There was so much to the cavern system, so much more than Aton had ever imagined. Surely this was the greatest of underworld domains anywhere in the galaxy. An independent man could live here in comfort, with challenge.

The mount's pounding thighs accelerated. Resume safe speed, Aton thought, and smiled. The wonders continued, more than the mind could assimilate in one swift trip. Some day he would have to return, to explore and exploit. There was sheer wealth here beyond calculation, and, more important, knowledge. A life spent here, recording for posterity the endless treasures of nature so much in evidence, would be well spent indeed.

Do not try to distract me from the minionette. *She* is my life, not this.

Would it ever be possible to map it all? This was a three-dimensional world, level upon level, climate upon climate, teeming with variety. A lifetime would hardly suffice.

Hour after hour. Progress slowed as the ascent became steep.

The glow from the walls faded and was gone, leaving him blind. Round rocks clattered away and down, dislodged by feet now blind and clumsy. This was the strangest section of all— too remote for illumination. It frightened him. He was helpless.

"The animals cannot stand the light of day," the half-woman's voice came from ahead. "We must stop."

The light of day!

"On foot. Another turn," she said. Aton could hear her dismounting, along with the zombies. He joined them. The animals, released, decamped, eager to get away from this area. "We shall not go beyond this point," she said. "You must go alone."

Alone! To the fate Chthon planned for him.

The loose boulders banged his bare feet. Aton maneuvered around them painfully, groped his way along the ragged wall, found the dread corner. He turned.

Light came down, not green but white. It was bright and beautiful, the bleak cave ugly. Freedom!

As he stared upward, he saw a silhouette. It was an animal of some sort passing between him and the light—an odd bird-like creature with a very long, cutting bill, hooked slightly at the tip. It had terrible talons on the wings, as they spread momentarily, and solid, pincer-like feet.

The chimera.

Was this the freedom Chthon had promised?

He could turn back, rejoin the zombies, give up his dream. Give up the minionette. Worship Chthon.

Or he could advance upon the chimera, a creature he could not hope to overcome, and die the death it offered. Eyeless and gutless, he could live for a few moments in freedom, on the surface of Chthon-planet: lovely Idyllia.

"I forgot *LOE!*" Aton exclaimed. "I left my book in the caverns, where the sieges of Myxo began." Yes, he would have to go back for it. . . .

Some other time. Behind the chimera he saw the minionette, beckoning. He went to her.

The great wings fluttered silently. The creature disappeared, and with it the other image, and the way was clear. Chthon had let him go.

"How can we know the dancer from the dance?"
WILLIAM BUTLER YEATS, *Among School Children*

Epilog:

Yes—we let him go.
We allow Aton to revisit life.
He was dead when he came to us,
His culture says.
But he was unfinished,
And we require him—complete.
We give him to our half-sane minion, Bedside,
And wait for his return.

Aton, Aton—did you search for evil?
Did you desert your father in his hour of need, to pursue a fond
        illusion?
Did you forsake honest love for incestuous passion?
Did you betray your fellows into decimation?
Did you finally bargain with hell itself, which you symbolized as
        Chthon?
You have been condemned:
Not by your father
Not by your first or second love
Not by your fellows
Not by Chthon.
Where is the evil for which you search?
How can you tell it from yourself?
How can you condemn yourself
For being what you are?
We had thought to salvage the good of your culture's philosophy
And destroy the evil of its being;
But we find them near of kin.
We had thought to recruit an envoy of extermination
To cleanse our galaxy of life.
But that envoy brings us *LOE*
And mocks our intellect with ethical conception.
(All we had seen before was your unsane element.)
How can we know life's destiny from ours?
Are we not near of kin in our quest for completion?
How can we condemn you
For sharing our ideal
In your inverted terms?

And thus we must accept you with your woman;
We must banish the chill from the shell,
And learn that in our mercy
Is our own nova.
For as we study the chill we discover a thing of wonder:
Not natural
Not inimical
Not accidental
But an agitation planted within our galaxy,
Whose side-effects on life are unintentional:
A signal.
A message to every intellect with strength to comprehend:
We are not alone in the universe.
The god-intellects are waiting for our reply.

An incredible quest comes full circle!

PIERS ANTHONY
FAITH OF TAROT

At last: after *God of Tarot* and *Vision of Tarot* comes *Faith of Tarot*, the concluding volume in Piers Anthony's magnificent epic trilogy. The Miracle Planet stands revealed in this science fiction masterpiece by the highly acclaimed author of *Macroscope*.

MS READ-a-thon—
a simple way to start
youngsters reading

Boys and girls between 6 and 14 can join the MS READ-a-thon and help find a cure for Multiple Sclerosis by reading books. And they get two rewards — the enjoyment of reading, and the great feeling that comes from helping others.

Parents and educators: For complete information call your local MS chapter. Or mail the coupon below.

Kids can help, too!